Blue Man

John L. Moore

BookLocker
Saint Petersburg, Florida

Paperback ISBN: 978-1-64719-350-8
Hardcover ISBN: 978-1-64719-351-5
Epub ISBN: 978-1-64719-352-2
Mobi ISBN: 978-1-64719-353-9

Published by BookLocker.com, Inc., St. Petersburg, Florida.

The characters and events in this book are fictitious. Any similarity to real persons, living or dead, is coincidental and not intended by the author.

Printed on acid-free paper.

BookLocker.com, Inc.
2021

First Edition

COVER ART: "Vast" by Margie Lucier

Library of Congress Cataloguing in Publication Data
Moore, John L.
Blue Man by John L. Moore
Library of Congress Control Number: 2021901480

Acknowledgments

Many, many thanks go to many people. First, Patricia Moore, David Aretha, and Becky McLendon for superb editorial assistance; to Lori Anderson Wills, Cathy Jones, Garris Elkins, Katie Rouse, Clo DiPilato, and Kristen Lim for comments and prayers; to Andrea Moore Ferguson for pointing me to the superb cover art by Margie Lucier, and to Margie for allowing its use; to Brett Badgett and Todd Engel for cover design; Rick Joyner, for aircraft information; to Debra Moore for loving a writer who happens to be her husband.

To Ray Hughes.
Minstrel, prophet, poet, teacher, historian, friend.

I'm going, I'm gone, back to Montana,
where the pines stand like angels,
and point to the throne.
I'm going, I'm gone, where the sky is forever.
You can stand anywhere and always hear home.

"Montana" (The Meadowlark Song)
by Ray Hughes
from *The Dark Nights Are Over*

Prologue

The tan-colored Jeep CJ-5 turned onto a gravel road north of Ely, Nevada, and traveled seven miles before switching onto a dirt road that kicked up dust the color of the vehicle.

Twelve miles later, the Jeep rolled to a stop at an encampment in the mountains. A lean, hard man in his early forties, aviator sunglasses shielding his eyes, got out of the vehicle and walked briskly up a hill to a clearing where nineteen young people stood, each with a barrel of sand in front of them.

Their instructor barked an order, and in perfect unison, each student shouted "ki-ayy" and dropped from a ready stance to one knee while driving a fist into the sand. Then, like a whip snapping, all nineteen rebounded to the ready stance.

"Repeat!"

The instructor saw his guest, called an associate over to handle the commands, and jogged to the visitor.

"Bill, this is unexpected," the sensei said. He was identical to the visitor except more muscled and had a shaved head.

The twin brothers hugged briefly.

"How are things going, Rob?" the visitor asked.

"Good, good. What brings you to our remote piece of heaven?"

"I thought I better see how the Company's dark money was being spent. How's this class?"

"Better than average. Most of these men were Special Forces career material."

"I count nineteen trainees and twenty barrels."

"The unused barrel was his," Rob said, pointing to the sleeping area where a wiry young man with shoulder-length hair was rolling up his sleeping bag.

"A civilian? You let a civilian in here? And a hippy at that?"

7

"Bill, remember, these are all civilians. This is a not a government operation."

"Where did you find him?"

"He was hitchhiking. I picked him up on the highway."

"He's packing up. Did he wash out?"

"Not exactly. He took everything we threw at him. He's just not ready. He hasn't found himself."

"We don't need people like him," Bill said sternly. "What if he talks?"

"He won't talk. He's one of us—he just doesn't know it yet."

"In my world, he'd be eliminated."

"I know, Bill, but that kid is special. He's your type. He has special senses."

"What abilities does he exhibit?"

"He's an empath, a synesthete, and a visionary."

"How old is he?"

"Nineteen."

"Where is he going?"

Rob shrugged. "He's going to the highway and stick his thumb out. That seems to be what he likes."

"It's twenty miles to the highway."

"That won't bother him."

"I think I'll give him a lift," Bill said.

Bill approached the young man as he was shouldering his heavy backpack. The kid looked at him curiously.

"Do you need a ride to the highway?" Bill asked.

"Are you going that way?"

"I can be."

"I don't want to put you to any trouble."

"No trouble at all. Throw your pack in my Jeep."

The young man put his pack in the back and climbed into the passenger seat. Bill started the Jeep, shifted, and they left.

"Have you been on the road long?" Bill asked.

"Fifteen months."

"Where are you going from here?"

"I don't know," he said, shaking his mane of long hair. "Wherever my thumb takes me."

"Why are you leaving this program?"

The kid shrugged. "It's too political or something. I don't fit in. Everyone is four or five years older than me and has military experience. Besides, I didn't like the name."

"The name? This program doesn't have a name."

"Yeah. Yesterday sensei announced that the program was called Righteous Sword."

"Righteous Sword?"

"Yeah." The kid shook his head. "I'm not into that, man."

"No," said Bill. "Neither am I."

"You're sensei's twin, aren't you?"

"We're distantly related."

"No, he's your twin."

"The sensei said you have special gifts."

"Ever since I was a kid. It hasn't done me a lot of good."

"Have you tried developing them?"

"I've stayed with gurus, psychics, warlocks. You name it. A lot of strange people."

"You didn't like them?"

"No, I didn't like them."

"Where are you from?"

"Montana."

"What do your parents do?"

"They're cattle ranchers."

They rode in silence the remaining miles until the Jeep came to a stop at the junction with Highway 93.

"Here you are," Bill said.

"Thanks," the kid said. He got out and lifted his heavy pack from the backseat.

"You're right about me and the sensei," the man said. "We are twins. But officially, he died in Viet Nam in '68."

"He deserted?"

"In a manner of speaking. He did desert his two baby daughters and I'm raising them."

"So, what is this really all about? What's Righteous Sword?"

"I'd rather you didn't call it that," Bill said. "This program is unnamed. Its reason for being is to combat communism within our nation's borders."

"Why did sensei let me in?"

"He sees something in you. So do I. I have an official program, but it is very selective. I look for people with extra-sensory perception and paranormal abilities."

"What do you train them to do?"

"I can't say. Tell me, young man, do you do hallucinogens?"

"I have."

"You would fit right in." Bill reached into his wallet and pulled out a card. "Here," he said, handing it to the kid. "My number is on this. If you're in eastern Virginia or D.C., give me a call." The man gave a little goodbye salute and drove off.

The kid looked at the card. It had the initials W.A.H. on one side and a phone number on the other.

Three days later, Ezra Riley was on an exit ramp of Interstate 27 south of Amarillo, Texas. The day was warm, and there was little traffic.

After an hour, a red Ford Fairlane slowed, and he saw the driver carefully checking him out. She pulled over and stopped.

Ezra grabbed his pack and walked to the car.

The woman rolled down the passenger window. "I don't normally pick up hitchhikers," she said.

Ezra hesitated, not knowing if he was welcome or not.

"Get in, get in," she said.

After putting his backpack in the back, Ezra took a seat in the front.

"Thank you," he said.

The woman was about thirty but looked older. She was tall and skinny, and her dark hair was knotted in a tight bun. She was the religious type, Ezra guessed.

"I've never picked up a hitchhiker in my life," the woman said. "But, the Lord told me to pick you up."

Oh-oh, thought Ezra.

"What's your name, young man?"

"Ezra Riley."

"Ezra? That's a Biblical name."

"I know."

The woman stared straight ahead. "The Lord has a word for you, Ezra Riley."

Ezra stayed quiet.

"You have a gift that will make room for you and bring you before great men."

She waited for Ezra to comment, but he didn't.

"That's Proverbs 18:16."

Ezra nodded.

The woman drove several miles. Then she added: "John the Baptist had a gift and it brought him before a king. The king cut off his head."

Ahead, Ezra saw an exit to a small town. He was hoping the woman would stop and let him out.

She did.

Before he could thank her for the short ride, she looked at him intently and said, "My name is Imogene Browne. If you ever want to know more about Jesus look me up. I live in Plainview, Texas."

1978

On a bitterly cold November day, Ezra Riley was on a bus returning to Miles City, Montana, for his father's funeral. Because of the weather, he'd left his wife, Anne, and their baby boy, Dylan, in California.

Ezra was anxious. He was the hippy returning to a grief-stricken mother, two sisters, and two surviving uncles to bury the father he never really knew.

Exhausted, he falls asleep.

In his sleep, he dreams.

He is alone in the ranch badlands when he sees an object on the distant skyline.

The object is coming toward him.

It is a coyote.

The coyote has no fear.

It approaches him with glaring yellow eyes.

It is evil.

Ezra is gripped in fear and cannot move.

The coyote comes close, and Ezra feels its hot breath.

The coyote speaks: "I own the land," it says. "And I shall soon own you."

1

Monday, November 1
Washington, D.C.

Davis Browne turned his collar up against the November chill and decided to take one more walk around the tree-lined block. The note he'd found in his locked office at American University that morning had made him cautious. Who used paper messages anymore? People who didn't trust the Internet, that's who.

The note read: Kafe Krazee, 10 o'clock, backroom.

Nothing on his desk had been disturbed, and the drop of Superglue on the drawer holding his Colt Combat Elite .45 was intact. He chided himself for being predictable. Every weekday at 10, he left the university and briskly walked eight blocks to this no-Wi-Fi coffee shop. The spacious front room—lit by large windows and crowded with plants—was popular with college students who found the unwired setting rebelliously fashionable. The backroom, quiet and windowless, was unofficially reserved for faculty. Browne made the trek daily to unhinge his damaged knees and fuel up on a single dark mocha.

Another reconnoiter completed, he stopped next to the shop to surveil his background in the window's reflection. A dark blue Lincoln Navigator parked on a side street caught his eye. Its windows were tinted, but Browne could make out a large, male form in the driver's seat. He sensed the driver staring at him. The SUV didn't sag on its axles, so Browne guessed it wasn't armored. Other than this, the usual customers and pedestrians busied the street: students, professors, a stray businessperson or two, city maintenance workers, and harried mothers with a need for caffeine. He glanced at his own reflection: clean-shaven, thinning blond hair, pale, calculating blue eyes. He thought by not wearing sunglasses, he'd appear more benign, but he didn't. He still looked like a government intelligence agent, even if he were an unemployed one.

At five minutes after 10, he walked into the shop, nodded at the baristas, mouthed *my usual*, and parted a sheer curtain open to the backroom. Four people sat singularly at scattered tables. Three were obviously professors. The fourth was a middle-aged woman whose stress was solvent. She had to be the contact. He went to her table and took a seat in a wrought iron chair.

"Good morning, Mr. Browne," the woman said. She did not offer her name. She looked like someone who badly needed a cigarette but never smoked.

"Good morning," Browne said. The woman's face was familiar, but he couldn't place her. She was short, buxom, and stylishly dressed in a black sweater and a gray tweed skirt and jacket. Her hair was tinted a light brown, and she wore reading glasses. Early fifties, he guessed. He knew better than to ask her name. The "lady in gray" would suffice for now.

"You wanted to see me?" Browne asked quietly.

"I understand you do some consulting," she said.

"When I have time. I'm employed at the university."

"No," she corrected him. "You have an office at the university. You do research and substitute teaching while you wait for a position to open up, but your last real job was at Homeland Security Investigations, and that ended a while ago."

Her acerbic tone helped him place her. She was an unofficial advisor to the United States President, a patron and power broker who stayed off-camera and behind the scenes. "The previous administration eliminated my DHS position," he said.

"That position is being restructured, but I am not here to debate your career status, Mr. Browne. I have an immediate situation that requires travel and discretion."

"You have my attention."

"Have you seen POTUS on television recently?"

"I try not to watch television."

"Have you heard rumors?"

"Some say he's not looking well."

A barista brought Browne's mocha and started to ask if he wanted anything else, but a sharp look from the lady warned her away.

"The President is well," the woman said. "But, he's exhausted. He's had the same reoccurring dream the past eight nights."

"Nightmares?" Browne asked. "Eight nights in a row?"

"Perhaps not a nightmare, no one knows. The President refuses to share the dream's content with his staff. But, it is disturbing and keeps him awake."

Browne cut her off. "I am not a psychoanalyst."

"One has been tried with no success."

"He has his own medical doctor. Surely he's been given something to help him sleep."

"Sleeping pills don't stop the dreams. They only make him more disoriented in the morning."

"There are plenty of psychics—"

"Not an option," she said curtly. "Bad optics."

"Preachers?"

"He's been prayed for."

"Hypnotists?"

She shook her head. "Not a consideration for security reasons."

Browne sipped his mocha and leaned back in his chair. "So, what do you want from me?"

"First of all, silence. This meeting did not happen. Should you take the assignment, you will speak to no one about it. And, if you don't take it, you will not talk about it."

He understood the threat. "Go on," he said.

She slid a folder across the table to him. As files go, it was thin: a quarter-inch thick. "This would be humorous if matters were less desperate," she said.

Browne laid a hand on the folder without opening it. "Who's in this?" he asked.

"A rancher in Montana."

He smiled. "And this pertains to the President's dreams? You have to be kidding."

"I wish I were." The lady looked at Browne thoughtfully. "I have an older sister," she explained. "In an anxious moment, I confided in her. She's an evangelical Christian. The emotional type."

"A Charismatic?"

"Yes, one of those. She follows preachers on the Internet and jets around the country to their conferences. My sister thinks the man in that folder can help."

"How so?" Browne asked.

"She says he has a gift for interpreting dreams."

"A cowboy in Montana?"

"He's a writer, too, it seems. He has had some minor work published."

"But still," Browne said, holding up the file. "A cowboy in Montana?"

"My sister is zealous, Mr. Browne, but sincere. I trust her."

And you are very *desperate,* Browne thought. He drummed his fingers on the file. "You want me to fly to Montana and check this guy out?"

"A private jet is waiting at Hyde Field."

"I don't know—"

"You will be compensated generously." She paused and arched her eyebrows. "And your daughter's tuition at Bennington is not inexpensive."

Browne frowned. The mentioning of family members was not fair play. "My standard rate is a thousand a day," he said. "But, this is hardly a standard case."

"Name it," she said coolly.

"Twenty."

"Done," she said. "If he seems legitimate, get him on the plane. But vet him all the way back. If you have doubts at any time, tell the pilots to turn back."

"You want him brought to the White House?"

"I will personally escort him."

"By tonight?"

"This evening."

"What if he isn't home?"

"He's home," the lady said. "We've had eyes on him."

Drones or satellite? Browne wondered.

"And he is alone," the lady continued. "His wife boarded a plane this morning for Brazil. It seems their third grandchild has just arrived. She'll be in Rio for two weeks."

Browne stared at the folder. He didn't mind flying to Montana. He had little to do at the university.

"If you do this, the administration will be in your debt," the lady said.

"And if it doesn't work out the way you want?"

"We will note that you are a team player, and you keep the $20,000."

Browne held up the folder again. "It's thin," he said.

"The basics are there. Tax information, credit card receipts, medical records. You will be hindered some in that he doesn't use a cell phone."

"No coverage where he lives?"

"Limited, I'm told. Consequently, this individual has no Smart devices at all, nor is he on social media."

"Not even Facebook?"

She shook her head. "Nothing. He's old school."

"He sounds like a dinosaur. How do we know the President will even meet with this *dream interpreter?*"

"I have influence."

"What if this cowboy doesn't want to go to the White House?"

"No coercion, he doesn't have to come. But if you believe he is legitimate, be as persuasive as you can be."

Browne nodded. Any easy $20,000, he thought, no matter how one looked at it.

"The issue of discretion applies to him as well. He must be made aware of that."

"I understand."

"There are concerns," the lady said, nodding at the folder. "The past few years, he's purchased a lot of ammunition, and it is Montana, after all. Make sure he has no ties to white supremacists, militias, or survivalist cults."

"That's what I do best," Browne said.

She slid a package across the table. "This is an encrypted sat phone. Keep your personal cell phone turned off."

"I don't have it with me."

"And your pistol?"

How did she know about it? he wondered. "Still in my desk," he said pointedly.

"Stay at this table for five minutes after I leave," the gray lady said. "When you go outside, an Uber driver will be waiting for you."

"I didn't bring anything with me. My laptop…"

"You won't need it. Everything you require is on the aircraft. My number is encoded into the phone. Call me as necessary."

He watched her rise and walk away. She was a compact package of gravitas, Browne thought. Someone who could make heads roll.

Browne finished his mocha and smiled. How a day could suddenly change. Now, who was this cowboy grandpa with the supernatural gifts?

He opened the folder.

A title page read: "Ezra Riley—Miles City, Montana—USA—b. 1952"

On the next page was a photo of a man on a horse.

2

Monday, November 1

Eastern Montana

Some said Ezra Riley could track a gnat through a sandstorm, but Ezra was not after a gnat. He was pursuing his favorite cow, and when he found her, he'd shoot her.

He called her the Wildebeest because she resembled the sub-Saharan antelope: short, thick horns twisting up like corkscrews from an oversized head with a thin fringe of hair dangling from her scrawny brindled neck. She was a mixture of three exotic cattle breeds: Corriente, Longhorn, and Scottish Highlander.

And she was a schizophrenic psychopath.

When the Wildebeest wanted to be gentle, you could scratch her back and feed her by hand. But, with her calf's safety at risk, she was as cunning as a coyote and meaner than a sackful of badgers.

Wildebeest first came to the Riley ranch after escaping a neighboring ranchette. After returning her three times, Ezra bought the cow and stamped his wife's brand on her as a joke.

The Wildebeest soon became a ranch favorite for her quirky personality and penchant for raising big calves. With each passing year, she became more skilled at hiding her babies during branding and shipping.

Ezra's other calves had now been weaned for a week, but he hadn't seen the Wildebeest and her calf for a month.

With Anne in Brazil, now was his time to find the Wildebeest, wean her last calf, and humanely put her down. Putting her through the sales ring was not a consideration. Her bones deserved to decorate the badlands.

Ezra pulled his big bay, Simon, to a stop on a high butte. A .30-30 Winchester carbine was scabbarded under his off-side leg, and a forty-foot nylon rope was strapped to the saddle's fork. A backup lariat was tied by rear saddle strings, and his cantle pack held a foot-rope, a small pair of binoculars, and a Smith & Wesson .22 revolver loaded with bird shot. A set of hobbles hung from a D-ring on his back cinch, and an extra pair circled Simon's neck. Every tool had a purpose, and he looked like a man riding to war.

Ezra shivered. The November day was pleasant, but there was *something* in the air.

He knew *something* was an impotent noun, but how else could he describe it? *Something* was coming. Of course, winter was coming. This was Montana, and weathermen, calendars, almanacs, and Ezra's aching joints warned that winter's promise was impeachable. After a scorching summer drought with triple-digit temperatures and suffocating dust and smoke, winter—as long and bitter as it might be—seemed like a respite. But, it seldom was. More often than not, winter brought months of snow and below-zero temperatures stretching into April.

Ezra stepped off his big horse to relieve himself. An enlarged prostate was a significant annoyance for an older cowboy on a tall horse. Simon rubbed Ezra's shoulder with his head. Ezra relieved himself, zipped up, ran two fingers under the headstall, and vigorously scratched behind the horse's on-side ear. Simon leaned into his hand.

"What do you think, Simon?" Ezra asked. "Do we find the Wildebeest today?" The bay answered by lifting his muzzle as an invitation to be scratched under the jaw. Ezra complied.

Ezra could not believe his luck. He'd been horseback since seven that morning, and now, six hours later, he'd hit the fresh tracks of a cow and calf in the roughs of Crooked Creek, an area he referred to as The Gumbo Jungle. The breaks were not tall and majestic here;

they were bleak and blunt. The land lay like mounds of coiled serpents with little definition between one and another. Some grew thickets of black sage, others were dotted with bristly greasewood, and all were veined by deep washes.

Ezra smiled. As he had no cattle pastured here, the tracks had to belong to the fugitives.

The calf was the problem. It needed to be corralled and weaned. If it was only the cow, Ezra might chase her down and put a merciful bullet between her eyes. He and his wife, Anne, loved the old girl, but with her teeth worn to the gums, she'd never make it through another rough Montana winter. A quick death was better than being bothered into a snowbank by coyotes and eaten alive.

He spotted movement in the distance. It was the Wildebeest running the Crooked Creek fence line. Her big steer followed awkwardly, spittle hanging in silver threads from its lips.

The fence was as tight as banjo strings, and Wildebeest was frustrated. She was too old to leap the four barbed strands.

Turn south, Ezra told her. *And I will beat you to the gate in Skeleton Coulee.*

She turned south.

Ezra nudged Simon into an enthusiastic lope. At Skeleton Coulee, Ezra dismounted, threw the gate open, remounted, and pointed the big bay toward Bobcat Flat. Simon snorted with disgust. Ezra poked him with his spurs, and the horse began lunging up the gumbo and sandstone slope. At the top, Simon's sides heaved like bellows. Ezra gave him his head and let him blow. "Sorry about that, ole boy," he said. "But, I promise you, this is the last year we chase the Wildebeest."

Moments later, the cow and calf appeared trotting eastward on the fence line. Fifty yards from the gate, Wildebeest stopped, stared at the horse and rider on the hill, then turned her head and gazed north.

Don't go that way, Ezra told her. *You might escape, but your calf will die trying to follow you.*

The cow looked back at her panting calf, then up again at Ezra and Simon. She chose the open gate.

Ezra patted Simon's neck. "We just might get her, big boy," he said.

He slid the horse downhill on its hocks. Horse and rider went through the gate, and Ezra didn't take time to close it.

Wildebeest is exhausted and lost, he thought. The game was all but over, and Ezra was sad to see it end.

He shadowed the pair from a graveled ridge as they trotted to Sunday Creek. Simon's chest was splattered with lather like the foam on a mug of beer.

The cow turned south at Sunday Creek as if pulled by a string to the Riley corrals.

Go through the next open gate and into the arena, Ezra commanded silently. He was lucky. She did.

Ezra gave Simon his head, and the giant bay took the bit and charged down the hill, through the creek and toward the gate. If Ezra could get the gate closed, the high woven-wire fence around the arena would hold her.

At the far end of the arena, another gate opened to pens constructed of bridge planking, telephone poles, and railroad ties. Ezra's father, Johnny Riley, had built them decades before to hold wild horses he sold as bucking stock. Ezra had kept them maintained.

Everything was working fine. As Ezra approached the open gate, he saw the cow and calf at the arena's end, almost entering the corrals.

Then, suddenly, a man appeared in the opening.

One man stood like an apparition in front of the trotting horned cow and her calf. The man froze. Wildebeest crested her neck and tucked her nose to charge.

"Get out of the way!" Ezra shouted at the stranger.

3

An hour earlier, a Gulfstream G200 touched down at the airport north of Miles City. While the jet was refueled, Browne took a taxi the three miles to the Riley ranch.

He looked for dogs when he got out of the cab in the ranch yard, but none were in sight. Browne knocked loudly on the house's front door, got no response, so he tried the knob and found the home unlocked.

"Hello," he called out. "Is anyone here?"

No answer. Perfect. He went in.

The house felt lived-in. Photos, mostly landscapes, covered the walls. Browne remembered that the rancher was a photographer as well as a writer.

The day's mail was lying on the kitchen table. Nothing of particular interest there, so he moved to the bookshelves. If you wanted to know about people, look at what they read.

Ezra and Anne Riley were book people. In the living room, two bookcases of hardcovers on holistic health. Those would be Anne's.

Another room by the back door held a wood stove, more photos, a couch and recliner, and a large bookcase with five shelves. Paperback fiction was on top, followed by hardcover fiction, various paperback Christian books, hardcover Christian books, and a row of nature books. He paid close attention to the religious texts: intercessory prayer, worship, inner healing, spiritual warfare, prophetic ministry, dreams, and visions. He was familiar with most of the books. His mother owned many of them.

Browne located the stairs to the basement. Here he found Ezra Riley's office. It was smaller than he'd imagined, with walls dominated again by bookcases and photos. Overflows of books were stacked in the room's corners. Their subject was primarily western history.

In a guest bedroom, he found more bookcases and a gun safe. He scanned the books first. All were on ministry topics. He noted the authors, filing the names in his photographic memory, then moved to the safe. The vault door was closed, but the angle of the handle suggested it wasn't locked. He pivoted the handle, and the door swung open. Inside was what his research had told him to expect: a row of lever-action rifles. Cowboy guns. All were working, functional firearms: Henrys, Marlins, Winchesters, a Rossi, and a Mossberg. An empty slot indicated one long rifle was missing. Also in the safe were three revolvers, a Ruger SP101 in .357 Magnum, a Taurus Tracker in .22 WLR, and a Colt .38. Riley, Browne noted curiously, did not appear to own a single semi-automatic.

Not wanting to be caught in the house, he moved outside. It was a typical ranch yard except for the lack of machinery. The Rileys were not farmers. Parked by the corrals was a 1978 Ford pickup, and Browne couldn't help but admire it. You didn't see such old trucks every day, and this one was apparently in running condition. He moved to an old bunkhouse. It had a porch built of thick planking and a roof supported by tall, twisted cedar posts. Nice touch, he thought. He opened the door to more books on shelves built from corral planks. He scanned the authors: Wendell Berry, Larry Woiwode, Tom McGuane, Ivan Doig, James Lee Burke, Vince Flynn, Will James, Charley Russell, Ernest Thompson Seton, Edgar Rice Burroughs, Frank Dobie, and more, many more. Ezra Riley's reading was prolific and eclectic. He didn't find more guns, nor militia material of any sort.

He left the bunkhouse and went to the barn. On the ground level, he found an enclosed tack room. Bridles, bits, lariats, and other assorted tack hung on the walls above four saddle-stands. One stand held a pile of saddle pads, and two had dusty saddles, but the rack nearest the door was bare. Riley, Browne reasoned, was horseback in the hills.

This presented a problem. Should he return to the airport and have the pilots look for him? His topo map of the Riley ranch suggested miles of rough country. Riley could be hard to find.

Good Lord, I hope he comes back soon.

He got his wish faster than he expected. Browne heard a noise from behind the corrals, so he jogged stiffly through the pens to an open gate that accessed an arena.

His eyes widened as he stepped into the open space. Coming at him was the strangest animal he'd ever seen. It was a cow, he thought, but he wasn't sure. It had a long, narrow head, horns that twisted upward, and fire in its eyes. A slobbering calf, its head bobbing with exhaustion, lumbered beside it.

"Get out of the way!" he heard someone yell, and Browne jumped behind the open gate.

Wildebeest came to a stiff-legged stop, stared at the gate, shook her horned head, wheeled on her hind feet, and stampeded back to the arena's opening.

Ezra spurred Simon to the gate. Simon, sensing the horned cow's charge, pranced nervously. From the saddle, Ezra fumbled with the gate's chain latch.

"Dang it, Simon, hold still," Ezra said. He got the chain free, gripped the gate, and wheeled the horse, trying to swing the gate closed.

The cow was upon them, horns down and aiming.

Simon yielded space and gave the cow the opening. Hooking at the bay as she raced by, one horn snagged the stirrup and nearly tore Ezra from the saddle.

The horse spun in a circle, collected itself, and stood, trembling. Ezra could only watch helplessly as Wildebeest and her calf escaped.

A long, hard ride for nothing. He had the cow and calf, and then he didn't. All because of some stranger.

Ezra turned Simon toward the man at the far end of the arena. Raw energy radiated in waves from both horse and rider.

The stranger stepped out to meet Ezra. He wore khaki pants, a polo shirt, and a lightweight MA-1 flight jacket.

Ezra pulled Simon to a stop. "Who the hell are you?" he demanded. "And what do you think you're doing?"

The man held one hand up. "Please," he said. "Step off your horse, Mr. Riley. We need to talk. It's a matter of national security."

4

The two men appraised each other.

Browne saw a clean-shaven cowboy who could pass for a decade less than his years. He seemed fit—Browne knew Riley had been a martial artist, weightlifter, and runner when younger—but he'd thickened some with age. He looked like the hills from which he'd ridden: a face burnt cedar red; short hair a sagebrush gray; cheeks as smooth as prairie except for crow's feet, deep as ravines, spreading from the corners of intense brown eyes. Angry eyes, at the moment.

Riley was no soft-skinned Sunday preacher.

Ezra saw a man brimming with arrogance, military without the starch, and exuding authority. A cop of some sort. Lean and muscled, but stiff.

"Who are you?" Ezra demanded. He remained horseback because being mounted had its advantages.

"My name is Davis Browne," the man said. "I am here in the interests of the government."

"Credentials?"

"I'm a civilian consultant. I have nothing besides a driver's license."

"Are you carrying?"

Browne opened his jacket wide. "I'm not armed, Mr. Riley. I apologize for the intrusion, but this is a serious matter concerning the President of the United States."

Ezra frowned, then scanned the yard. "Where's your car?"

"I took a cab." He saw Ezra's dubious look. "From the airport," he added. "A private jet is waiting for us there."

"Us?"

"Yes. Give me ten minutes at your kitchen table," Browne said. "If you do not believe me, I'll be on my way. But, if you do, you might be in the White House with the President this evening."

In the White House with the President? The guy had to be a nut, Ezra thought.

"I'm not in the mood for this," he said.

Browne shook his head. "This is very real, Mr. Riley. I am who I say I am, and I need a few minutes of your time."

In my house? Ezra lowered his right hand to the walnut stock of his .30-30.

The stranger noticed the movement and subtly shook his head.

"No need for that," he said.

Ezra didn't answer.

"Ten minutes," Browne said.

The writer in Ezra was intrigued. "Okay, but I have to take care of my horse first."

"That's fine. I'll wait here."

Ezra led Simon to the barn and unsaddled the big bay. The horse shook its muscled body, then rolled in the dust while Ezra poured a can of grain in a tub.

The cowboy looked at the agent and nodded toward the house.

Browne took a seat at the kitchen table.

Ezra grabbed a Michelob Amber Bock from the refrigerator. "Want one?" he asked. Browne declined.

Ezra sat down opposite him. He'd removed his jacket, but not his hat, chaps, boots, black scarf, or spurs. "So," he said. "What's this about?"

Browne got to the point. "I understand you interpret dreams."

Ezra frowned. "This is about dreams?"

"Believe me, Mr. Riley, I am as surprised by this as you are. It seems the President has had a reoccurring and disturbing dream. He's hardly slept for eight nights."

Ezra's eyes widened. Eight nights? "How did anyone hear about me?"

"I'm not at liberty to explain that, but you do interpret dreams, don't you?"

"I have in the past."

"Does that mean you don't do it anymore?"

"Not like I used to. Maybe a few times a year."

"Would you be willing to fly to Washington and see the President?"

Ezra laughed. "Right now?"

"Right now. Before the President goes to bed."

"We can get there that fast?"

"It's a three-hour flight for a Gulfstream G200. It cruises at 530 miles-per-hour." Browne watched Ezra calmly process the situation. He was intrigued by the old cowboy's lack of surprise.

"I'll go," Ezra said plainly.

"It's not quite that simple. First, I have to vet you. And, none of this is happening. You can tell no one about this."

"Not even my wife?"

"Discussing this on a phone call to Brazil is not a good idea."

Ezra's eyebrows raised. "You know where Anne is?"

"Where she is *going*, actually," Browne said. "And congratulations on the third grandchild."

Ezra frowned. "What else do you know?"

"You had a few scrapes with the law when you were a young hippy hitchhiking around the country. Do you maintain any radical ties?"

"That was the '70s. Everyone was radical."

"No drug use anymore?"

"Not for decades."

"There is some concern about your stockpile of guns and ammunition—it appears you like lever-action rifles and revolvers." Browne did not admit he'd already been in the house.

"Yes, I like lever-action rifles and revolvers."

"No semi-automatics?"

"Too hard to clean."

Browne changed course. "I'm curious about your writing. You've published five novels, a collection of essays on ranch life, and a book about western history. But no books on dream interpretation."

Ezra shrugged. "I don't consider myself an expert on the subject."

"You used to speak several times a year at religious conferences. You don't anymore. Why?"

"I don't like flying." Ezra took a long drink from a chilled glass. The dark ale cut the dust from the day. "Airports depress me."

"Who do you interpret dreams for?"

"A few friends."

"Would I be correct in saying these friends are prominent in national ministry?"

Ezra looked at him warily. The fact that he was close to several notable Christian leaders was not well-known. "For friends," he repeated.

"You should know there is no financial payment involved in this."

"That's fine with me."

"Are you willing to go?"

"I am."

"You don't seem especially impressed with this situation, Mr. Riley."

Ezra shrugged. In his mind, he was still pursuing the Wildebeest in the hills. "I've not been impressed by much for a long time."

"Did you vote for the President?"

"I did not."

Browne, of course, knew that. "Do you still hold any ministry credentials?" he asked.

"Not anymore."

"Why not?"

"No need."

"Do you belong to any organizations? For example, are you a member of the Republican Party?"

"I belong to the American Quarter Horse Association and the NRA."

Browne smiled. "I already knew about those two. Are there any associations you belong to that I may not know about?"

Ezra finished his beer. "I'm not a joiner."

"Are you involved with any militias?"

"No."

"Would you tell me if you were?"

"Yes."

Browne looked at his watch. "I am putting you on the plane, Mr. Riley. But, I have the discretion to disqualify you at any time."

"I should take a shower."

"You can freshen up on the jet. There are plenty of toiletries."

"But my clothes—"

"Don't worry. From what I understand, the President's appearance is worse than yours, but you could remove the chaps and spurs."

Ezra peeled off his shotgun chaps and unbuckled his spurs.

"Pocketknife, too," Browne said.

Ezra laid his quick-assist Kershaw on the table.

"I am surprised by your lack of excitement, Mr. Riley."

"At my age, I take things as they come."

"You'd rather be chasing that odd-looking cow?"

Ezra nodded.

Browne smiled. "Your priorities are fascinating, Mr. Riley."

"Cows and horses, Mr. Browne," Ezra replied. "Cows and horses."

5

The interior of the Gulfstream was opulent: plush leather, stainless steel, chrome, and mahogany. Two sets of chairs faced each other, each holding what Ezra believed was called an information station. A kitchenette, lavatory, and large couch completed the cabin. Browne directed Ezra to a chair, then took the one opposite him. They strapped themselves in.

Browne took a file folder from a leather briefcase. "Before we take off, I need you to sign this. It's just a standard non-disclosure form," he said. He handed a sheet of paper and a pen to Ezra. "By signing this, you agree never to talk about this evening to anyone, nor write any articles or books implying this occasion took place."

Ezra paused, stared at Browne, then signed the paper.

Browne pressed a button on the cabin's wall. "We are good to go," he told the pilots. The jet powered up and began taxiing down the runway. Browne put the paper away.

Ezra looked out a window, hoping to glimpse the Wildebeest if the jet banked over the ranch. A sighting might save him time, for whatever happened this evening, he'd be horseback again in the morning.

Browne took a notepad from his briefcase. "We need to continue our talk."

"With all due respect, tell me about yourself first," Ezra asked.

"What?"

"The more I know about you, the more you will learn from me."

"That's not how this works."

"Do you have something to hide?"

Browne shrugged. "Okay. Briefly. I was raised in Texas, an only child. My late father had a vending machine route. My mother, who is alive and living on her own, was a homemaker. I'm a graduate of the Air Force Academy with a bachelor's in criminal justice. I served eight years, then resigned my commission and went to Duke University, where I got my master's."

"What happened to your knees?"

Browne smiled. "That's very astute, Mr. Riley. I try to hide the stiffness. I joined a parachute club at the Academy. On my first jump, my knees blew apart when I landed. I've had seven operations. Four on the left knee, three on the right."

"Yet, you served."

"Desk duty. That's the reason I got out."

"What's your master's in? Psychology?"

"I'd rather not say."

Ezra gave him a hard stare. "And what type of work have you done the past few years?"

Browne's smile was thin and tight. "We're not going there, Mr. Riley. This situation is not about me. It's about you. And I get paid whether I clear you or not."

"And you need the money," Ezra said.

"Everyone needs money."

"But, you need it because of Atlantic City."

The color drained from Browne's face. "How did you know that?"

"You have a gambling problem."

"How did you—"

"You came for a person with gifts, didn't you?"

"How do I know this a spiritual revelation?"

"I'm an old cowboy, Mr. Browne. You can't believe I have access to your personal information through human or electronic sources."

"This is just weird," Browne said.

"This entire trip is weird, so let's assume I'm gifted, but am I mentally balanced? That's the question, isn't it?"

"Yes, it is."

Ezra enjoyed seeing Browne off-balance.

"You think you should be lucky," Ezra continued. "This leads you to the gambling tables, but you haven't been lucky, have you?"

"I'm not sure you should see the President."

"But you want me to because you want favor with this White House."

Browne glanced at the satellite phone on the stand beside his chair. He was tempted to call the lady in gray. This was not turning out as he expected.

"I don't know who's on the other end of that satellite phone," Ezra said. "But, if you make the call, will it really change anything?"

"What do you mean? I can tell the pilots to turn back," Browne insisted.

"You can," Ezra admitted. "But you won't."

"My money is guaranteed."

"Yes, but you're a high-stakes gambler, Mr. Browne. You're not used to folding early."

Browne had no retort. The old cowboy was right. To end the game now was too simple; it could cancel future employment possibilities and leave this story unfinished. He stared out the window at a black void as the Gulfstream glided eastward as silently as an arrow.

"Will you treat the President with respect?" Browne asked.

"Yes."

"Why should I believe that?"

"Because I respect the office, if not the man," Ezra said.

And I respect the One who has given me the gifts, he thought but did not say.

6

The gray lady did not look out the windows as the Sikorsky S-76C helicopter touched down in remote western Virginia.

The few visitors to this secluded estate, set like an island in a sea of state forest lands, knew the rules. It was allowable to view the granite manor, stables, and swimming pool, but it was forbidden to peer north into the thick evergreens.

The lady knew what was behind the veil of trees. Above ground were satellite dishes and antennas, but below the Virginia soil was a complex containing a gymnasium, living quarters, and a small "chapel." The chapel had gold-plated walls and a pyramid-shaped quartz crystal from Malaysia that stood nine feet tall and weighed six thousand pounds.

This subterranean sanctuary is where Blue Man lived. The lady in gray had never seen him. She hoped not to but knew it was inevitable that she would.

She walked briskly from the helipad to the house, entered without knocking, and traveled down a marbled hallway to a large study behind oak doors. She felt small under the towering mahogany bookcases, Oriental tapestries, and mounted heads of wild sheep and goats that stared down with yellow glass eyes. She seated herself in an ebony chair with crushed velvet padding and waited.

Moments later, a slender, elderly man, supported by a cane carved from African Blackwood, entered silently and took a chair across from her. His thinning silver hair was oiled and combed back; his eyes were a watery blue.

"Your man is in the air?" William Anderson Hall asked.

"He is."

"Does anyone know the content of the dream yet?"

"No, and I have to be careful not to inquire."

"Do you believe the President will share the dream with Riley?"

"I think so. There is growing desperation amongst the staff."

"Blue Man is unsettled."

"Unsettled? Does he know the dream?"

"No, it doesn't work that way. He is concerned about Mr. Riley."

The gray lady was surprised. "He doesn't, I mean, *you* don't believe this cowboy is for real?" she asked.

"You doubt your sister's evaluation?"

"She's sincere but prone to hyperbole."

"Blue Man isn't, and he is restless."

"But, Riley is a nobody."

"A nobody? How is it he has the ears of several influential preachers in the nation?"

"Perhaps they find him entertaining?"

"Or perhaps he's accurate."

Hall's concerns bothered the lady. "If this cowboy interprets the dream, isn't that what we want?" she asked.

"Yes, we need to know the dream."

"And Riley's interpretation?"

"Only if it is correct, and who would know? The dream itself is crucial. Riley is only a tool."

"But, the President has been very secretive, and Riley has signed a confidentiality contract."

"You must be in the room when Riley is told the dream."

"In the room? I can't guarantee that."

"You are the person delivering the interpreter."

"Yes, but I'm not *that* close to the President. He hasn't told the dream to his chief of staff. I don't think he's even told the First Lady."

The old man sighed deeply, but the exhale was hardly heard.

"This could be a problem," he said. "Blue Man provokes nightmares by activating repressed memories and anxieties. Judging by the President's reactions and secretiveness, whatever is buried in his subconscious is serious and, therefore, of value to us. We don't have to know the dream, but it would be beneficial."

"If we don't learn the dream, what was this all for?"

"It was a field test for Blue Man, and he has proven his worth."

"Then do we even need Riley now? Should I have the plane turn back?"

"No, no. There is still a chance we can benefit. I am actually interested in Riley's interpretation, and who knows, perhaps the President will allow you to stay in the room. We have to let it play out."

Hall brought an arthritic hand, lined with lavender blood vessels, to a forehead speckled with liver spots, then waved the hand as if shooing a fly.

"But, Browne is another matter," he said. "We have a lot invested in Browne, but there is a time to cut one's losses."

"Immediately?"

"No, we will play him a while longer. He may be of further use." He closed his eyes as if resting.

The lady rose and left. She did not need to be told when a meeting was over.

Moments later, a soft rap sounded on the study door.

"Come in," Hall said softly.

A lithe form entered and seemed to glide across the floor to a chair in the shadows. Blue Man moved as lightly as lint.

"Are you feeling okay?" Hall asked.

A barely perceptible nod came from the head in the shadows.

"I need you to shift focus."

Another nod.

"In a few more hours, Mr. Riley will be meeting the President. Starting now, please concentrate on Davis Browne. Can you do that?"

A nod.

"And some focus on this cowboy, as well?"

Another nod.

The old man gestured, and Blue Man rose and moved like air toward the door. As his hand, the color of glacial ice, touched the handle, the old man's voice came from behind him.

"I am very proud of you," Hall said. "Very proud."

Blue Man nodded and left.

7

On the eastbound jet.

"What are you thinking?" Ezra asked.

"Excuse me," Browne said.

"You seem lost in thought."

"Nothing important," Browne said, looking down at the blank note tablet.

Ezra smiled. "You want to get this job over with, don't you?"

Browne nodded. "Damn straight. You scare the hell out of me."

"You didn't expect that."

"From an old cowboy from Montana? Hardly. But, I have to continue questioning you."

"Your employer will want a full report?"

"Definitely."

"Let's keep your employer happy," Ezra said.

"Okay," Browne said. "Tell me why you have no denominational ties and seldom attend church in your hometown."

"The first question is easy. I believe the age of denominations is over."

"And the second?"

"Not so easy, and I am hesitant to go into details."

"That answer alone could cause me to disqualify you as a lone wolf."

"Your job is not to determine if I am a loner, but if I am a wolf."

"Are you?"

"No."

"Do wolves admit they're wolves?"

"Good point. But while I might make you uneasy, do you believe I'm delusional or deranged?"

"Delusional, possibly," Browne said. "But I have no reason to believe you're dangerous."

"Are my gifts real?"

"You've given me a taste."

"Would you like another?"

"Sure," Browne said. "Showing is better than telling."

"Then, let's discuss your mother."

Browne's head snapped back. "My mother?"

"Yes," Ezra said, and his weathered faced softened with compassion.

Browne's lower lip slightly trembled.

"Your tenth birthday," Ezra continued. "What is it about your mother and the day you turned ten?"

The exhausting day had caught up to Anne Riley. She was halfway through a thirteen-hour flight to Rio, and while she was excited to see her three grandchildren—Gabriella, Garris, and the new baby, Gavin—she was worried about her husband.

Ezra Riley could be so stubborn!

She had offered, again, to buy him a cell phone.

"You can buy me one, but I won't use it," he told her.

She'd begged him not to ride alone in the hills, particularly not to look for the Wildebeest.

"The old cow and her calf can wait until I get back," she'd insisted, but Ezra had only smiled.

It was a game, she realized. Every fall, the Wildebeest would disappear with her calf, and every fall, Ezra would ride until he captured them.

He was too old for games!

She sighed, leaned her chair back, and closed her eyes. She was saddened that Ezra was not with her. He'd not seen Gabriella since she was four, and she was now twelve. He'd not even met Garris, let alone Gavin.

Anne loved ranch life but hated the work toll. She and Ezra could never go anywhere together for more than a day or two. Anne's parents had never understood that. People didn't realize one couldn't leave a ranch and its livestock to tend to itself.

Not that Ezra liked traveling. He didn't. He preferred horses and cows to planes and people.

Some people need more than sagebrush. Dylan had said that when he graduated from college. It saddened Anne that their only child had come home but three times in twenty years. He and Kristen had lived in Rio de Janeiro for seven years and now talked about moving to Melbourne, Australia.

She wondered if Dylan was trying to stay as far from Eastern Montana as possible. He'd never liked the harsh environment of the Northern Great Plains. Forty below zero in the winter. One hundred in the shade in the summer. As one of the world's premier software creators, he could live wherever he chose, and Dylan liked big cities with temperate climates, concerts, fine restaurants, and exciting society.

Anne sighed, then slipped softly to sleep.

She did not stay there.

An image shook her awake.

Ezra, not on Simon, but in a plane.

And on the horizon, a dark cloud, shaped like a fist and poised to strike.

8

My mother looks like a witch, Davis Browne thought, *only taller than most.* He imagined the wicked witch in *The Wizard of Oz,* surrounded by imprisoned Munchkins.

Fourteen of his classmates were crowded into the small Browne home on a quiet street in Rockwall, Texas, and the boy's dream had become a nightmare.

He was awkward at ten: long legs, big hands and feet, buckteeth, and a sprouting cowlick at the back of his head that refused to bend to water, oil, or gel.

He hadn't any friends.

This tenth birthday party was his mother's attempt to provide them. She had designed and sent invitations to the twenty-nine kids in his class and even phoned parents, promising that presents weren't necessary, just their children's presence.

His father was on the road again, filling vending machines, practicing his preaching in the car, staying in cheap motels, and calling at precisely six o'clock in the evening to report in. Neither the son nor the wife worried about him. He was cautious, capable, and faithful. The father was not one to mess around with strange women, drink, or gamble. Howard Albright Browne was a staunch Southern Baptist who only desired another church of his own. He'd pastored two, and both had failed. As one council member had said, "Howard Browne is a good, solid man, but he couldn't preach water out of a garden hose if you turned the spigot for him."

His mother was a different matter. Imogene Archibald Browne could preach, teach, screech, play the piano and organ, and sing off-key with enthusiasm, and would have converted the pope to Protestantism if granted an audience. The same council member had said of her, "Imogene could suck the oxygen out of a dumpster fire."

The house was crowded that day, not just with children but with boxes. It was always filled with boxes: Amway, Avon, Mary Kay, Herbal Life, Tupperware, Shaklee, Nature's Sunshine. There was not a multi-level marketing company that didn't know Imogene Browne by her first name. She was fervent with all, successful with none.

Between the boxes of miracle cures and beauty aids were stacks of books and tapes. Hal Lindsey, Kenneth Copeland, Kenneth Hagin, and Jimmy Swaggart were her favorites. In this clutter, his mother seated his fourteen classmates on the floor and preached beginning in Deuteronomy, then skipped to Jude, Genesis, Esther, and Acts, and ended, naturally, in Revelation. In case their memories failed them, Xeroxed notes were handed out.

"You will remember this as the best day of your life," she told them.

The worst day of my life, thought ten-year-old Davis when he caught Heather Adams' eye, the one girl in the class who was kind to him. Her face was a study in misery. *Why me?* She seemed to cry out. *Why did you do this to me?*

His mother never saw him leave. The boy slipped out the back door and ran like a breeze for blocks, fighting back the tears, not knowing or caring where he was going. He ran to exhaustion, then staggered on. In the running, he found liberation. The oxygen coursing to his brain brought a strange and pleasurable peace. If he were to have no friends, "the run" would be his friend.

He ran daily after that. When his parents argued, he ran. When his mother's cassette player blared teachings, he ran. In middle school, a coach noticed him and coaxed him onto the cross country team. Davis was a standout. He trained with the high school varsity and repeatedly beat them. As a sophomore, he won district and divisional titles and placed second at state. Running, his coaches told him, would be his ticket to a good education. What, exactly, did he want to do?

A Discovery Channel program on skydiving provided the answer. He wanted to jump out of planes. An appointment to a military academy became his goal, and he did the applications himself, sending countless letters to his state's senators and courting help from high school administrators.

His parents saw his tenacity but misinterpreted it. "Our boy, Davis," he overheard his mother telling a neighbor, "will be a great preacher someday."

Davis becoming a preacher was one thing his parents agreed on, but they argued about the denomination.

His father wanted him to be Southern Baptist and dragged him to Baptist churches on Sunday mornings.

His mother insisted on the Pentecostal Assemblies and took him to Assembly services on Wednesday nights.

He found the Baptists stiff and boring. His cheeks grew raw from the pinches of blue-haired old ladies. His mother's church was a circus with a carousel of itinerant evangelists in white shoes, matching leather belts, and diamond pinkie rings. He imagined them returning to expensive hotel rooms, tall glasses of whiskey, and stacks of the congregants' cash.

When his military appointment was announced, his high school and the city were proud. Davis Browne, the standout harrier, was going to the United States Air Force Academy in Colorado Springs to compete in cross country and track.

For the first time in his memory, both parents were speechless. Neither suspected he was serious about the military.

If his tenth birthday had been the worst day of his life, the day he left for the Academy was his best. His parents insisted on driving him, and they argued the entire way, but Davis didn't hear them. In his mind, he sailed under silken parachutes while gazing down on colorful continents and rippling seas. These would be his overseas assignments, all painted in the primary colors he'd studied on globes.

Istanbul, Turkey, his orders might read.

How far was that from Plainview, Texas? Davis would ask.

Not far enough. Not even the moon could be far enough.

9

When Ezra Riley mentioned the birthday party, Browne had closed his eyes to defuse his emotions. His eyes popped open now. "How did you do that?" he said.

The rancher was surprised at the question. "Do what?" Ezra asked.

"You made me live it?"

"Live what?"

"I was there. I could see it all again in vivid colors. I knew the names of the kids. I could even smell that god-awful perfume my mother used to wear. How long was I gone?"

"You had your eyes closed for only a few seconds."

"A few seconds? That can't be."

"That's all it was."

Browne looked at Riley suspiciously. "Have you done this to people before?"

Ezra shook his head. "I didn't do anything."

"I was there, but not there. I was at our house at the party, but I could see myself watching everything. It was as if I were two people."

"Two people?"

"Me and the young me. I wasn't in him, but I knew everything he was thinking. For an instant, I was afraid he would see me."

Ezra was intrigued. Browne was terrified.

"You can't do this to the President," Browne said. "Neither one of us would see the light of day again. We'd be buried so deep in some third-world prison the worms wouldn't find us."

"I didn't do anything," Ezra insisted.

"You triggered it!"

"It must have been a stress reaction. The birthday party was traumatic, and you buried the memory, but for some reason, it came to the surface rapidly, like a trout rising for a fly."

"I still think you did it," Browne said.

"I gave you a word of knowledge about a party and your age. Nothing more."

"Damn," Browne said, shaking his head to clear it. "That shook me. I don't know where we go from here. You're no charlatan; you're worse than that. I hope the President doesn't have any buried traumas."

"I'm only meeting with him to interpret a dream, that's all."

"A reoccurring dream," Browne emphasized. "One that has tormented him and kept him awake for eight nights. What if the interpretation is disturbing. Can you refuse to tell him?"

"I don't get interpretations if they're not meant to be told."

Browne let out a big sigh. "Twenty thousand isn't enough," he said softly.

"Excuse me?"

"Nothing, nothing," he said. He glanced at his watch. "Look," he said, "I don't really have the justification for ordering this plane back. The lady in—my employer," he corrected himself, "would need an explanation, and she'd see through any excuse I could come up with. But, you can turn the plane around. All you have to do is say you don't want to go."

"But I want to go," Ezra said. "Under one condition."

"One condition. What condition?"

Ezra untied the black silk scarf from around his neck. "I need to be blindfolded," he said. "Beginning now and up until I am actually in the President's presence."

"Blindfolded? How's that going to look? Why do you want to be blindfolded?"

Ezra lay the scarf across his lap and smoothed out the wrinkles. "Up until a couple hours ago, I was horseback chasing a wild cow. Suddenly, I'm on my way to the White House to meet the President. I've had no preparation for this, no time to pray. I have one fear. I'm afraid of being wrong."

"But, blindfolded?'

"This is heady stuff," Ezra explained. "If I look out the plane's windows and see the nation's capital or the White House, my ego might take over. This old cowboy is not going to make an absolute fool of himself. I need to see nothing until I am with the President."

"But, we're an hour from Washington."

"I still need to do it now," Ezra said.

"You're going to step off this plane with a black scarf around your eyes?"

"Unless you have a better idea."

"You insist on not being able to see?"

"I insist."

"I'll get you special dark glasses," Browne suggested. "We'll tell the Secret Service you hurt your eyes."

"I did? How?"

"Snow-blinded."

"Montana doesn't have snow yet."

"Welding. You hurt them welding."

"I wasn't welding; I was riding."

"Think of something!"

"Just tell her the truth," Ezra insisted. "You said she had a sister who knew about me. Ask her to call her sister."

"And when you meet with the President, are you going to wear the glasses?"

"No, I'll take them off when I am with him, but I will put them back on when I leave."

"Put them back on? Why?"

"Why? Because you never know. Maybe I'll be coming back."

"Coming back?" Browne exclaimed. "To the White House?"

"Could be. Will you be flying back to Montana with me?"

"Me? No. As curious as I am to see how this turns out, my job is simply to get you to D.C."

I hope I never see you again, Browne thought.

You will be seeing me again, Ezra thought.

10

His boots were on the tarmac; sounds of traffic, commerce, and human busyness stirred the air, but Ezra saw nothing; the black scarf wrapped about his eyes did its job.

More than its job. The perfume of sage, leather, horsehair, and sweat had soaked into the silk, shielding the cowboy from the odors of aviation fuel, asphalt, and smog.

He could hear Browne talking to someone. A woman.

Soft footsteps.

"Neither black glasses nor a sleep mask could be found at short notice," Browne told Ezra. "My employer wants to know if you still insist on wearing a scarf."

"I do."

Browne's hand on his left arm guided Ezra to a vehicle; its engine's deep, soft rumble reminded him of a giant cat's purring. He imagined it a long, black limousine.

Browne opened a back door and positioned Ezra to step in. Habit told Ezra to remove his black hat. He felt for the car's roof, bent his knees, and settled onto a cushioned leather seat. The texture of the leather spoke of quality.

"Good luck, Ezra," Browne said, surprising himself with his sincerity.

The door closed solidly. This was a vehicle built with purpose.

The opposite door opened. The scent of lotion and the slight tremble on the seat's suspension told Ezra it was a woman. Middle-aged, short, and stocky, but not fat. Her movements were not awkward.

Ezra was relieved she didn't speak to him. He didn't want a conversation.

Two men were seated in the front, a driver and a guard; their alertness rippled through the air.

As it entered an expressway, the limousine purred to a confident stride, reminding Ezra of Simon when the gelding was young.

Ezra sensed the woman's nervousness and knew she was staring at him from the corners of her eyes. That almost made Ezra smile.

The big cat of a car swerved gently left, and the flow of traffic slowed. Ezra sensed the traffic made room for the limousine as if the sea were parting; the mundane was making way for the exceptional.

A checkpoint—no words were spoken—then another checkpoint. A window opened, then closed. The big cat purred forward.

A gradual but final stop. Doors opened. Ezra sensed fresh air.

"Careful, sir," a man said. Taking Ezra's arm, he assisted him from the limousine.

Ezra put his black Stetson back on.

"This way, sir." A man took each arm. Strength and decisiveness radiated from the two protectors.

Angels, Ezra thought. *They're like angels.*

A door opened. The echoes were shallow, the footing was smooth. A narrow hallway and a linoleum floor. A back way, perhaps even a secret entrance.

He suspected the woman was gone. Left behind.

A door. A room with a sterile, medical smell.

"Please, wait here," he was told, and he heard his guardians leave.

Ezra took a deep breath. He felt anxious as if mounting a colt for its first ride.

Someone was in the room before him, or had the person been there all along?

"Please remove the blindfold," he was told.

Ezra unknotted the scarf and let his eyes adjust to dim, greenish lighting.

The President of the United States stood just feet away. He seemed smaller than Ezra had imagined, his shoulders slouching as if the world was caving in on itself and melting toward its molten core.

"You're Mr. Riley?" the President said.

"Yessir."

The President started to speak again, but Ezra held up a hand and was surprised by his own voice's steadiness and authority.

"Mr. President, please," Ezra said. "Do not tell me the dream. Allow me to tell it to you."

11

Tuesday, November 2

Ezra awakened in his bed sore, stiff, and thinking about the Wildebeest. Where could she be? A pilot might locate her, but by the time the pilot contacted him, the cow could be elsewhere. Besides, using a plane wasn't fair.

Plane?

He thought of Anne. By now, she had arrived in Rio and was holding their second grandson. What had they named him? Gavin?

Plane?

Jet!

A flash of him standing before the President.

A dream?

No, not a dream. Ezra remembered not taking off his black hat in the presence of the President.

His mother would have been shocked at his rudeness.

The clock on his bedside stand, barely visible behind a stack of books, read 6:35. He'd overslept. Days were short, so Ezra dressed quickly, made a hasty breakfast of poached eggs on toast, and did the dishes. He was not one to let dirty dishes pile up.

As he stepped out the front door, a pickup pulled into the yard, and a tall fellow with a thick, gray mustache stepped out of the truck. He wore a floppy brown hat, a big, crooked smile, and a heavy Carhartt coat, its pockets crammed with little notebooks and pencils.

"Mornin', my good friend," the man said. It was Barney Wallace, former bronc rider, full-time cowboy cartoonist, and Ezra's longtime friend.

"Good morning, Barn Wall," Ezra said. "What gets you up before the milk cows and cats?"

"I thought I'd better stop by and see how my little buddy was doing. You've been a full day without Anne. Did she arrive okay?"

"As far as I know."

"You didn't call her?"

"She'll call and leave a message."

Barney nodded at Ezra's apparel. "Chaps and spurs…you going riding? Don't tell me you haven't caught the Wildebeest yet."

"Not exactly. I had her penned yesterday, but some jughead stepped in front of the gate and spooked her off."

"That wasn't me, was it?" Barney joked.

"Not this time."

"Who was it?"

"Some salesman trying to sell me something I didn't want to buy."

Barney reached into a coat pocket for a notebook. "Shoot, this will make a cartoon. What was he selling?"

"Adult diapers, I think."

Barney scowled. Only his nose kept his thick eyebrows and mustache from colliding. "Diapers?"

"Yeah. Depends."

"Depends on what?

"Depends on whether you need 'em. Where's your horse, Barn Wall? I could use some help today."

"Wish I could, little buddy, but Mrs. Wallace has a honey-do list for me today."

"And you're at it this early?"

"The first thing on her list was for me to get out of her way," Barney said. "So, I'm going to a horse sale in Broadus. By the way, where were you last night? I tried calling to see if you wanted help today."

"I was in the White House with the President."

"Sure, you were." Barney snickered. "Did you get to meet the First Lady?"

"No, maybe next time."

Barney looked around the yard. "When are you going to get a new dog?"

Ezra shrugged. "Since Casey died, I haven't really wanted one. You know how it is; once you have a great dog, you know you'll never replace him."

Barney got back in his truck. "Yup, I know exactly what you mean," he said. "Mrs. Wallace says that about me all the time. She calls me irreplaceable." He gunned the motor. "Or maybe it's erasable," he laughed, and the truck rattled away like it had a trash compactor under its hood.

William Anderson Hall was in the study when the Gray Lady arrived. Hall appeared rested, but the woman's face showed she had slept little.

"How did it go?" Hall asked.

The woman sat and straightened her wool skirt. It was gray like the one she'd worn the day before.

"Riley must have interpreted the dream," she said. "The President slept well, and he appears refreshed this morning."

"You weren't allowed to stay in the room?"

"No. Riley was secreted into the basement. He and the President were alone."

"Did the president tell anyone the dream's content or Riley's interpretation?"

She shook her head. "Not that I know of."

"It concerns me that the President seems invigorated after meeting with Riley. Why would that be? Does anyone in the White House know about this meeting?"

"No. The only people who know about Riley are you, me, Davis Browne, the two pilots, the driver, and the bodyguard."

"So, Riley and Browne are loose ends, but we know nothing more of the dream itself?"

"That's correct."

Hall brought a crooked finger to his thin lips. "That's not good," he said. "I want to know the dream."

The lady in gray hesitated, then said the name. "Blue Man. Can he tap into Riley's memories?"

"I don't know," Hall said. "Memories repressed due to guilt or trauma are not the same as memories suppressed by honor. Riley has given his word. We made a mistake in having him sign a confidentiality statement."

"But what was the alternative? We couldn't have the information leaking out."

Hall rubbed his head. "Yes, I know," he said. "But Riley could be a tough nut to crack. I don't know that Blue Man is ready for the attempt."

"Maybe Riley can be bribed?"

"Bribed? Not a chance. He's an honorable man."

The woman waited.

"Abducting Riley would not be difficult," Hall said. "But that takes this operation to a different level."

"Maintenance could do it."

"That requires another private jet landing at a small airfield in rural Montana. Too conspicuous."

Hall thought for a moment.

"I wish Browne were capable of torture and extraction," he said.

The gray lady raised one eyebrow. "Davis Browne is not a killer," she said.

"Not yet, but he would like to be."

"Can't we use him some other way? He's Riley's only contact. Perhaps Browne can convince Riley to tell him the dream."

"I doubt it. Browne is not exactly personable."

The old man knew he had to make a decision.

"We'll use Browne. We know what triggers him."

"How will you use him?"

"For Blue Man to access Riley's memories, Riley's consciousness must be fractured. We will crack Browne first. His psyche is constructed of cardboard. He can't withstand Blue Man, your ploys, and tempting bait."

"Bait?"

"Boys like their toys. If you remember his file, Browne's Christmases were miserable, and he gambles because he wants nice things. We shall build on his secret agent fantasies. Guns, night scopes, knives, and an appropriate vehicle. For Montana, it should be a pickup truck. Make sure it is a special truck."

"I will arrange it immediately."

Hall smiled. "And don't forget money," he added. "Untraceable cash. He will be drunk with happiness."

"And that will be enough?"

"Enough to distract him," Hall explained. "Blue Man will do the rest."

"You believe Browne can be manipulated into kidnapping and torturing Riley?"

"Blue Man will drive Browne temporarily insane and Browne will do something rash, something shameful. We will cover his guilt with money."

"I'm still concerned about Browne's lack of experience with violent operations."

Hall smiled. "It is true Browne's fantasies exceed his realities, but that is precisely his weakness. We will let him believe he has become what he has always wanted to be."

Davis Browne, too, had overslept. He knew he would—it had been a long night—but he didn't care. It was not as if he had a real job at the university. No one would miss him.

He turned over in his bed to look at the clock and saw a person instead. A large man sat in the chair beside his bed.

Gray Lady's driver.

Browne reached for the nightstand and his suppressed Sig Sauer.

The driver raised a finger and shook it back and forth. Browne pulled his hand back.

The driver handed Browne a card. It read, "Hyde Field. Noon. Pack clothes."

Again. More work? More money? But what now?

When Browne looked up, the big man was gone.

12

Dusk.

Ezra walked head down, the brim of his felt hat pointed at the ground like a shovel blade, the right arm bent, a leather headstall hanging in its crook. A silver bit with slobber chains jingled as he moved, bow-legged, tired but not defeated. His flannel-lined denim jacket was buttoned tight, the bottoms of his shotgun chaps barely brushing dry manure. He was home, he was hungry, but the Wildebeest was still in the hills.

It had been a long ride and a lonely one. Ezra missed a dog's companionship, but he hadn't the energy and patience to train a new pup. He missed the company of good friends, but except for Barney Wallace, few men Ezra's age seemed up for long hours in the saddle.

Comfort had not been part of Ezra's upbringing. His father, Johnny Riley, had ridden for the CBCs—Chappel Brothers Cannery—a legendary wild horse outfit that swept feral horses from the plains in the 1930s. CBC cowboys were rawhide tough during hardscrabble times, and Johnny Riley changed little afterward. By the time Ezra was eight, the boy was following his father on day-long rides in the badlands, his stomach aching from hunger and the jostling of a trotting horse; his lips and mouth parched from sucking on the ends of leather reins.

He'd rebelled after high school, grown his hair, written poetry, and hitchhiked thousands of miles throughout the United States and Canada. He'd met Anne during an antiwar demonstration at the University of Kansas, where he dropped-kicked a cop through a plate-glass window. He and Anne later married and lived in California. When Johnny Riley's proud Irish heart suddenly stopped, Ezra's grief-stricken mother asked him, Anne, and their baby son, Dylan, to come home.

Ezra stepped into the tack room, turned on an overhead light, then paused to breathe in the atmosphere. He'd always found solace here amongst the lariats and bits; the headstalls and cinches; hobbles and reins. Still warm from use, his saddle sat nearest the door, the blanket draped over it to dry. The smell of horse sweat perfumed the air. It gave him peace. He could sleep here if there were a bed.

The house, in contrast, would be empty, dark, and lonely. A message on the answering machine from Anne would say the flight was long but good, she was fine, the baby was beautiful; was Ezra okay? She hated that he never carried a cell phone. Yes, coverage was spotty, but still, a man his age, alone in the badlands horseback, no one knowing where he was. Not carrying a phone was foolish.

Ezra smiled to himself. He'd die before he owned a cell phone.

He'd spent little time that day thinking about the night before. Yes, he'd flown to the White House where he secretly met the President. And yes, he'd interpreted the dream that had tormented the man for eight nights, but Ezra wasn't awed or impressed with this.

He'd only done his job. It had been a unique experience, nothing more.

Next time, he hoped he'd be better prepared. Maybe he wouldn't have to blindfold himself with his scarf and forget to take off his hat.

Next time?

Ezra chuckled out loud. What were the chances of him returning to the White House?

Only miles away, Davis Browne rested in a motel. This time, to cover their tracks, the pilots had flown him to Billings, where an F-250 pickup truck, boxes of gear stuffed into the rear seat, had awaited him. Two hours later, he was in Miles City posing as an out-of-state deer hunter. He'd purposely left a fluorescent orange vest visible on a gun case when he wheeled it from his truck.

In his room, he'd unpacked the cases with the joy of a kid at Christmas. The long case held a Nosler Custom Model 48 Long-Range Rifle chambered in .28 Nosler, with a Shilen Match-Grade stainless barrel and Timney trigger. Mounted on the receiver was a Swarovski X5i rifle scope in 3.5-18x50. Two boxes of Nosler Custom Ammunition completed the kit.

The padded square case held a Swarovski SYR 25-50 spotting scope and Swarovski 8x42 EL Range-Finding binoculars.

Another case contained a Nighthawk Mongoose Silver .357 Magnum revolver, Speer Gold Dot ammunition, Buck hunting knife and hatchet, laptop, and three disposable cell phones.

Browne disdained revolvers, but he held the Nighthawk tenderly as if it were a newborn. He'd heard of this custom handgun but had never seen one. It was a work of art. Why his benefactor had provided a premium revolver rather than a more practical semi-automatic eluded him, but why quibble?

In a padded envelope, he found $10,000 in banded hundred-dollar bills for other necessary expenses.

Better than any Christmas I had at home, he thought.

He showered quickly, then reclined on the motel bed, a terry-cloth towel wrapped around his waist, awaiting the call.

A burner phone hummed precisely at seven.

"You've settled in?" the voice asked.

It was the Gray Lady, as he expected.

"I have," he said.

"We are going to make this worth your while."

"That's nice."

"Fifty thousand a day."

"That's very nice. What do you want me to do?"

"Surveil our subject. Keep your cover, but find out everything you can."

"Do I make contact?"

"No. Not yet."

"I assume things did not go as you hoped last night?"

"You will assume nothing, Mr. Browne. All you need to know is the subject is an existential threat."

Browne started to speak but paused. *An existential threat?*

"To the country," the Gray Lady added.

"I understand," he said, but he'd didn't. How could an old cowboy be a threat to the nation?

"The man in Washington is weak, and the subject said something that triggered him," she explained.

"Okay."

"We must keep them from having contact again. We can monitor electronic communications, but we need eyes on the subject."

"He's going to be horseback. I have no way of following him in the hills."

"We know that. There will be limited air support. Your concern is the residence."

That wouldn't be easy, Browne realized. The Riley house sat in a broad valley, and he owned the land surrounding it. There was little cover save for cottonwood trees and rolling hills, and Riley would quickly notice a stranger's truck.

"Prove the subject is a threat," the woman said.

"I can do that," Browne said. For $50,000 a day? Certainly.

"Look for journals," the woman commanded. "Riley is a writer. He may have written about his recent trip."

Would he dare? Browne wondered.

"We are concerned about what he told the President privately. We need to know the dream and its interpretation."

Browne could not believe it. One day he flies a cowboy, sworn to secrecy, to Washington; the next day, he's ordered to discover the secret?

"One more thing."

"Yes?"

"Destroy this phone immediately."

"Roger that."

"Oh, and the toys, including the truck, are yours to keep."

Browne smiled. Christmas in November.

The lady hung up.

Using the hatchet as a hammer, Browne pounded the burner phone into bits and flushed the pieces down the toilet.

In the bathroom mirror, he smiled at himself. Now more than ever, he was a dangerous man.

13

Wednesday, November 3

That night in the motel room Davis Browne had a dream.

He was six years old, in his bedroom, under the covers, the door shut, a child not wanting to hear but hearing. His parents argued below, in the living room, the hallway, the kitchen, the words following the steps.

His mother snarled doctrine; the father growled Scripture; she hissed venomous rebukes, which he backhanded with guttural contempt.

Bloody religious combat: stabbings from Philippians, bludgeoning from Leviticus, mortar rounds of Genesis, sniping from Acts, the heavy artillery of Revelation.

His home was a circus, a zoo without cages. Lions and tigers and bears.

He curled into a twisted, aching ball and brought fingers to his lips. He was too old, and it was shameful, but the thumb in his mouth worked like a magic cork. It plugged his wishes inside.

He wished the arguing would end and for happy birthdays and Christmases. But most of all, he desired a world without religion.

Without religion, he might not be a six-year-old boy crying and sucking his thumb.

Browne didn't remember the dream in the morning, though a restlessness nagged the back of his mind, like a black cat hissing in shadows. He blamed his exhaustion on jet lag, but he perked when he remembered the paydays.

A lot of money. Every day.

Browne filled a Thermos with coffee at a truck stop and drove north. It was still dark, a good hour before daylight, but there were lights in the Riley house—one in the kitchen and one in the basement. Riley was up, had made coffee, and was in his office. Past the Riley mailbox, the highway rose gradually to an approach at a pasture gate where he parked his vehicle. He uncased his binoculars and waited.

Riley left the house with the first glow of daylight and walked to the corrals.

Still hunting the weird-looking cow, Browne thought.

Twenty minutes later, Riley left on horseback, rode north up Sunday Creek, then turned on a pasture road and trotted east. Browne waited five minutes, then drove down the hill, past the mailbox, and found a place to park a quarter-mile away. He emerged from the truck with a small backpack and the .357 Magnum on his belt. Bad knees or no bad knees, Browne jogged lightly through the cottonwoods to a creekbank at the edge of Riley's yard. He rested there for six minutes, his ears poised for any alerting sound. Hearing nothing and having caught his breath, he rose and tested the house's back door. Unlocked.

The kitchen sink and counter were clean. A quick look in the trash showed eggshells and coffee grounds.

Browne moved quickly to the living room. A stand at the end of a couch held a Bible and notebook. Bible verses in a woman's cursive. Anne Riley.

The land-line telephone showed one message. Ezra had already listened but hadn't deleted it. Browne turned the volume down, then hit play:

"Hi, my love. How are you doing? Everything is fine here. Gavin is beautiful. Everyone sends their love. I will be checking email often, so please let me know when you are back in the house. I'll email you photos later. Love you."

Email? Who uses email? Old cowboys and maybe the Gray Lady, Browne thought. The idea of that combination made Browne smile.

He turned the volume back up on the answering machine and eased downstairs, his left hand on the railing. He turned to the guest room on the right and first checked the gun safe. It was the same as before. He then moved to the closet beneath the staircase, an area he hadn't previously checked. Browne pulled the string on an overhead light and saw stacks of Rubbermaid storage tubs.

Ammunition, he guessed.

He was wrong. Each contained piles of notebooks, filled with notes Riley had taken for his books, and others held completed manuscripts. The title pages of the documents showed these were books Riley had written but never published.

Perhaps in these, he thought, *I will find clues to why Riley is considered dangerous.*

Then he heard the upstairs door open.

Browne closed the closet door and switched off the light. Heavy steps sounded above him with the slight tinkling of spurs. Riley was back. Heavy footfalls above him seemed to strike his head as the cowboy descended the stairs. Then Browne heard the gun vault open. A weapon was stored and another removed.

The two men were inches apart, separated by cheap paneling and two-by-four framing. Browne held his breath and inched his fingers toward his holstered revolver. He was thankful he didn't wear aftershave. The safe door closed, and Riley's footfalls were labored climbing the stairs.

Then Browne heard tires on gravel.

The steps paused as Riley stopped to listen.

A vehicle had pulled into the yard. Ezra finished climbing the stairs, and the front door opened, then closed, as Ezra went out. Browne slipped from the closet and made arrested steps to a basement window. He saw Ezra standing in the yard talking to an older cowboy with a bushy gray mustache.

"I didn't think I'd catch ya here at the house," he heard the visitor say.

"Traded the .30-30 for my .357 Magnum," Ezra said, tapping the revolver on his hip.

"You're making the Wildebeest too much of an obsession, Ezra."

"Obsession! Where's your sense of adventure, Barney? I thought you'd be coming with me by now strapped down with Colt six-guns."

"I don't want to shoot the old cow. I like the Wildebeest."

"Well, so do I, but she doesn't have a tooth left in her head."

There was a quiet pause.

"I came to check on ya," the man called Barney said. "Anne called me this morning."

"Anne did?"

"She's worried about you, Ezra. You need to take a cell phone."

"I don't own one."

"Here, take mine." Browne saw the taller cowboy rustle in his coat pocket.

Ezra held his hand up. "Forget it. Thanks, but I'm not taking a cell phone."

"You're stubborn as hell."

"I know it."

"Are you at least going to call Anne when you get in tonight?"

"Yeah, yeah," Ezra said dismissively, walking to the corral.

"Shoot, I'd come with ya," Barney called after him, "but I've got cartoons to mail off today."

Browne couldn't hear Riley's reply. Moments later, a pickup rumbled away. He waited a few minutes to give Ezra time to ride off, then Browne turned on the light, stuffed his backpack with manuscripts, eased up the stairs, and stealthily went down the outside steps and disappeared into the sagebrush and cottonwoods of Sunday Creek.

A cowboy cartoonist Ezra's age?

That had to be Barney Wallace. Browne had found references to him in his research.

He had two things to do. He had to read and return the manuscripts, and he had to meet Barney Wallace. Or, *Barn Wall*, as Ezra called him.

Unpublished stories and a cartoonist, one or the other, would likely provide answers.

14

It had been seventy years since William Anderson Hall had died and come back to life on an operating table in a Chinese prison. Those moments floating above his corpse had changed his life.

And charted his future.

Now he sat in a chair of polished Bocate wood and stared through bulletproof glass across his estate, to a forest wall of Virginia pine, red spruce, and eastern redcedar. Behind the evergreens, his creation, Blue Man, began his morning regime.

He watched his niece, dressed stylishly in shades of gray, enter the room, and for a moment, he considered her with affection. They seldom used each other's first names, and he had to remind himself she was Isabel Elizabeth Hall, the second child of his late twin, Robinson Alexander Hall. Though he'd never married, Hall adopted her and her sister in 1968 when their mother died of cancer and his brother, a Special Forces colonel, was killed during the Tet Offensive.

"You seem pensive," Hall noted.

His niece seated herself, smoothed the wrinkles from her skirt, and emitted a low, soft sigh. "We have a development," she said.

"You have heard the content of the President's dream?"

She shook her head. "No."

"Then what is it?"

"The President did not tell Ezra Riley the dream."

"He didn't? But you said—"

She held up her hand to stop him.

"I know," she said. "Ezra Riley did interpret the dream. But first, he *told* the President the dream."

Hall knitted his arthritic fingers together. "Riley told the President the dream?" The old man unknotted his hands and brought a knobby forefinger to his temple. "That is an interesting development," he said. "You have this on good authority?"

"From the President himself. He asked me to convey his thanks to the cowboy in the black hat, though he did say it in somewhat of a sarcastic tone."

"Perhaps you should," Hall said thoughtfully. "Was he curious about Riley? Did he act like he might want to see him again?"

"No, he didn't. I suspect he wants to keep Riley a secret from the press. But he did ask me to thank my sister for suggesting him."

Hall's sparse gray eyebrows lifted. "And what was your reply?" he asked.

"I said I would, of course, but what if he wants to meet her?"

Hall rested his chin in a bony palm. "I don't think we need to worry," he said. "The President has far more important matters on his mind. Can you stay close, or will your continued presence draw suspicion?"

"I think I should back off," she said. "I don't have an official position in the President's administration."

Hall nodded. "I agree. It has taken years to put you where you are. We mustn't risk that access through overexposure."

"Does this new information create problems?"

Hall appeared lost in thought as he gazed out the window. Finally, he turned back to her. "Yes, it presents problems. If the President believes Riley is prescient, he may consult him in the future, even though the press would have a field day with a cowboy Rasputin in the White House."

"Do we still try to learn the dream from Riley and activate Browne for the job?"

"Yes. Knowing the dream would be very helpful, and Browne harbors fantasies of being what I was, an agent of death from the sky."

"Davis Browne could never be you. You survived a Chinese POW camp, the Bay of Pigs, and three tours in Viet Nam."

"I was never in Viet Nam."

"What? But you said—"

"That story was a cover. I was in Cambodia and Laos."

"Still, you have served your country well."

"My work is not complete," he barked. "Stay focused on the task at hand. I am concerned that Riley's interpretation somehow nullified the effects of the memories."

"I apologize," she said, lowering her head.

He waved an arthritic hand. "It's okay. I didn't mean to snap at you. There are things I do need to tell you; things we need to discuss. But, first, we must take care of the Riley problem. I didn't spend my life serving my country to be stopped now."

"Our country owes you much."

"My country owes me nothing," he said. "But it would benefit her if her government would listen to me."

Her. America, to Hall, was a lady. His lady.

His head bobbed as if his neck could not support his passion and vision.

"You're getting tired," she said. "Do you have anything else for me?"

Hall gestured to the estate beyond the windows.

"Yes, there is something I want you to see." He pulled a remote control from a pocket, pushed buttons, a wall cabinet opened, and a television screen appeared.

"Observe," he said.

Rows of boxes appeared on the screen, all displaying rooms in the underground complex where the Blue Man lived.

He highlighted one, and for the first time, she saw him: the Blue Man in his sanctuary. He seemed to consist of a powdered silver

75

smoke that floated softly in the chamber's air, but that was an illusion; not the colors nor the floating, but the substance. He wasn't smoke. He was flesh.

But he was blue, and he was floating.

The Blue Man was levitating in the air.

"He's mine for now," Hall said. "But the coming days will be taxing. I may not survive. But you will."

She looked at him in trepidation.

"Then Blue Man will be yours," he said.

15

Barney Wallace bounced down the Post Office steps with a grin as wide and crooked as a badlands ravine. In his left hand, he clutched a small stack of mail orders for next year's calendar. In his right hand, he held the sunglasses he'd been missing the past week. The postal workers, against all official regulations, regularly put Barney's lost items—delivered by merchants from a surrounding area—in his P.O. drawer unless they were too large to fit. In that case, the employees shelved them in the back with personal items. The head postmaster, a double-dipping GS15, seldom left his office, so Barney's special treatment went unnoticed.

Barney was considered a local treasure, like a strongbox discovered in an ice jam whose rusted padlock remained unbroken so the contents would remain a mystery. The citizens thought it better to imagine stolen silver and gold than face disappointment with sand, gravel, and river debris. To Barney, it would have made no difference. A pile of river rock was as interesting to him as the clutter and glitter of O*ro y Plata*—Gold and Silver. Montana's official motto.

"Barney! Barney Wallace!"

He heard the voice but at first didn't know from where it had originated. He glanced skyward. Since he was a child, he'd heard that if you split a magpie's tongue, it could learn to talk. Barney harbored a secret hope that someday a garrulous *Pica pica* of the *Family Corvidae* would alight on his shoulder and whisper in his ear the secrets of the universe, or at least, where he'd recently lost his wallet, car keys, and reading glasses. But he couldn't see a magpie, just a slender, blond-haired stranger cutting across the street, against traffic, with a hand of greeting extended.

Davis Browne had gone undercover many times, but he never excelled at it. *Too opinionated and obstinate to create empathy* is how his superiors regarded him. Still, this was Miles City, Montana. How cleverly deceptive did he have to be?

"Barney Wallace! I'm so glad to meet you," he said, gripping the cartoonist's hand.

"Uh, glad to meet you, too, uh, Mister..."

"Davis. Benny Davis. "I'm from Wisconsin," he said, pumping Barney's arm like a pump handle. "I'm here on a deer hunt, and the one thing I was hoping is that I'd meet the famous Barney Wallace."

"Well, shoot, I..."

Browne gestured across the street to an espresso shop. "Please, permit me to buy you a cup of coffee."

"But I don't drink—"

"Coffee! No, of course not. I've read all about you on your calendars. You drink unsweetened tea." He took Barney by the elbow and started him across the street. Barney clutched his mail and sunglasses to his chest to keep from dropping them.

"Look," Browne said as they approached the shop's counter. "A stack of your calendars, and they're free. If I get a couple, will you autograph them?"

"Well, shoot, yeah. Be glad to."

They sat at a small, circular table, Browne with a cup of single-shot mocha and Wallace with his tea.

"Where did you say you were from?" Barney asked.

"Wisconsin. The little town of Granton in the center of the state. Not much around, just corn, dairies, and cheese. But, there's a farm supply store there that carries your calendars. I've been getting them and your books for years. *Grafitti on a Barn Wall.* How did you ever think of that title?"

"Well, actually, I didn't."

"Your wife, Henrietta? She thought of it, didn't she?"

"No, it was a friend of mine, Ezra—"

"Ezra Riley! Dang, ain't this a small world? He's the other person I'd love to meet."

"I just came from his place."

"You know where he lives? Do you suppose if we went out there, he'd autograph a book for me?"

"Well, he would, I suppose, except he won't be home."

"He's not home?"

"No, he's horseback in the hills chasing an old cow that he doesn't really want to catch."

"But he'll be back later?"

Barney liked people and commonly saw the best in everyone, but this stranger was making him suspicious. First of all, he didn't look like a Wisconsin deer hunter. He looked more like a tax auditor pretending to be a Wisconsin deer hunter.

"What did you say your name was again?"

"Benny Davis."

"I didn't know I had calendars for sale in Wisconsin."

"The store manager said he gets them from a friend in Wyoming, some big tractor dealership in Cheyenne, or something like that."

"Oh."

Browne leaned forward, doing his best to appear interested and sincere. "Tell me, how do you get all those wild ideas for your cartoons?"

"Shoot, most of those things have happened to me."

"Did you go to art school?"

"No, I began by doodling on my school papers at a one-room country school. When the school teacher sent me outside as punishment, I'd carve figures into a nearby sandstone bluff. It's a state park now."

"They made your school into a state park?"

"No, just the sandstone bluff. Archaeologists from the Forest Service determined those drawings were Native petroglyphs.

"Petroglyphs! And you never told them any different?"

"No, shoot, I didn't want to disappoint them. Those boys spent a lot of money and time going to school to get as smart as they are."

Browne paused. As entertaining as this was becoming, it wasn't helping his investigation.

"Ezra Riley," he began, changing the subject. "He's a darn good writer, isn't he?"

"Yeah, he's the cowpony of words. He can gather 'em up, then herd 'em where they're supposed to go."

Browne lowered his voice as to sound secretive. "Do you know anything about him interpreting dreams?"

Wallace raised his bushy eyebrows, and his gray mustache curled at the edges. "No, no. I don't know anything about that."

"I've heard he interprets dreams for famous preachers all over the country."

"That could be. I dunno. I interpret pizzas."

"You interpret pizzas? That's funny. You must be a spiritual man, too. There are a lot of churches in your cartoons—"

"And outhouses."

"Yes, and outhouses. But a lot of churches. You must be a Christian man."

"Well, I go to church, but I don't know how—"

"And Riley? Does he go to your church?"

Wallace caught the sterile, impersonal use of Ezra's surname. Was this guy really a fan?

"I don't think Ezra goes to church much," Barney said.

"He doesn't go to church, but he speaks at conferences across the country?"

"Well, sometimes Ezra rides different pastures than I do." Wallace's suspicions were increasing. The best thing, he thought, was to have Ezra meet this character for himself. Ezra was naturally suspicious.

"I could take you out to the Riley ranch this evening," Barney offered. "I'm sure Ezra would be glad to sign a book or two for you."

The suggestion caught Browne off guard. He'd forgotten how generous small-town people could be. "No, no," he said. "I'd hate to bother a busy man like Ezra Riley."

"Shoot, I bother him all the time."

"Yes," Browne said, pushing himself from the table. "But, you're his friend, Barney Wallace. I wouldn't want to intrude." He glanced at his smartphone. "Say, look at the time. I must get going. It was quite an honor to meet you, Mr. Wallace." Browne left the shop.

Barney watched the character walk quickly to a late-model Ford truck, and then Barney looked down at the table.

Browne had left the two calendars Barney had signed.

Well, shoot, Barney thought. *If that fellow can't hunt deer better than he can collect autographs, he's going back to Wisconsin empty.*

16

After coffee with the cowboy cartoonist, Browne returned to his motel room unsettled. If Ezra Riley was a threat to national security, how was it his close friend, Barney Wallace, was so likable? Even his Internet search on the cartoonist moments before meeting him had shown nothing negative.

Barney Wallace, the epitome of uniqueness, was liked and respected, though occasionally laughed at, which he seemed to take graciously.

Browne dealt with casts of bad actors pockmarked with *tells*: shifty eyes darkened by anger, nervousness, fear, or dulled by stupidity, drink, or drugs; shoulders that slouched; faces scratched with stubbly beards; soiled clothing and body odor.

White trash, but those were foot soldiers.

Leaders were polished to a glossy slickness and carried airs of arrogance and stale aftershave.

Right-wing groups had not been his jurisdiction—he'd been a field inspector for border security—but Browne had investigated and infiltrated patriot organizations, militias, and Christian sects on his own. Pro-Life activists were also fair game. He pounced on them like a coyote on field mice.

Internal terrorist groups were the FBI and ATF purview, so Browne avoided those agencies diligently. Yet, he stumbled, and it proved embarrassing. Tipsy in Tonopah, Nevada, Browne moved on a stunning brunette, assuming she was a cocktail waitress. He tried impressing her with tales of his undercover daring.

She turned out to be a sheriff's deputy and former ATF agent who understood jurisdictional lines. Browne's stories didn't pass her smell test.

A report, an investigation, and a reprimand followed. Browne was dismissed when other discretions came to light.

Emptying his backpack on the bed, the former federal agent began going through Riley's manuscripts. Ten notebooks handwritten in spiral-bound notebooks, all in-depth studies of various books of the Bible: Proverbs, Psalms, Amos, Jonah, Judges, John, Acts, Ephesians, James, and Titus, to be exact.

Titus? An entire notebook on Titus?

Browne picked up the study on Proverbs and settled onto a pile of pillows. Being a professional, no matter how long it took, he would go through each looking for hidden codes or ciphers.

It would be tedious, but after all, he was making $50,000 a day.

Ten hours later, his mind felt like a wad of wet tissue. He rose from the bed, his knees creaking, eyes burning, and neck sore; he stretched and then put the Bible notebooks carefully into his backpack. His rumbling stomach demanded food. Browne splashed water on his face, ran a comb through his hair, grabbed a jacket, and crossed the street to a truck stop cafe, thinking he deserved a Montana steak with a baked potato on the side.

The burner phone in his shirt pocket vibrated while he waited for his meal. It was the Gray Lady.

"Have you found anything?" she asked.

"I took some notebooks from his basement this morning and spent the day reading; nothing suspicious or incriminating so far."

"We have new information here. I am not at liberty to share the details, but the report is alarming."

We? thought Browne. He was becoming concerned with who *we* were.

"Can you give me something?" he asked quietly. Two truck drivers in stained baseball caps settled heavily into a booth beside him.

"Where are you?"

"I'm in a truck stop having dinner."

"That's not secure. Step outside."

Browne caught the eye of his waitress, gestured to his phone and the door, making her understand he was stepping out but would be back. He left his jacket in the booth.

"Okay," he said after stepping around to the back of the building. "I'm outside and alone."

"Riley claims he traveled for several years when he was a hippy."

"Yes. He hitchhiked throughout the US and Canada."

"Actually, he spent that time with a mystical Christian sect in the mountains of Nevada."

"I'm aware of his karate training in Nevada."

"This was more than karate. Riley went through rigorous mental and physical conditioning to develop his psychic powers. He was one of dozens of young men and women selected by the cult leader."

"Who was the leader, and what was the sect?"

"The sect was called Righteous Sword. Its leader is alive but very old. We choose not to release his name."

"I've never heard of this group."

"We just learned of it ourselves."

We again.

"What are their goals?"

"Terrorism against abortion clinics, migrants, and gays."

"But they can't be active. Not after fifty years."

"The ones that survived the training are still active, including Riley."

Browne paused. This news was a lot to absorb, and he was chilled and hungry.

"You're telling me there are sleeper cells of elderly right-wing extremists in the country?"

"The older ones are the leaders. They control younger followers."

"What do you want me to do?" he asked.

"What are you capable of doing?"

"Anything."

"We need to know the dream, and we need it by hook or by crook, do you understand?"

"Copy that."

The Gray Lady heard both bravado and reluctance in his voice.

"The bonus will be seven figures," she added. "Now, destroy this phone and return to your meal. Your steak and potatoes are getting cold."

Gray Lady put her phone away. She had just taken a significant risk. Browne's hatred for conservatives and patriots was easy to manipulate, but Gray Lady hadn't had time to have false evidence planted in Ezra Riley's home. Would Browne believe Riley was a domestic terrorist? And riskier still, Righteous Sword did exist, but not as she had painted it for Browne, and Riley had a weak connection to it though he probably didn't remember it.

Don't worry, she told herself. Browne would believe what they wanted him to believe, what *he* wanted to believe.

No matter the day's warmth, Montana's November evenings came with a biting chill. Ezra hunched into himself as he rode toward a sunset aflame in burnt orange with splashes of turquoise striping the sky. The colors lay like a scarf on the shoulders of silhouetted hills.

Again, no Wildebeest, but what did it matter? The day had been salubrious, the fresh air was quickening, and he was astride Q-Tip, a young horse with promise.

Old cowboys didn't need and shouldn't ride young horses, but good horses grew old too quickly. He missed them: Gusto, Shogun, Shiloh. Wasn't it yesterday that he and they were young? Now his bodied carried a list of surgeries done, surgeries needed, and wounds healed. He had an artificial hip, reconstructed finger, rebuilt foot; carried aches from a broken leg, six cracked ribs; and still needed operations on his shoulders and elbows.

The good news was he didn't need knee replacements. Yet.

Age was a poor partner, but Ezra had no thoughts of retirement. As long as he could throw a saddle on a horse and his leg over the saddle's cantle, he was going to work if he had work to do. He was not the type to ride for recreation. Riding for work re-created him.

Two different forces fought for his attention. His flesh was weathered and worn, but rawhide tough for its age: a crumbling cabin on an expansive canvas of prairie. But his inner man was a library of sandstone and cedar with Anne's lilting piano concertos echoing in its chambers.

Anne.

What was the time difference between Montana and Brazil? Three hours, four? By the time he unsaddled Q-Tip, it would be ten o'clock in Rio. He'd email Anne and suggest she call him in the morning.

No, he would call her tonight. She'd be awake worrying about him.

Why would she worry?

17

Thursday, November 4

Hall was surprised when he again heard the sound of helicopter blades. The last thing he did each night was check in with each of his five employees: the cook/housekeeper and the security team's four members. He'd done that and was ready to go to bed when came noises on the helipad.

Soft footsteps meant the housekeeper was going to the front door. Moments later, a woman was escorted into his study.

"Mary Margaret," Hall said pleasantly.

"Uncle William," the woman said, and she took a chair opposite him.

"To what do I owe this pleasure?" the old man asked.

Mary Margaret Hall was a year older than her sister, taller, less buxom, and not prone to wearing gray. Her attire was a scarlet blouse under a blue vest and black slacks fitted into riding boots.

"I had coffee with Isabel last week," she said.

"That's good. Sisters should see each other."

"She told me she'd had a dream two nights in a row and asked if I knew someone who could interpret it."

"And did you?"

"I think you know," she said pointedly. "I gave her the name of a man in Montana, but I had no contact information for him. His phone number and email address had changed since I met him."

"And would you like my help in finding this man?"

"Please, no games, Uncle. I think you know what I am talking about."

"And what could that be, my dear niece?"

"Don't play me for a fool. Remember, you tried recruiting me before you enlisted Isabel."

"You should have come aboard."

"Oh, yes," she said, gesturing with her hands as if defining the estate. "Then, I could be a part of your dark practices."

"What is dark to some is light to others."

"I am not questioning your motives, Uncle. A love of country has always guided you."

"And hatred of communism."

"Yes, and while I share those sentiments, your continued exploration and exploitation of the occult—"

He stopped her with the raising of a gnarled hand.

"It is not the occult, Mary Margaret. It is the undeveloped regions of the human mind."

"No, it is the occult, and it is perilous. It saddens me that you've entangled my sister in this web."

Hall's frail shoulders shrugged.

"I will not try to change your mind," he said. "I haven't the strength for it. But, you still haven't informed me as to the reason for this visit."

"I phoned Isabel today to let her know I had a land-line number for the man in Montana and asked if she wanted it. She didn't. She said the dream hadn't returned, and she no longer considered it important."

"So all is fine."

"No, Uncle, it isn't. I don't think Isabel ever had a dream. You are behind this, but I don't know why. Why would you want a dream interpreter?"

He smiled weakly. "And why would I?" he asked. "It doesn't make any sense at all, does it?"

"It's one of your psychic field experiments, isn't it? MKUltra reborn, or perhaps Stargate revisited?"

"No, dear niece, I am much too old for those endeavors."

"Isabel is lying to me, and only you could command that."

"I'm sure it was a simple misunderstanding. No offense, Mary Margaret, but neither of you are as young as you once were."

She rose from her chair. "I have my resources, too, Uncle William. Hall money is old money and well-dispersed."

"And what is that supposed to mean? I would advise you do not interfere in matters that don't concern you."

"My sister concerns me," she said and turned to leave.

Mary Margaret Hall had made up her mind. She was going to Montana.

Hall watched his older niece leave the room. It saddened him that Mary Margaret was not on the team. She would have been such an asset. But Hall carried a greater sadness regarding both nieces.

They did not know the truth about their father, and he could not tell them.

With her golden locks and long, athletic legs, Brittany descended the grassy hill with the grace of a woodland elf.

Davis could not believe how beautiful she was. It was a sunny day in Boulder, Colorado, with the scent of lilacs in the air and a flicker of breeze teasing the overhead leaves.

The bride wore a modest white wedding dress with a short train and carried six red roses in her hands. Two bridesmaids assisted her.

Davis stood ramrod straight. An officer at attention. First Lieutenant Davis Browne, USAF, with his best friend, a fellow graduate of the Academy, at his side.

The ceremony was more than they'd first planned. Brittany said the two of them and a justice of the peace was plenty. Then she thought of her sister and best friend. He thought of his buddy at the base. Officiating was a female Unitarian pastor from Brittany's yoga class.

There was no *dearly beloved*, or *do you promise to love, honor, and obey.*

They'd written their vows. Actually, she had had to write his, too. Romantic expression was not Davis Browne's strength.

The ceremony almost over, the pastor loudly joked, "Now does anyone object to these two being married?"

"I do!" cried a voice from the hill.

Browne looked up. Silhouetted against the sky was the angular frame of his mother.

She stabbed her heels into the grass to descend, her torso weaving as if she might fall, a black purse dangling from one arm. She held a hat on her head with the other hand while descending upon them like a large black crow, smiling because her actions were justified but stern, too, because justice was an immense responsibility.

"Davis," she said, standing between them. "If you marry this woman, you know you will be unequally yoked."

"Mother," he implored.

"No offense, dearie," his mother said, turning to Brittany. "I'm sure you are a lovely girl, that yoga nonsense aside, but this is eternity we are talking about."

"Mother!"

The ceremony concluded.

They were married, but more trouble followed.

He awoke sweating. This dream he remembered.

18

Friday, November 5

Anger boiled in his stomach, and murder was on his mind. Browne rolled over onto his back and stared at the ceiling. What a night. Freight trains of bad dreams, their boxcars loaded with painful memories, had rumbled through his mind, leaving him exhausted in body and soul. He glanced at the clock: 7:15. He'd overslept.

He threw off the covers, pulled on his jeans and sweatshirt, not bothering to shower though the hours of torment had caked his body in dried sweat. He had to get to the Riley house, replace one bundle of notebooks, and look for more. With a touch of a key fob button, his truck rumbled to life in the parking lot. He grabbed his go-to bag—a handled canvas case that held his essentials: handgun, ammunition, binoculars, phone charger, false identity papers, zip ties, flashlight, stun gun, pepper spray, and duct tape. *Why the heavy revolver?* he wondered as he hefted the bag. A lightweight Glock would have made more sense.

Maybe they want me to kill that wild cow for Riley to get on his good side, he joked to himself.

A corner kiosk provided the coffee and roll, and Browne was on his way.

Killing the cow. *I wouldn't mind doing that,* Browne thought, driving north. That beast had scared him enough in the gate the other day.

The other day. What day was that? Just two days ago? Three? Time was a blur. His mind was fuzzy.

He parked on the highway in sight of Riley's house, not worried about attracting attention. He'd seen several vehicles stop nearby trying to get cell reception. The binoculars didn't show any movement. Riley was gone or not up yet. If he were still in the house, that would be a problem.

He got out of the truck, locked it, shouldered his bag, climbed over a four-strand barbed-wire fence, and jogged to the creek. The Gray Lady was getting impatient. He had to take chances.

Counting the horses in the corral told him Riley was gone. One horse was missing. But, before trying the house, he slipped quietly through the corrals and checked the tack room. Yes, Riley's saddle was gone.

I should have all the time I need, he thought.

There were three large pastures on the Riley ranch and five smaller pastures near the house. Riding north, Ezra trotted through the creek pasture first, where he wintered his cattle after December 1.

Next came the Gumbo Jungle, where he'd concentrated his efforts the past few days.

He was on his way to the Summer Pasture, where his cattle still grazed. He now regretted not taking his pickup and horse trailer. It was going to be a long day. It would have been smarter to jump a horse into the trailer, haul it north to the corrals on Deadman Creek, and save himself many miles and a few hours, but he hadn't thought of it.

Ezra was on automatic pilot. Anne had called early and was upset about him riding alone, so he'd left the house in a huff, saddled, and mounted, not thinking there was a better way of doing things.

Oh, well. A long day made for a sweeter night.

But, Ezra knew Anne was right, or at least half-right. The cow was obsessing him, and he couldn't explain why. He and the Wildebeest went through this every year, but this time around, the chase was different. Yes, he would shoot her and put an end to their annual event, but something heavier loomed in the atmosphere.

Today he rode Quincy, a tough roan gelding that made up for his lack of personality with a bottomless well of stamina.

"You're tougher than I am," Ezra whispered to the horse as they jogged down a pasture trail. The roan cocked one ear back as if asking the human what he wanted.

It was late in the morning when he arrived in cattle. Ezra had ridden this far, thinking the Wildebeest might try to blend back into the herd, seeking safety in numbers, a chance to catch her breath.

The cattle grazed contentedly or lay chewing their cud. The sight of Ezra horseback didn't bother them. Unlike his neighbors, Ezra never used motorcycles, UTVs, or four-wheelers to gather his cattle. He did it the old, slow way, and his herd was quiet because of it.

The roan settled into a brisk walk through the red-hided cattle, and for a moment, Ezra Riley was so captured by *where* he was, he lost track of *who* he was. The day was cool and beautiful, the cattle fat and glossy, and he owned all the land he could see. Though thousands of acres, his ranch was not large by Montana standards but was paradise compared to city life. He paid for these hills with blood from injuries, sweat from hard labor, and tears from family troubles that seemed inherent with land and relations.

The land is *where* he was, and readers of his writing would add that land is *who* he was, but Ezra was more than anyone knew except Anne.

Ezra Riley was the man chosen to fly across the country and meet privately with the United States President.

He wasn't thinking about that now. He enjoyed the cattle, badlands, prairie, encompassing blue skies, and soaring hawks, and then he saw the calf.

The Wildebeest's steer calf was lying in a small circle of ruminating cows. It stared at him, hoping not to be seen. A ripple of energy was exchanged between the calf's eyes and Ezra's. The calf rose, slightly trembling as if not knowing if to run or stand.

"So, where's your mother?" Ezra asked aloud.

The steer looked about nervously.

The roan horse fidgeted, not knowing why Ezra was speaking.

"Did she leave you, or did you leave her?"

The calf stiffened with tension, so Ezra eased his horse away. Let the calf lay. Let it rest. But what had happened? Was the Wildebeest dead? Did she bring the calf here for the steer's sake, or had she abandoned it for her survival?

It was an intriguing mystery.

Ezra pointed Quincy home. He'd leave the calf to settle, or "locate," as ranchers said. Soon, he'd corral it, but until then, he would continue to ride, searching for the Wildebeest.

The game continued.

Journals.

Manuscripts.

Letters.

Browne dropped a trove of materials taken from Riley's stairwell onto his motel room bed. He sorted them by priority and settled in for long hours of reading.

It was hard to concentrate, because dollar signs danced in his head. A seven-figure bonus. He ignored what he might have to do to earn that money and thought just of the tax-free cash. He would pay his daughter's tuition in whole, move to a hamlet in Costa Rica, and for once, avoid the casinos in Atlantic City.

The stacks of paper in front of him were intimidating.

He had one tempting alternative.

Why not forge a dream and interpretation by using Riley's computer and printer?

Perhaps in this pile of writings, he would find an old dream journal and slip his counterfeit in as if Riley had included it as a hasty afterthought.

It was an option but a dangerous one. Whoever the money-man was behind the Gray Lady, his power and reach had to equal his wealth. He, or she, or they, wouldn't see the humor in a bogus dream.

No, first, he better go through each journal, notebook, and letter.

Two notebooks were more detailed Bible studies: Joshua and Amos. Boring. He'd save those for last.

Other binders held notes Riley had taken for magazine and newspaper articles. Browne found nothing interesting in them.

He promptly dismissed folders containing American Quarter Horse pedigrees and histories.

All that remained were four padded envelopes containing loose-leaf pages of manuscripts Riley had submitted to publishers.

The first text was Riley's views on the need for small-group home churches to replace brick-and-mortar denominational structures. The attached rejections ranged from standard form letters to caustic handwritten comments from editors. The letters were dated 1989.

A contemporary western novel set on the Riley ranch was the second rejected work. One editor wrote: *While the writing is exemplary, the lack of romance and no pronounced Christian message does not meet our readers' current needs.*

The contents of the third package held promise. Titled *12,000 Miles on My Thumbs*, it was the record of Ezra's hippy hitchhiking days. Browne put it aside. It would require a close look.

The fourth manuscript was a novel titled *Cleansers*. A synopsis attached to the cover letter described the book as a thriller set in the future. A bundle of twenty-three rejection letters, dated from 1994 to 1997, were bound by a rotting rubber band that broke when Browne touched it.

He began with the hitchhiking journal. If Riley had joined a radical cult in Nevada, here, he might find implicating clues.

He had to find something.

Three hours later, Browne's cell phone vibrated.

"What are you doing?" the Gray Lady asked.

"I just finished a manuscript Riley wrote in 1978 about his days on the road."

"Did you find anything?"

"No. The book is well-written. I enjoyed it. He is very detailed about his travels throughout the US, Canada, parts of Mexico."

"No mention of Righteous Sword?"

"No. He did visit what he called a 'martial arts monastery' in Nevada briefly, but he didn't stay long."

"Remember, Riley writes fiction. This manuscript could be an elaborate cover-up."

"I don't think so; he comes across as truthful and sincere. I do have a novel manuscript to read next, and I'll compare styles."

Browne could tell the Gray Lady was displeased.

"We're getting nowhere reading Riley's books," she said.

"What would you rather I do?"

"There is one consideration," she said thoughtfully. "What if you approached him directly and said the President regretted not having a copy of the dream and its interpretation? Ask him to give the information to you so you can take it back to the White House."

Browne deliberated. "I don't know if Riley trusts me enough for that."

"Tear up the non-disclosure form in front of him, and tell him if he'll give you the details, he can share the story with his wife, but no one else."

"That might work. He's conflicted about keeping secrets from Anne."

Anne? the Gray Lady thought. That sounded too familiar.

"But, I don't understand," Browne said. "If Riley is the threat you say he is, why would he cooperate, and why would we believe him?"

"We need the dream," she insisted. "Once we have it and Riley's *supposed* interpretation, then we will make judgments about authenticity."

"There might be one problem," Browne said. I met one of Riley's friends and used an alias. If he happened to stop by while I was there..."

"Don't let that happen. Pick a time when you are sure he'll be alone and be direct and expeditious."

"Can I continue digging before I approach him? I still think there is something to be found."

"We need to wrap this up soon. Find something, get Riley to give you the information, or be ready to go to the next level. Do you understand?"

Browne swallowed nervously. "I do," he said.

"Now destroy your phone."

"I'm running out of phones."

"Look underneath the seats in your truck," the Gray Lady said. "Your needs have been taken care of."

Browne drew a hot bath, dropped the phone in the water, then disrobed. He was exhausted, confused, and entangled in constricting webs he couldn't explain.

He suddenly didn't feel dangerous. He felt endangered.

A hot bath, a nap, and then he'd begin the novel, *Cleansers.*

In Browne's afternoon rest, a lion crawled from the closet, climbed onto the bed, lay heavily on Browne's chest, and took his head in its massive jaws. Fangs sank into each temple. The beast's rancid breath was the only air reaching Browne's lungs.

He couldn't scream, but he did. He heard his voice yell, "Mother!"

A tall, dark female figure came through the motel room door and hovered above the lion and the boy.

"There are no monsters in your closet, Davis. I took authority over them in Jesus' name."

Yellowed fangs cracked his skull.

"Dad! Dad!"

A black mist took the form of a bear with a human head.

"Don't cry, Davis. Big boys don't cry," it commanded.

The female figure turned and hissed at the bear.

The bear growled.

The lion crunched.

Davis, the boy, died.

Browne came to life with a stabbing pain of light blinding his eyes; his stomach clenched, and the taste of bile rose in his throat. He rushed to the bathroom and vomited, again and again, and again, into the porcelain toilet bowl.

Exhaustion had finally caught Ezra Riley. He walked from the barn to the house, his head down, feet dragging as if in mud, and his heart wishing he had a dog.

A good dog to share his labor, one that would walk beside him faithfully even when tired.

The house was cold. He needed to start a fire in the woodstove. Now is when he missed Anne the most, not just for the chores she did happily, but for the warmth of her eyes and smile.

And a hot meal already prepared and on the table would be a blessing, too.

He stacked crumbled newspaper, kindling, and cottonwood sticks in the firebox, tossed in a match, then sat on a bench and pulled off his boots.

The light on the answering machine was dark. Anne hadn't called. At the workroom sink, he washed his hands, splashed water on his face, and dried with a soiled towel. He hadn't done laundry yet.

Anne had left a large kettle of homemade soup in the refrigerator. He poured the last few cups of the soup into a bowl and stuck the bowl in the microwave.

He did not see the headlights coming down the lane.

He did hear the knock on the door.

Who in the world?

He shut the microwave, walked down the hallway, turned on the porch light, and opened the door.

A car drove up and stopped. A man got out of the driver's side, came around the car, and opened the passenger door, and a lady stepped out.

She ascended the front steps gracefully despite her long winter coat and boots and stopped at the landing where Ezra was standing.

"Ezra Riley," she said. It was a statement, not a question, and her hazel eyes carried the suggestion of purpose.

She extended a gloved hand. Ezra took it cautiously.

"My name is Mary Margaret Hall. Do you remember me?"

Ezra shook his head. His wife was in Brazil, and a strange woman was on his doorstep. Hospitality was the rule in eastern Montana, but this had the makings of a set-up.

"A prophetic conference in St. Louis fifteen years ago," she explained. "You did a class on dream interpretation. You were not one of the main speakers, but you privately interpreted dreams for four of us: the conference host, two keynote speakers, and me."

"I remember now," Ezra said.

"May I please come in?"

"And your friend?" Ezra asked, nodding at the well-built driver.

"Peter is my pilot as well as my driver, and he is here for your protection."

"My protection?"

"It would not be wise for you to be alone with a strange woman when your wife is out of town," she explained. "Peter will stay inside by the door so that we can talk privately elsewhere."

He nodded and stepped back to grant them access. How did everyone know Anne was out of the country?

He took her fur-lined coat and hung it on a hook next to his chaps and spurs. He offered to take Peter's, but the man declined.

Ezra and the woman moved down the hall to the main parts of the house.

"Were you having supper?" she asked.

"Just nuking some soup."

"Don't let me stop you from eating. You look hungry."

"It can wait," he said, bidding her to a seat.

The woman looked around the room, appraising the photos and books.

"What can I do for you, Ms. Hall?" Ezra asked.

"Please, call me Mary Margaret, and I am a straightforward person. Have you flown on any private jets lately?"

Ezra tried to hide his surprise. "And if I say yes?"

"If you say yes, I should apologize, for I am at fault."

"You are?"

"Last week, my sister called wondering if I knew anyone who interpreted dreams. I thought of you, though I've heard nothing about you in years. I gave her your name. I regret that now."

"Why?"

"So you were on the jet?"

Ezra nodded.

Mary Margaret Hall sighed and stared at the floor.

"I am sorry you are involved," she said.

"Involved with what?"

"With what, I don't know. But with whom I know too well. Have you heard of my uncle, William Anderson Hall?"

"No, sorry."

"Uncle Bill is an elderly man who spent his life in the military and the Central Intelligence Agency. During the Korean War, he had a near-death experience that sparked an obsession with the paranormal. Are you aware of Duke University's Parapsychology Laboratory?"

Duke, thought Ezra. Davis Browne said he went to Duke.

"Yes, I am," he said, drawing himself from thoughts of Browne.

"And MKUltra Subproject 58?"

"Yes. The Duke projects were Army, but MKUltra was CIA."

"My uncle was involved with both and more. When he was forced to retire in 1995, he recruited first me, then my sister, to continue his research. He had raised us, so we had an allegiance, but I refused. Unfortunately, my sister, Isabel Elizabeth, was won over. Have you met my sister, by chance?"

Ezra thought of the woman in the limousine.

"I may have," he said. "What does this have to do with a jet?"

"The jet was my uncle's."

Ezra didn't want to react, but his chin subtly jerked, and she noticed.

"Can you tell me where you went?" she asked.

"No."

"Nor who you went to see?"

He shook his head.

"Yes, this certainly sounds like Uncle Bill. I have a friend at Hyde Field. He told me the flight plan for Uncle Bill's jet was Miles City, Montana. It returned that evening, then departed again."

Ezra sat stone-faced.

"I can only guess who this might involve," the woman said. She waited for Ezra to respond.

He didn't.

"I won't ask you to break your word," she said. "And it's not important who you went to see. What is important is for you to understand who you are working for."

"Working for?"

"Yes, whether you took money or not—and knowing you a little, I am sure you didn't—by getting on the jet, you put yourself in my uncle's employ."

"What are you saying?" Ezra asked.

"I am saying your life is in danger."

Ezra looked down at the floor, then looked out the room's picture window. It was dark outside, and a string of cattle trucks, lit up with running lights, roared by on the highway. He always liked seeing the trucks this time of the year. The lights reminded him of Christmas. Then he turned to the woman and saw the conviction and concern in her eyes.

"I thank you for the warning," Ezra said. "I guess I've known it would always come to this."

"What would?"

"My life. If we are fortunate, we are an arrow released by a Master Archer. We might buck the wind for years, but eventually we hit the mark."

"Are you prepared for what is unfolding before you?"

"I don't know what's unfolding," Ezra said. "Can you shed some light on it for me?"

"All I can tell you is that Uncle Bill has spent the past thirty years at a remote estate in Virginia. I've only been there twice. What goes on there, I can only guess."

"The Lord knows."

"Indeed." She looked at him thoughtfully. "May I ask you what happened, Ezra? You once spoke at conferences, wrote articles for Christian magazines, and had a growing prophetic ministry. Then, suddenly, you disappeared."

"The church world wasn't for me," he explained. "Too much drama and self-promotion. I realized my cowboy culture had more common sense and integrity than the church, and in it, I could be myself."

"And how has this worked for you?"

"Spiritually, it can be a desert."

"Are you in a good local church?"

"No."

"You're more than a dream interpreter, Ezra. You have seen miracles, walked in the miraculous, and now you are hiding in the hills? Are you a Samson or a Jonah? Samson allowed himself to become bound and blinded. Jonah refused to give the word of God to people he didn't like."

"Did you come here to interrogate me?"

"You're right, I'm sorry. But I would like to know why you disappeared from the Body of Christ."

"As I said, too many games. I'm not into gamesmanship."

"Come back and be an example. You were ahead of your time, Ezra. You may find that things have changed."

"Life has changed for me in the past few days. I am better off in the hills."

"Yes, maybe you are," she said. "A mile down the road, I had Peter stop the car, and I tried to call so as not to surprise you. There is no cell coverage here," she said.

"That's one reason I don't own a cell phone."

"That's excellent. I would advise you not to get one anytime soon."

"Because your uncle could trace me?"

"Undoubtedly."

"You came a long way, Ms. Hall—"

"Mary Margaret, please."

"Mary Margaret," he corrected himself. "You came this far to warn me about your uncle?"

"Not entirely. I had to know if I had responsibility for the situation you are in. I had to come."

"If it is in my power, I absolve you of responsibility."

"Thank you. Would you consider leaving here with us and staying at my estate in Vermont?"

Ezra smiled. "I thank you for the offer, but there is a certain wild cow in the hills that requires my attention."

"I expected that," she said, rising. "I will leave you to your soup."

He walked her to the door and helped her with her coat. Peter had stepped out and was standing by the car.

"Thank you for seeing me," she said.

Ezra took her hand. "You came a long way to warn me, Mary Margaret. I do appreciate it."

She nodded. "You are very welcome, Ezra Riley. But, do me one favor."

"Yes?"

"Stay alive," she said. "We need you."

21

Saturday, November 6

"Your sister came to see me."

The Gray Lady's teacup rattled in her hand.

"Mary Margaret came here?" she asked.

"Yes," said William Anderson Hall. "And since you didn't convince her the dream was yours, she flew yesterday to Montana."

"She went to see Ezra Riley?"

"We can only assume so."

"Is this going to be a problem?"

"I don't think so," the old man said. "She's likely to warn Riley about us, but what can he do? What is the latest from Davis Browne?"

"I have a small concern about him," said the Gray Lady. "I called Browne this morning, and he didn't answer."

Hall waved his hand disparagingly.

"Blue Man is turning Browne inside out," he said. "Browne not responding is a good sign."

"If you say so. You said you had something to show me?"

"Yes," said Hall, reaching for the remote. With a touch of a button, the cabinet opened, and the small boxes appeared again on a screen. He highlighted the one that showed Blue Man making fluid, almost weightless movements in his exercise room.

"Shaolin Kung Fu," Hall explained. "One hour of *katas* every morning, followed by an hour of Kundalini yoga."

"He's very graceful," the Gray Lady noted.

"He's hardly flesh and bone. Blue Man is almost pure energy, and it is time you heard his story."

The Gray Lady reached for the teapot, freshened her uncle's tea, and put a single sugar cube in the cup. She knew he'd need his energy.

"Toward the end of my service, government interest in the paranormal waned. Technology took over," Hall explained. "I lobbied to retain psychic research programs, and they did, but half-heartedly."

He took a sip of tea, holding the cup tenderly in shaking hands.

The Gray Lady had heard this part of the story many times. It was a preface to every tale her uncle told.

"The challenge in today's warfare is weapons becoming microscopic," Hall continued. "Computer viruses, biological viruses, drones the size of honeybees; I understand robots have been miniaturized to where they can enter a person's bloodstream."

He took a tissue from a stand and wiped his lips.

"Military developments are one thing," he continued, "but the civilian world is more threatening. Technology is leading to artificial intelligence replacing all but an elite cadre of humans. Billions of idle people will subsist on welfare and enforced sedation."

None of this was new to Isabel, but she didn't dare interrupt him. Her uncle repeating himself had become more common, but alerting him to it would only rile his anger.

Hall coughed hoarsely into a tissue.

"Communism disguised as globalism must be defeated at any cost," he continued. "I saw this coming sixty years ago. We were on the right course with psychic warfare, and results were proving our case. But politicians are materialists. They want products they can hold in their hands to show the taxpayers where their money is spent.

"To win any conflict, we must hit the nerve center, the brains of the leadership; drive them mad, influence their decisions, cause doubt within the ranks. Blue Man can do that. I have prepared him for this.

"Thirty years ago, the agency dismissed two capable psychics; a man and a woman in their thirties. I persuaded them to have a child and deliver the baby to me."

Isabel squirmed in her chair. She never enjoyed hearing this part.

"You've never seen him in the flesh, Isabel. He's a beautiful creature, but you know so little about him. You have avoided his sanctuary, and Blue Man must stay underground. He can't meet you outside—he's never been in fresh air."

This Gray Lady did not know.

"But why?" she asked. "Does he have a disease?"

"He believes he does, or a *special condition*, to be more precise."

"This condition is why he is blue?"

"I made him blue to guarantee his focus. Blue Man has argyria."

"Silver toxicity?"

"Yes. From colloidal silver. It is mixed in his morning drink."

"He doesn't know this?"

"Of course not. His handlers do all of the food preparation."

"Did you do anything else?" Gray Lady asked tentatively.

"Yes. Blue Man is surgically mute. He hears, but he cannot speak."

"How does he communicate?"

"Sign language, written language, and he is a telepath."

The Gray Lady's eyes widened. "He can read and send thoughts?"

Hall raised a hand in caution.

"His telepathy is not for social interactions," he explained. "Blue Man's skills are weaponized for extraordinary circumstances."

"Like the President."

Hall nodded.

"But, how does he send energy to distant places?"

"His meditation chamber was carved from the world's largest natural crystal," Hall said. "This crystal, along with other gems and minerals, serves as an amplifying transmitter and receiver. On a smaller scale, his chapel may be the most beautiful in the world, if not the most expensive."

"Does he weaken? Can Blue Man get tired?"

"Of course. He is human."

"How high can he levitate?"

Hall chuckled. "That caught your eye, did it? What you saw the other day is nothing. Blue Man's best elevation so far is four feet."

"Four feet!"

"Yes, it is wonderful to watch."

Isabel Elizabeth Hall sat with her hands resting in her lap. She'd known about Blue Man for years but never dared imagine what type of creature he was. "Is he happy?" she asked.

Hall's brow furrowed. "He does not know what unhappiness is," he replied.

"Does he leave his sanctuary at all?"

"Blue Man is locked in for his protection—he believes his condition makes him susceptible to diseases outside cleansed environments."

"But he's been in this study."

"Yes, rarely. He's told this room is mostly sterile and whatever contaminants might exist will strengthen his immune system. He knows to stay away from other parts of the house."

"If he can't go outside, how does he come here?"

"There's a tunnel, my dear."

"A tunnel?"

"When I need him one of the handlers brings him to me."

"And he accepts his handlers?"

"They raised him. And they double as my security force," Hall added.

"Does he use computers?"

"Blue Man has no access to any technology, including cell phones and television. He has learned to be dependent on his sixth sense."

"What does he do in his free time?"

"He has no free time."

The Gray Lady turned her head and stared out the window at the grove of evergreens.

"Will he like me?" she asked.

The old man looked at her curiously. Blue Man liking her had never been a consideration. He shrugged his frail shoulders. "Blue Man understands duty. He knows you are next in command and will accept your leadership."

"He will accept me without question?"

"Of course, you have not met him, but I have told him much about you. He will be eager to accept your leadership. I think you should stay here a few days," he said, changing the subject. "I may need your assistance to see things through."

She knew it wasn't a request. Her uncle rose, and as Isabel watched him leave the room, she noticed he leaned more heavily on his cane than he used to.

Later, in her room, she had time to think. Was she, like Blue Man, only one of William Anderson Hall's creations? Her doctorate from Yale, business accomplishments, political connections, and access to the Hall family's vast wealth suggested a woman of achievement and power, but what had *she* accomplished? What actual weight did *she* carry?

She wondered, *Is Blue Man more my brother than Mary Margaret is my sister?*

22

Davis Browne sat naked in the bathtub, shower curtain drawn closed and a weak stream of tepid water dripping onto his head. He did not sleep the night before; instead, he drank coffee and energy drinks and read Ezra Riley's novel manuscript, *Cleansers*, three times.

The book and the caffeine shook him to his core, left him doubting his sanity and confused about his next step.

The novel's plot concerns a federal agent who discovers a scheme to reduce the world's population using a virus that reads human intelligence; people with an IQ under 100 die.

The novel was mediocre, and Browne could see why the book idea died after twenty-three rejections. The science was sketchy, the prose lacked confidence, and the characters were hollow. It was the worse writing Ezra Riley had done, in Browne's opinion.

Though lousy writing, the story rattled him for two reasons: the main character was called Benny Davis, Browne's undercover alias, and a dream had alerted this character to the plot.

Synchronicity or coincidence? An almost thirty-year-old manuscript using Browne's alias and a dream of international consequence?

Who was Ezra Riley, and more critical to Browne at the moment, who was the power behind the Gray Lady? Someone who owned private jets, had unlimited cash, and had access to the White House, not to mention Browne's own office and apartment, could do anything, couldn't they?

When would they decide that he was expendable?

The .357 Magnum revolver lay on the floor beside the bathtub, but Browne knew it was merely a prop. If *they* wanted him dead, it would happen. Fancy six-guns weren't going to stop them.

And if the supplies were all props, what was the motivation? Was he being set up?

How many people knew Ezra Riley went to the White House? Himself, Gray Lady, the pilots, the limousine driver, and the bodyguard. And Ezra Riley. He and Ezra were the outliers, the loose ends.

How did he get into this? He knew how and regretted it. Greed, ambition, and debt were the tines on the trident that had skewered him.

How could he get out?

He didn't have the cash to disappear. He needed much more, not only for his escape but also for his daughter's. How much? Ten million? A completed mission guaranteed him a seven-figure payment.

Why not eight figures?

Why would they pay him at all?

No one would miss him if they killed him, and theirs was the power to erase any memory of his existence.

Sleep deprivation and stimulants had his mind racing in circles.

Pregnant pauses on the phone. Browne laughed to himself. What a silly phrase to suddenly think of, but it was true. The Gray Lady used pregnant pauses to infer suggestions.

She'd said *by hook or by crook.*

Then she'd paused. The pause meant: *Get the dream and its interpretation even if you have to lie, cheat, torture, and kill.*

Why him? He'd done no *wet work* in his job, no *dark ops* except the innocuous ones he'd created for his gratification.

His was a blemished record; he knew that. No job promotion or career advancement was coming. Those promises were lures.

A burner phone buzzed again. The Gray Lady was calling; he wouldn't talk to her because he had nothing to report, only questions he was afraid to ask. What was he supposed to do, tell her he'd found something crazy in a poorly written manuscript? Admit he was sitting naked in a bathtub with water dripping on his head?

If they wanted the dream's interpretation in the first place, why the non-disclosure form? Why wasn't Ezra told delivering the President's nightmare to his handlers was part of the deal?

It wasn't the non-disclosure contract, Browne suddenly realized.

It was the President. It had to be. Of course. The President would have sworn Ezra to secrecy. *They* knew that and knew Ezra would honor authority.

But the dream wasn't a priority, and its meaning certainly wasn't—that was Ezra's opinion, nothing more.

"There's a bigger picture," Browne said out loud, the acoustics in the bathroom amplifying his voice.

"They don't want to help the President," he said, more softly this time. "This is about *them*, whoever *they* are."

But what if he were wrong and basing conclusions solely on finding his alias in an unpublished manuscript?

The water dripped, and his mind spun.

23

Sunday, November 7

"So, what's new, Ezra, my friend?" Barney Wallace asked, climbing into the passenger seat of Riley's 2005 F250. The men had loaded their horses in the stock trailer—Barney's mount was a half-draft Clydesdale—and were trailering to Deadman to corral the Wildebeest's calf.

"Not much," Ezra said. "Except, a nice lady arrived on a jet to ask me about my time in the White House."

"Shoot, no wonder Anne's worried about you."

"Speaking of my lovely wife, she isn't behind you being here early this morning, is she?"

"Nope, my wife is. She told me I could help you gather your last calf, or I could stay home and help her scrub floors."

"Hard choice."

"I tossed a coin."

They pulled off the county road, traveled two miles down a pasture trail to the corrals, unloaded their horses, tightened the cinches on their saddles, and got mounted. Barney had brought a mounting block to get astride his mammoth animal.

"Are we going to head-and-heel this calf and drag it into your trailer?" Barney asked.

"No, we're going to trail it in with a couple of cows and sort it off in one of the small pens."

"Shoot, Ezra, you don't want to do anything fun anymore," Barney joked.

"Neither do you, Barn Wall. You're just bluffing. Your friend, Ben Gay, told me you wanted to take it easy today."

"Shoot," Barney said. "That reminds me, I met a fan of yours named Ben. Or Benny. A deer hunter from Wisconsin."

"A fan of mine?"

"Of your books. Well, and of my calendars, too."

"And where did you meet this man of questionable taste?"

"I was coming out of the Post Office when he saw me. He took me across the street for an iced tea."

"That's nice," Ezra said. He wasn't concerned about fans of books and calendars.

The two men rode quietly through grazing cattle, looking for the Wildebeest's calf and the Wildebeest, should the old renegade show herself. Ezra was on Q-Tip, choosing the smaller young horse over Simon.

"You been watching the news?" Barney asked.

"No, since I've been to the White House, my life has been in turmoil."

"White House!" Barney laughed. "You're going to need a better storyline when Anne gets home."

"So, what's on the news?" Ezra asked.

"Death, destruction, and delirium all over the globe."

"I thought you just watched cartoons."

"Those were the cartoons. The news is worse."

"If I didn't know you better, Barn Wall, I'd say you were concerned."

"Well, shoot, I'm wondering if the Rapture's about to take place. What do you think?"

"The Rapture? That's pretty deep thinking for you, Barney."

"I'm no theologian or Eskimo-ologist, but the days look dark to me."

"Eskimo-ologist?"

"Yeah. Someone who studies the End-Times."

"You mean eschatologist."

"Yeah, that too. I didn't think it was just for Eskimos."

Ezra shook his head. "You never cease to amaze."

"I think I see the calf."

"Where?"

Barney pointed toward the East Fork of Deadman Creek. "Down there in the brush with a few head of cows."

"Perfect. Let's get off this skyline and circle around behind them. We'll take the bunch of 'em to the corrals."

They reined their horses west and trotted down a long, grassy coulee.

"Shoot, this is the life," Barney said. "And to think I could be scrubbing floors."

"Do you ever think about your last day horseback?" Ezra asked.

"Whadya mean?"

"You know. The last day you saddle up and ride."

"Geez, you're gloomy," Barney said. "I'm gonna get Raptured before then."

"What's with this Rapture business? You've never been one to talk about religion."

"The pastor's been hittin' it hard the past few Sundays. He said we better make sure our canteens are full of oil or something like that."

"Lamps."

"Lamps what?"

"Lamps full of oil. It's the parable about the wise and foolish virgins."

Barney chuckled. "Yup, I thought virgins were in the story. You know any?"

"What?"

"Virgins."

Ezra shook his head and urged Q-Tip into a slow lope. Knowing when to take Barney Wallace seriously was one of the more challenging tasks in his life.

Barney galloped his half-draft up beside him. The giant horse rumbled along like a semi-truck hauling melons.

"The way I figure it," Barney continued, "we're either going to be in a shooting war soon, or the Lord's coming back. What do you think?"

Ezra reined Q-Tip in. "I think we better slow down a little and not spook this calf into the next county."

"The Mark of the Beast," Barney whispered. "That's next."

"Could be," Ezra said.

"I wish someone would stop the planet and let me off. I miss the days when crooks robbed banks with six-guns and rode out of town on horses."

"You weren't alive then, Barney."

"Yeah, but I miss 'em anyway."

The bedded calf stood up and eyed the riders anxiously. It was nervous but stayed with the cows as the cowboys trailed the herd placidly to the corrals. Once penned, Barney watched the gate while Ezra used Q-Tip to sort the cows until the nervous calf was alone. Barney ran the steer down an alley, jumped it into the trailer's front compartment, and slammed the trailer gate shut.

"Gotcha," he yelled.

They loaded their two horses into the back compartment. Barney's half-Clydesdale took up most of the room.

As the truck and trailer pulled onto the county road, Barney shouted, "Davis."

Ezra stared at him.

"Davis," Barney repeated. "Benny Davis. That was the Wisconsin deer hunter's name."

Benny Davis, thought Ezra, that sounded familiar, but *Davis*?

"What did this guy look like?" Ezra asked.

"Mid-forties, kinda slender. Blond hair."

Davis Browne.

"What did he talk about?"

"Oh, calendars. And outhouses and churches. He asked if you ever went to church. I thought he was a little odd."

"In what way?"

"Suspicious-acting. One of those guys who thinks he's smarter than he is."

"He didn't seem like an out-of-state deer hunter?"

"No, more like a tax auditor reading your checkbook. Why?" Barney asked. "Do you think you know him?"

"Just curious," Ezra said. "As you've noted, we're living in dark days."

"There was one thing really odd about him. He wanted to know if you interpreted dreams."

"He what—" Ezra's eyes left the road for an instant, and the right tires spun in the loose gravel of the shoulder.

"I told him I didn't know about dreams, but I interpreted pizzas."

Davis Browne is back. How long has he been here, and what is he doing?

Ezra remembered Mary Margaret Hall's warning: "Your life is in danger."

24

Monday, November 8

Davis Browne, carrying two hard cases, entered the sporting goods store and walked straight to the gun department. Looking around, he saw the rifle racks were half-empty, the handgun displays were meager, and ammunition shelves were bare. It was not a good time for trade-ins, but he was determined to get it done.

The department manager, a trim young man with a goatee and a smile, came over. "Can I help you?" he asked.

Browne put his cases on a workbench and opened them.

"I need to make a trade," he said.

The manager looked the weapons over. "That's a Custom Nosler 28 with a Swarovski scope and a Nighthawk Mongoose revolver," he said. He whistled softly. "There's a lot of money laying here. We would have to trade you four or five guns for similar value."

"I don't care about similar value. I need something more practical."

"How many guns are you thinking?"

"I only need two."

The manager studied his customer and noted the red, swollen eyes and stubbled beard.

The young man shook his head. "I don't know," he said. "You have ten thousand dollars in value here."

The guns appeared new, and the clerk was afraid they'd been stolen.

Browne brought his wallet out and laid his driver's license and concealed carry permit on the table. "Run a background check on me," he said. "I'm a retired federal agent. I won these guns in a raffle, but I'm not a hunter."

The employee grimaced. It all seemed dicey to him.

"You need to talk to my boss," he said. "If you can wait here a minute, I'll go get him." The clerk turned and walked toward an office.

Moments later, an older man with swept-back gray hair walked up.

"So, what do we have here?" the owner asked.

"He has a Nosler 28 and a Nighthawk Mongoose .357," the clerk said. "Neither looks like they've been fired."

The older man handled the rifle, then laid it back in the case and picked up the revolver.

"A Custom Nighthawk Mongoose Silver," he said, admiring the fit and finish on the gun. "The finest revolver made in my book."

"I had a winning raffle ticket," Browne said nervously.

"And what were you hoping to trade for?" the owner asked.

"A semi-auto nine and an AR."

The owner looked at the employee. "Run his name through the system." The young man walked away.

"My background is clean," Browne said. "I'm retired Homeland Security."

The store owner looked at him curiously.

"And what are you doing in Montana?" he asked.

"I came out to hunt, but it's not my thing."

"We have a few ARs, but our handgun inventory is down. There's not much to choose from."

"Do you have any Glock 19s?"

"Not a one."

"Any Sigs?"

"Nope."

"What do you have?"

The owner looked down the aisle at the handgun display.

"Looks like I have a couple KelTechs and a Taurus."

Browne frowned. "That's it?"

"I don't know where you've been, mister. But there's been a huge run on guns and ammunition the past year. We have more stock than most dealers. There's a pawnshop down the street. You might try there."

Browne looked appreciatively at his guns. "That would be casting pearls before swine," he said.

"Well, it's up to you."

"I'll take an AR and the Taurus."

"That's only $1,800 worth from my end," the owner said. "I can't come up with thousands to boot."

"Straight across," Browne said. "No boot."

The storeowner raised his eyebrows, then looked down at the Nosler and Smith.

"If you throw in some ammo," Browne added.

"Now that could be a problem. We don't have a single box of 9mm or .223."

"I'll toss in the ammo I have for the Nosler and the Nighthawk."

"I dunno," the owner said, scratching his head.

Browne leaned closer. "The scope on the Nosler is worth more than your Taurus and AR," he whispered. "You're clearing thousands here. You must have a private stock of ammunition. I just need a couple boxes of each."

"You seem to be a little desperate," the owner said cautiously.

"Not desperate, wise. My former employment created many enemies."

"Anyone around here?" the man asked.

"I'm not free to say, and you don't want to know."

The young employee came back. "His background is clear," he said.

The older man studied Browne's face thoughtfully.

"Okay," the owner told the young man. "He's taking the Taurus and his pick of an AR. Get the paperwork started." He turned back to Browne. "It'll take me a minute to go home and get your deal-sweetener."

Browne nodded and smiled. He'd awakened that morning convinced Ezra Riley would be killed and the murder pinned on him. *That won't be as easy now,* he thought, since he'd traded the guns the Gray Lady had provided him.

Next, he had to do something about the truck.

But first, he had to make a call. Browne stored his new weapons in the pickup and crossed the street to Walmart, where he bought a cheap cell phone.

What was the number? He'd created an alphabetic code for a former girlfriend who was a reporter at the *Washington Post*. What was it? Yes, he remembered. He punched in YOUARESEXY and hoped the number was still active. One ring, two, three, four, five...

"Hello?"

"Cecily! This is Davis Browne. Please, don't hang up."

"Davis Browne," she said. There was sarcasm in her voice.

"Don't hang up. This is important."

"I should hang up. What do you want?"

"Cecily, listen. Would you believe me if I told you someone high in government has taken advantage of my stupidity?"

There was a pause before she said, "Yeah, I can believe that."

"It's true. There's a woman close to the President. Short, stout, mid-fifties, not unattractive, dresses in grays and blacks."

"Yeah, so? We call her the Gray Lady."

"You know her?"

"Sure. Her name is Isabel Hall. She's a wealthy patron who floats in both parties. Her money gives her access."

"What else? Who is she connected to?"

"No one that I know of since her uncle died."

"Her uncle?" Browne asked.

"Yeah, c'mon, don't tell me you don't know about William Hall."

Wild Bill Hall!

"Bill Hall, the master spook?"

"That's the one, but no one ever called him Bill. He was William Anderson Hall or Mr. Hall to the few who ever talked to him."

"He *was*?"

"Was. Hall has been dead for over ten years."

"Are you sure?"

"Yes, I'm sure. What's this about? Are you sober?"

Browne scanned the parking lot, wondering if he were in the crosshairs of an assassin at that moment. No, too public. It would be later, somewhere more remote.

"Davis? Are you still there?"

"Cecily, do some checking at Hyde Field for private jets coming and going the past few days."

"Private jets come and go there all the time."

"Ones connected to Hall."

"The Hall family is a web of corporations, NGOs, nonprofits, and foundations. Tracing anything back to Isabel Hall could take months. And why should I? What's the story here?"

"The story is about a secret visitor to the White House, to the President himself, a few nights ago."

"What secret visitor? Who are we talking about?"

"I can't tell you just yet," Browne said. "But it's true. I accompanied him."

"You accompanied him?" the woman asked incredulously. "Is this another of your secret agent fantasies?"

"I didn't go to the White House with him, just to Hyde Field. The Gray Lady took him from there."

"This sounds hinky, Davis."

"It's true, I swear. Just check it out, please."

Browne returned to his motel room. He needed to change motels. He needed to get rid of the truck. No, he had to replace the fancy new pickup with something else. No, he didn't need to change motels; he had to get out of Montana. His mind spun so rapidly it made him dizzy, so he lay down on the bed, his jacket still on, the Taurus semi-automatic pistol in the coat's right front pocket. Just in case.

He was instantly asleep, and the dream hit him like a fist to his forehead.

25

"Preacher's kid, preacher's kid! Sissy, sissy, preacher's kid."

Davis Browne clung to his stack of schoolbooks while the bullies pushed him, but the burden of the weight toppled him. The books scattered onto the sidewalk, where the bullies gleefully kicked them, until the leader, Anton, planted a shoe on Browne's ribs, forcing the air from the boy's lungs in short, sharp gasps.

"Pussy preacher kid," Anton growled. "Go to church with mommy, go to church with daddy." He stepped on Browne's hand and ground it into the cement.

They left laughing. Davis struggled to his feet, picked up his books and papers, and stomped home. His mom had come to the lunchroom at noon with his Bible to remind him to study for the Wednesday night service at the Pentecostal Assemblies.

Anton and his pack had laughed and then caught him after the final bell.

Davis ran home.

He would do something about this.

No one was home, so he rushed to his parents' bedroom, climbed onto a chair, and grabbed a shoebox on the closet shelf. Davis unwrapped a snub nosed .38 Special from oil rags, checked the cylinder to assure it was loaded, stuck it in his waistband, and ran back out the door.

No one could run like Davis Browne. Through the clutter, trash, and barking dogs of the poor neighborhood, he sped like Achilles. Knowing where Anton lived, Davis knew he could catch Anton walking alone, down the railroad tracks, to the place the bully shared with an alcoholic father and three brothers.

He saw Anton ahead, lumbering like a bear.

The big boy turned and laughed in surprise when he saw his skinny victim running on stilted legs.

"What do you want, preacher boy? Another whipping?" he mocked.

Then, as an eastbound freight train rumbled by, Davis pulled the .38, still running, huffing and puffing, and unable to draw a good bead, and fired.

The gunshot sounded like a crisp crack against the low thunderings of the train.

Anton's eyes widened, and he turned and ran.

No one could outrun Davis Browne.

He shot as he ran. A second shot, a third—he was gaining quickly—a fourth, a fifth.

He was on the bully's heels now, aimed at his head, and pulled the trigger.

Click.

The revolver only held five rounds.

Anton kept running, screaming, crying, having not heard the firing pin fall on an empty chamber.

Davis came to a staggering stop, watched the waddling Anton lumber on in panic, then turned and jogged home. Arriving ahead of his mother, he reloaded the revolver and was wrapping the gun in the rag when he had a sudden thought.

Why not kill *her*?

Why not kill his mother?

Killing her would end most of his problems.

A stabbing headache jarred Browne awake on the motel bed; sweat was stinging his eyes and salting the edges of his mouth.

He trembled with horror and excitement.

Somehow, the Taurus pistol that had been in his coat pocket was gripped rigidly in his right hand.

After Barney left, Ezra unsaddled Q-Tip, grained the horses, then packed a reclining lawn chair and a space heater into the narrow tack room. With a concrete floor and wooden walls, the room was solid and warmed quickly. He considered sleeping there.

The house, in contrast, seemed large, cold, dark, and hard to defend.

Was he actually thinking about tactical defense?

Yes, and he should be.

Mary Margaret Hall had warned him his life could be in danger, and she was undoubtedly in a position to know.

The absurdity and gravity of the past five days had caught up to him. Yes, he had clandestinely gone to the White House and interpreted a dream for the United States President.

What had seemed like a duty to God and patriotism to his country now seemed reckless. He'd assumed the jet was provided by the administration or by a friend of the President.

But was it? On whose side was William Anderson Hall, a man who had dedicated his life to harnessing unseen powers? During Ezra's days of hitchhiking and drug use, he'd crossed paths with many in the New Age, the occult, and even Satanists, his innate spirituality drawing these people like a magnet.

He missed Anne.

He didn't want to put her in danger, but she was his anchor. Anne could speak peace to turbulent waters.

He missed having a good dog as an early-warning device.

Ezra decided to sleep in the tack room. He went to the house for a sleeping bag, pillow, and blankets. He left lights on in the basement so people would think he was home and grabbed a revolver, a lever-action carbine, a tactical flashlight, and a box of ammunition from the gun safe.

After being casual for days about his trip to Washington, he bordered now on paranoia.

What role did Davis Browne play in this? he wondered. Why had he given an alias to Barney, and what was the connection between Browne and Hall and Duke University?

Ezra moved the saddle horses to the corral closest to the tack room and tossed a hay bale in a rubber tub. Not having a dog, perhaps they'd alert him should a stranger approach the barn.

The tack room door had locks on the inside and the outside.

He could lock someone out.

But they could also lock him in.

26

Worry kept the Gray Lady awake. She seldom slept in her uncle's small mansion, and the bed, pillows, and country stillness were uncomfortable to her.

For months she'd seen the old man slowly failing—expected from one of ninety-four years—but why did it have to be now after an operation had been launched?

Was dementia, even senility, interwoven in the planning of this mission?

Isabel Elizabeth Hall had a condominium in Georgetown and a cabin in upstate New York. Within her social world, she enjoyed prestige, power, and privilege. Her aged uncle could pass at any time. What would she do if he died with this operation underway and a human experiment housed underground on the estate?

Could she lean on the estate's five employees?

Would they know what to do with the Blue Man?

Would they agree to kill him if that was the only way out of this deadly dilemma?

William Anderson Hall had never lacked confidence in his abilities and beliefs and didn't understand fear, but he had two concerns.

His nieces.

He should have made Isabel Elizabeth aware of the Blue Man long ago but feared her reaction. Isabel was loyal to him and her country, but she'd never ventured into war zones, endured torture, or slit a throat while holding a person's face in her hand. Isabel wasn't built for field operations. Her skills were infiltration and influence. The younger niece was intelligent and dedicated, but she was a stranger to horror.

Her older sister was another matter. Hall did not know what to do about Mary Margaret, and her appearance here had caught him off guard.

Mary Margaret had been his first choice for a successor. She was formidable. If it had come to slitting throats, she would have rolled up her sleeves and done it.

But an *ecstasy* had intersected her path, and she'd never been the same. And only Mary Margaret was brazen enough to challenge him.

There was no doubt his older niece loved him, but her higher allegiances would not be deterred. Her loyalty was to her faith, not to family blood, and if human justice was involved, her ideals could lead to his betrayal.

Despite her religious idiosyncrasies, Hall was fond of Mary Margaret.

He sincerely hoped he would not have to dispose of her.

When she was certain her uncle and the servants were asleep, the Gray Lady slipped from her bedroom and padded softly to her uncle's study. First, she ran her hands along the burnished bookshelves searching for the Blue Man's tunnel entrance. Not finding it, she surmised it was elsewhere, perhaps in a closet.

The Panic Room, she thought. Of course, William Anderson Hall didn't call it a Panic Room because he never panicked. But the house held a heavily fortified room where the former intelligence agent kept weapons, cash, and who knows how many secrets. But the room was locked, and she hadn't been trusted with the combination. It was an odd quirk of her uncle's; he preferred combination locks to padlocks.

Did any of the staff know of the tunnel's entrance or the combination to the Panic Room?

How much did the staff know about Blue Man?

Four men were assigned to him and stayed in a cabin near the sanctuary. Gray Lady had only glimpsed them a few times, and they seemed imposing. No doubt they were former government contractors with strong loyalties to William Anderson Hall. One looked like he might be Cuban.

The housekeeper was as shy as a mouse. At the sound of Isabel's helicopter, the woman scurried to her hole, but Isabel suspected she was foreboding in her unique way. *Domestic* was not a term that described her uncle's house help.

There were no cameras or listening devices in the study; Isabel was sure of that, but she didn't dare rifle through her uncle's desk or files. If everything wasn't locked tight, it was likely booby-trapped.

Why am I even down here? she thought. Nothing good comes from spying on the world's best spy.

Then she was drawn to the windows, parted the curtains, and looked toward the pines where a sanctuary lay under the Virginia sod.

Blue Man.

Blue Man had called her.

Bill Hall was not asleep. He was sitting in bed reading the journal he'd removed that day from his walk-in vault.

He heard Isabel get up, and it pleased him. He wanted a little more spunk from his younger niece. She was formidable in the business realm and affable amongst politicians but only dutiful in covert operations.

He didn't know what she was doing, and he didn't care. If he got up and confronted his niece, it would only scare her.

He had other concerns. Hall knew his strength was weakening, but he was determined to live long enough to see Isabel through her transition to becoming Blue Man's manager.

He looked down at the journal. Another matter was more complicated.

Should he reveal the truth to Mary Margaret and Isabel?

Or should he take the history with him to the grave?

27

"Ezra! Wake up!"

A pounding sounded on the tack room door.

Ezra sat up startled and reached for his flashlight and revolver.

"Come on, Ezra, open the door."

"Who's out there?" Ezra demanded.

"It's me, Davis Browne. Open the door. It's an emergency."

Ezra, sleeping in his clothes, pulled on his boots, coat, and hat and pushed the chair out of the way. "What do you want?" he asked.

"We need to talk," Browne said.

"Are you armed?"

Browne paused, then said, "Yes."

"Put your hands up high, and I'll open the door." Ezra knew his high-lumen tactical flashlight would blind Brown.

Ezra opened the door. Browne grimaced as the light hit his face.

"My revolver is aimed at your chest," Ezra said. "Tell me why you're here."

"Can't we go in the house?" Browne asked. "It's chilly out here."

Browne was right, Ezra realized. The night was cold. "Okay, but walk ahead of me and keep your hands up."

"This isn't necessary," Browne insisted.

"Yes, it is." They walked across the ranch yard to a house lit up with lights. Browne had been in there looking for him, Ezra realized. They went up the stairs, through the front door, down the hall, and to the kitchen, where Ezra told Browne to take off his coat and sit at the table.

"Hand me your coat," Ezra said. Browne did, and Ezra could feel the weight of the pistol in the front pocket. He lay the jacket on the kitchen counter, then sat between Browne and the coat, his handgun still leveled at the former federal agent.

"What are you doing back in Miles City?" Ezra asked.

"I was doing my job," Browne said. "You can put the gun down, Ezra."

Ezra didn't. "Why did you tell Barney you were Benny Davis?"

"Like I said, it was my job. She paid me to investigate you."

"Who's *she*?"

"A woman who contacted me in D.C."

"Isabel Elizabeth Hall?"

Browne's eyebrows knotted with surprise. "You know about her?"

"I do, and I know about William Anderson Hall. What's your role in all this?"

"They hired me to vet you before taking you to the White House, then right away, they hired me again saying you were dangerous, that you belonged to a violent cult."

"What violent cult?"

"Righteous Sword."

"I've never heard of it."

"Neither have I. I don't think it exists."

Ezra lowered his revolver to his lap. "So why are you here tonight?"

Browne looked sheepish and Ezra almost felt sorry for him.

"I brought back some of your stuff I took," Browne said.

"What stuff?"

"A storage tub of manuscripts and letters."

Ezra looked at him sternly, and his hand started to raise the revolver.

"I've been in your house three times," Browne said. "You really should lock your doors. I was looking for proof that you had dangerous affiliations. I don't know what happened in the White House, but the Gray Lady said the president seemed upset."

"The Gray Lady?"

"That's how Isabel Hall is known."

"The President was a little upset," Ezra said. "That's all I can say about that."

"The Gray Lady and her uncle want to know the dream and your interpretation."

"Why?"

"I have no idea."

Ezra looked at him more closely. "You look like hell," he said.

Browne shrugged. "I can't sleep, and if I do, I have terrible dreams. This afternoon—"

"You dreamt about your childhood?"

Browne gave him a flat look. "Yeah, how did you... No, don't answer that."

"A dream about something that actually happened?"

Browne nodded. "When I was twelve, I took shots at a bully. I missed him five times, thank God, but then I came home and planned on shooting my mother."

"Obviously, you didn't."

"No, but I wanted to."

"You've been played."

"I think they've been playing me for years. I left the Air Force because I got a scholarship to Duke to get my master's. Then a job with Homeland Security fell in my lap. I lost that job, but a position at a university opened up, and I've sat in an office there doing next to nothing for years."

"They had you on ice," Ezra noted. "Besides bringing back my manuscripts, what else do you want?"

"Two things," Browne said. "First, I want to know how you came up with the name Benny Davis."

"*I* came up with the name?"

"He's the hero in your unpublished novel, *Cleansers*."

Ezra grinned. "So that's it. I thought the name sounded familiar. I haven't read that novel in twenty-five years. I forgot all about the name."

"You used my alias," Browne said. "And the plot of the novel is about a dream."

"That is interesting," Ezra said. "But it's just one of the Lord's little jokes. The novel was terrible. I hated it."

"So, that's it? Just a divine coincidence?"

"That's all. What's the other thing you want?"

Embarrassed, Browne looked down at the table, then looked up bashfully. "I want your old truck," he said.

"Old Yeller? You want my '78 Ford?"

Browne nodded. "I'll trade you a brand new Ford—less than five hundred miles on it. I have a signed title."

"Why?"

"They can track me in that new truck. I need an old one with no GPS, no computers, no bugs."

"I like Old Yeller."

"Will it get me to Texas?"

Ezra thought for a moment. "Sure, it will get you to Texas if you take it easy."

"You can have whatever else is in my truck, too. There's a pair of binoculars and a spotting scope."

"You think the Halls are after you?"

"I know they are. Even if I got the dream and interpretation from you, I think they'd finish me."

"I can't tell you the dream."

"I know, and I'm not going to ask you to."

"What do you plan on doing?"

"I'm going to see my mother," Browne said. "I need to see her. It's been five, six years since I've even talked to her."

"Then what?"

"I know someone in Mexico. I have some cash the Halls paid me and some money back in Washington. More than enough to get me there."

"Will they be expecting you to go to your mother's?"

"Maybe, but I won't be there long. I think my hatred for my parents and religion is why they recruited me."

"Hating religion hasn't helped you, Davis."

"I know, but I do hate it. It robbed me of my childhood."

"In my writings, have you read my story of the little blue roan horse?"

Browne shook his head, confused. "I don't think so."

"When I was ten, my father made me break a blue roan pony named Ribbon Tail. That horse was born mean. It hated people and refused to leave the corrals. I couldn't do anything with it. My father yelled at me, my uncles and sisters mocked me. At night my mom lectured my father about that horse, wanting him to get rid of it, but he refused. His son was going to break that horse, and that was all there was to it."

"So, what happened?"

Ezra laughed. "I shot it in the ear with a .22. and killed it, but that's not the point of my story. The point is I could have hated horses forever after that, and I wanted to, but I didn't, and horses have been a huge part of my life ever since."

"What made the difference?"

"The Lord sent a good horse, a paint I called Gusto. My dad bought him as a yearling. That horse was from the Lord. He was everything Ribbon Tail wasn't. Ribbon Tail was evil. Gusto was grace."

Browne shifted in his chair. "What does this have to do with me?"

"Don't discount Jesus because your parents went to religious extremes, Davis. Jesus is bigger than religion."

Browne pursed his lips. "I guess I'll have time to think about that on my way home to Texas."

"You'll have lots of time to think," Ezra joked. "Old Yeller will be in the slow lane all the way south."

"Sorry about asking for the truck. I know you like it, and a $60,000 new one isn't a replacement."

"I'll get by. It will stay parked in the yard. The Halls know where I live, but, finding me in the hills isn't easy if I'm horseback."

"They'll be coming," Browne said. "Or sending someone, more likely."

Ezra nodded.

Browne handed him the title to the new Ford, then the two went outside and put Browne's few belongings in Old Yeller.

"The tank is full, and you have a spare and a jack," Ezra said.

Browne extended his hand. "Thank you," he said. "For everything." Then the ex-agent climbed in the front seat, and the old truck slowly rattled away.

Ezra watched the taillights diminish in the darkness.

"Dang," he said to himself. "I'm going to miss that truck."

Half a mile up the highway, sitting in the darkness on the shoulder of the road, a person in a dark sedan watched the old pickup truck leave Ezra Riley's ranch.

28

Mary Margaret Hall pulled onto the blacktopped parking lot of the Range Riders Museum, which sat on several acres west of Miles City across the Tongue River Bridge. She was immediately impressed with the site's cleanliness and the number of historical structures.

Hall hadn't finished her Miles City assignment; she didn't know what was left to do and how long it would take, but she would know when she was released.

Her family wealth enabled prayer missions and ministry trips to Haiti, Mozambique, Mexico, Peru, and Romania. Miles City, Montana, was another mission field on the map, but one that she shared responsibility. She regretted giving Riley's name to her sister.

Hall's pilot liked his employer's randomness. He relished the downtime to read and catch up on paperwork, and Ms. Hall paid very well.

Mary Margaret parked her rental car and walked to the unlocked museum door. A bell tinkled as she entered.

An older man in a work apron emerged from a back room. "Can I help you, ma'am?" he said but added, "The museum is closed for the season."

"May I walk through the displays quickly?" she asked. Mary Margaret wore authority comfortably, like a royal shawl upon her shoulders, and her smile was confident but warm.

"I guess it wouldn't do any harm," the man said. He was curious about this stranger who'd disarmed him with style. "Is there anything, in particular, you are interested in?" he asked.

"What is through those doors?" she asked, pointing straight ahead.

"That's our Hall of Pioneers. It's a bit cool in there. We don't heat it in the off-season, but you can take a look if you want."

He led her into a spacious room with walls lined with scores of black-and-white photographic portraits of stalwart-looking men and a few sturdy women.

Hall scanned the faces with appreciation and amazement.

"We have big doings in here sometimes," the man said. "Banquets, weddings, special ceremonies, and the like."

"Are you the curator?" she asked, not taking her eyes from the men who appeared to be staring down at her.

"No, just a volunteer," he said. "I'm building new displays for our Pioneer Women addition."

Mary Margaret looked at him closely. He was trim and erect and looked capable of long hours of labor. "How old are you, if I may ask?"

"I'm eighty-six," the man said.

She smiled. "You certainly seem to have inherited the vigor of the pioneers on these walls."

"Keep the body moving is my motto. That way, age has a hard time catching up with you."

Plaques under the photos described each settler's profession: Pioneer Rancher, Sheepman, Sheriff, Buffalo Hunter, Wolfer, Cowboy.

"Tell me," she said, still following the faces as if meeting each soul. "Do you know a man named Ezra Riley?"

"Sure. Known Ezra for years. We went to the same church for a long time."

"But you don't go to the same church anymore?"

"Oh, no, I'm not sure Ezra and Anne attend anywhere."

Mary Margaret pulled her collar tight. The room held that dank chill that crawls into one's bones. "Did something happen?" she asked.

"Well," the man paused, not knowing how to answer.

"I don't mean to pry," she said. "I've met Ezra; he is the reason I am in Miles City." She lowered her gaze from the portraits to the handyman. "I'm in ministry myself, and I'm an admirer of Ezra's ministry. I first met him many years ago at a conference in St. Louis."

"He's a gifted fellow," the man said. "A good writer and speaker."

"And dream interpreter?"

"Yes, that was part of the problem."

"The problem?"

"Why don't we go to the room where I'm working," he said. "It's much warmer in there." He led Ms. Hall out of the Hall of Pioneers. She followed him past old saddles, bits, spurs, photographs, paintings, sculptures, military uniforms, native headdresses, artifacts, a collection of Bull Durham tobacco pouches, and other items so numerous Hall could hardly separate one from another. They entered a room enclosed by plastic sheeting. Sawdust and tools littered the floor, and a space heater glowed invitingly.

The man offered the lady a folding chair, and he leaned against a sawhorse.

"Ezra was in our church for several years before the first pastor left," the man explained. "We didn't have any denominational help, so Ezra filled in. He preached on Sundays, taught on Wednesday nights, and he and Anne did some counseling out at their ranch. He refused to do weddings and funerals, though.

"We got another pastor, but he didn't last long. His hands were too soft, and his head too full of Bible School ideas. He didn't understand the people around here. You know, hard-working, blue-collar folk. That young man thought preaching was a white-collar position with career advancement. He particularly didn't like Ezra."

"I can imagine a stark difference," Mary Margaret said.

"Then another preacher came. He represented a big denomination and promised lots of help from headquarters, like the financial assistance we sorely needed. But there was a catch. The denomination wanted the deeds to the building and land. Ezra was dead set against that.

"Then there was Ezra's beliefs. He and Anne are Charismatics. They speak in tongues, believe in supernatural healings, deliverance from demons, words of knowledge, and prophecy. All that stuff."

"Do you believe in those things?" she asked.

"I sorta do," the man admitted. "But the church needed help, and that denomination was dead set against Holy Rollers."

Holy Rollers? Mary Margaret had not heard that term in decades.

"The issue to join this denomination came to a vote by the board," the man continued. "It passed 3-2. The new guy became our pastor, and he sent Ezra an official letter saying Ezra was banned from the church property and would be charged with trespassing if he showed up."

"A restraining order? That was harsh."

"I think it hurt Ezra and Anne. Anne had been leading worship there for years, and Ezra didn't grow up in a close family. The church was his family."

"Do you still go to that church?"

The man shrugged. "Yeah, I do, but not as often as I should. It just doesn't feel like home anymore."

Ezra swung a leg over the cantle and gently lowered himself to the ground. Dismounting Simon was like stepping off a roof. He needed smaller horses. Even Q-Tip and Quincy were taller than he liked.

Maybe I've gone full circle and need to ride Shetlands again, he thought.

Ezra rubbed the bay giant behind each ear, and the horse responded by lifting its head for a good scratching under its jaws.

"I thought we saw her today, ole boy," Ezra said. He'd glimpsed what he thought was the Wildebeest in his neighbor's cattle, but riding the pasture turned up nothing.

"She's a shape-shifter," Ezra said. "She changes into a coyote and crawls into a hole."

Simon shook his head, rattling the chains that attached the leather reins to the bit. The bay was tired of idle conversation.

"I miss Ole Yeller," Ezra said, wondering how far Davis Browne had gone in the past twenty hours.

A wave of melancholy washed over the cowboy. He knew life could never be routine again. Ezra disdained boredom, but if his life was at risk, as Mary Margaret had suggested, the mundane was welcome. Going home to a dark, silent house was uninviting, knowing someone could be waiting in the shadows.

The days of long rides ending with his wife's smile and a hot meal seemed ages in the past.

He looked about at the land he had worked so hard far, digging countless postholes by hand and pounding innumerable steel posts into the hardpan soil. What he'd accomplished was done through muscle and sweat. Ezra didn't like machinery, let alone technology, and had worn his body beyond its expiration date. Only his momentum kept him going. If he slowed down or stopped, the clock in his chest would stop ticking.

Time. That is what it was all about.

Time was winding down.

Not just for him, but all things temporal.

Ezra shook off the contemplations and pulled himself back into the saddle. Simon's ears perked, his stride lengthened, and energy coursed through his 1,350 pounds when Ezra reined him toward home.

As dusk settled, the evening chilled. Ezra threw hay to the horses and crossed the graveled ranch yard with a carbine in his arms—a Mossberg tactical .30-30 with powerful lights mounted on two Picatinny rails.

I should have locked the house.

Old habits die hard.

Nearing the ranch house, he saw headlights slow on the highway, then turn down his lane.

Visitors.

29

In the headlights, Mary Margaret Hall saw a cowboy with a rifle, and for a moment, she recalled the portraits in the hall at the museum.

Riley's set jaw, piercing eyes, and determined brow was a monument to men who stood against blizzards, drought, injuries, and falling markets. He wore chaps, jeans, a heavy coat, and silver spurs twinkled on his heels.

She remembered first meeting him in a Fort Worth motel lobby long before their encounter in St. Louis. She and two friends couldn't open the plastic case that held highlighters. One suggested asking the front desk for scissors, but Mary Margaret saw a lean, muscled cowboy standing by the front door as if awaiting a ride.

"What we need is a sharp knife," she told her friends, and she walked across the lobby to the man in the cowboy hat.

"Excuse me," she said. "You look like the type of man who'd carry a pocketknife."

He turned and looked at her with a startling intensity in his eyes. His face, deeply tanned and weathered, was kind, but the eyes cut straight through her. He reached into a front pocket and handed her his knife. She brought it back moments later and thanked him. He nodded, then stepped through the door and into a taxi.

Years later, in St. Louis, Mary Margaret recognized his photo on the conference brochure's back page. The text said Ezra Riley was a Montana writer who'd teach a single morning session on interpreting dreams. He later ministered privately to the conference leaders.

What a tangled twist of fate, she thought.

"I thought you two were gone," Ezra said, opening the door to his house.

"I couldn't leave just yet," the woman responded.

Ezra took off his hat, chaps, and spurs.

Hall's pilot gestured to the wooden stove. "I'll start a fire for you, if you wish," he said.

Ezra thanked him, then guided Mary Margaret Hall to the living room.

"I'm sure you have things to tell me," Ezra said.

"I do, but first I must ask you something. The other night a shiny new truck passed me while I was driving and praying. It pulled in here. Twenty minutes later, an old pickup left here and I passed it on my way back to town. The drivers were the same person."

"It was the same person."

"Would you care to tell me more?"

"He is, or was, an employee of your uncle's."

"What did he want?"

"To get to Mexico untraced. Why are you still in Miles City, Mary Margaret?" He'd not noticed before that she was uniquely attractive. Not beautiful in a standard way, but elegant and refined; a woman groomed by wealth and education.

"The Lord hasn't released me to leave."

"You're a prophetic intercessor?"

"You understand what I am?"

"I'm married to a prophetic intercessor. Your singular mission is to go wherever sent and pray however long it's necessary."

"It's too bad your wife's not here. You could use her now."

"It's not safe. What has the Lord shown you?"

"This region is similar to where I live in Vermont. The people are philosophical and stubborn, but here they are considerably more conservative."

"Excuse me, but it doesn't take revelation to realize that. What specifically have you been shown?"

"There is death on the highway."

"Whose? Mine?"

"No, your threat is in the hills."

"The man who left in the old truck?"

"He has death attached to him, but it won't happen here."

"Who then?"

"I don't know. He's not here yet."

"Someone sent by your uncle?"

She cocked her head, and a long strand of auburn-colored hair fell across her face. She whisked it back.

"My uncle officially is dead. He faked his death years ago and retreated to a fortress in a Virginia forest. I've no idea what he is up to."

"How evil is he?"

"How evil can deception be? He has good intentions. In many ways, you and he are similar. Patriotism guides Uncle Bill, but his methods are dangerous."

"Why are you so different?" Ezra asked. "What broke you out of the family mold?"

"When I was twenty, I was diagnosed with stage four breast cancer, given six months to live, and told to get my affairs in order. And yes, even at that age, I had considerable *affairs*. I was dying at home, just my private nurse and me. I had occasional visits from my teenaged sister.

"One evening, as I lay in bed, Jesus came into my room, smiled, touched me, then left. An hour later, I was downstairs enjoying a full meal.

"I was completely healed."

"Neither you nor your sister ever married?"

"No. My life has been dedicated to the Lord and hers to Uncle Bill."

"Is your work here in Montana finished?"

"Yes, we'll be flying home tonight. I hope I've been some help because I am responsible for your involvement."

"No, you're not. It was meant to be. I'm not concerned about your uncle."

"You should be concerned about my uncle," she corrected him. "And my sister. Their motives may be honorable, but the forces behind them want to destroy you."

"Noted. Not being concerned won't mean not being cautious."

"I know why you went to Washington, Ezra. It's not revelation from God or reports from my political sources. It's simple logic. You were sent to interpret a dream for the President."

Ezra's face didn't flinch.

"I won't ask you what the dream was, or your interpretation, but should we be preparing for war?"

"Preparation is always wise."

"What will be your response, Ezra?"

"If they come for me for the sake of Christ, I will surrender peacefully and pray to be a witness of His love."

"If they come in the name of politics?"

"If they come to take my land, cattle, horses, and guns, I will resist."

Mary Margaret rose to leave but stopped and looked at him intently. "I'll pray you'll know the difference," she said.

30

Wednesday, November 10

Ezra not only slept in; he slept through Anne's phone call.

He emailed her, made coffee, started a fire in the woodstove, then settled into a chair with a loaded .30-30 at the ready.

He turned the television on and browsed through the religious channels, deciding if he'd be a Baptist, Seventh-Day Adventist, or a Charismatic this morning.

Catholic. The Catholic station awed him with the cathedral's beauty and the loveliness of the acapella singing. The liturgy was heavenly, so Ezra turned the volume up and closed his eyes. There was value in ritual and tradition, Ezra thought, providing it didn't obstruct the power of the Holy Spirit.

He didn't hear Barney knock, nor did he hear his friend come in.

"Ezra, did you become a Catholic?"

Ezra jumped in the chair and reached for the rifle.

"Whoa there, cowboy," Barney said. "I didn't mean to startle you. I knocked, but you couldn't hear me."

"That's all right," Ezra said. "Have a seat. I was just enjoying the music." Using the remote, he lowered the volume of the television.

"That's the Catholic station," Barney said. "I'm Catholic."

"Barney, you've been attending an Evangelical church for thirty years."

"Yeah, but I was baptized Catholic."

"Sprinkled, you mean."

"No, I got dunked. I think the priest was trying to drown me. He must have been part Baptist."

"So, what brings you over this morning, Barn Wall?"

"Nothing in particular. Whose new pickup is sitting in the yard?"

"Mine."

"Yours?"

"I traded Old Yeller for it."

Barney's eyebrows rose to his brow line. "You did? Who would do that?"

"Benny Davis, the deer hunter."

"You're putting me on. You just traded for the day or something, right?"

Ezra reached for the piece of paper near his coffee cup. "Here's the title," he said.

Barney carefully examined it. "Shoot," he said. "This is the real deal. I don't get it. Why would he do that?"

"It doesn't have a computer chip, so they can't track it."

"Ole Benny's on the run?"

"Benny's on the run."

"Who's after him?"

"I can't say."

Barney thought for a minute. "Are they after you, too?"

"Probably."

"What are you going to do with the truck?"

"Sell it to you."

"I don't want it."

The two old cowboy friends sat quietly, weighing the irony of the moment.

"Did you ever think you would turn down a brand new F-250?" Ezra asked.

"I'm reconsidering the deal," Barney said. "What do you want in exchange for it?"

"I'll take a sackful of barn cats."

"I don't have any barn cats."

"How about twenty pounds of stout French roast coffee beans?"

"You know I don't drink coffee."

Ezra yawned. "I guess I'll just have to keep it then."

"You look tired. Riding every day is wearing you out."

"We're old, Barney."

"No, we're just old for being cowboys. If we were accountants we'd be in our prime."

"You and me as accountants; something about that doesn't add up."

"So who is this Benny Davis guy? Do you know him?"

"I can't say."

"Are you growing pot, again?"

"Barney, that was fifty years ago."

"Ezra, you're edgier than a roomful of razor blades. I want to know what's going on."

"No, Barney, you don't. The less you know the better."

"This has something to do with your ministry work, doesn't it?"

"In a manner of speaking."

"You think this Benny Davis character will come back for his truck?"

"I hope so. I miss Ole Yeller."

"And all this has you watching Catholic TV?"

"The country is getting weird, Barney."

"Ain't that the truth." He opened his heavy Carhartt coat to reveal a .45 Colt Single Action Army revolver. "I always have a gun in a vehicle, but I'm carrying concealed from now on."

"You're feeling a sense of impending judgment?"

"I don't know about that," Barney said. "But I think the proverbial barnyard excrement is about to collide with the rotating cooling device."

Isabel Hall met her uncle downstairs for breakfast. He buttered his muffin with shaking hands and drank weak coffee.

"Did you sleep well?" he asked.

"Fine," she said, lying.

"We have a development at Hyde Field. Do you know a journalist named Cecily York?"

"From the *Post.* I believe I've met her." Isabel had a bowl of hot oatmeal in front of her but had no appetite.

"She was making inquiries last night about private jets flying to Montana. I don't think she found anything determinative, but it shows someone is talking. It has to be either Browne or Riley. Have you heard from Browne yet?"

"No, he's still not answering."

"Then it's him. Get a fix on his truck. Let's find out where he is."

Gray Lady nodded.

Hall gestured at her bowl. "You're not hungry this morning, Isabel?"

"No, I often don't eat until noon."

"Breakfast is important. You should eat breakfast. Now then, what were we talking about?"

"Dealing with Browne."

"Oh, yes, Browne. Take care of him."

"And after that?"

"After that? You and I have thirty years invested in this project; you get close to leaders and compile information, and I train Blue Man. We will continue toward our goal."

Hall ate his muffin carefully with his fingers, then wiped his hands daintily on a napkin.

"We must continue," he said. "Globalism is on our doorstep. The Communists have been patient. It has taken them decades, but they own most of the world leaders, including our own. They all have dirty secrets. Drugs, bribes, human trafficking…who knows what else? Blue Man will reveal it all."

"So, what, or who, is next?"

"Riley first," Hall said.

"Why Riley?"

"I want the dream, but if we can't pry it out of Riley, we still have to test him. How is Riley prescient? How did he know the dream before the President spoke a word. Is he someone's creation, and if so, whose?"

"You want to test Blue Man against him?

Hall slammed his fist on the table, but it made little noise. "Riley was a hippy, don't forget that. His short hair and cowboy boots mean nothing."

"You think he might be a Communist?"

"I don't know what to think. That's why we have to find out."

"And after we find out?"

"We eliminate him. He's a dangerous loose end, much more problematic than Davis Browne."

"If we're cutting loose ends," the Gray Lady said, "is Mary Margaret one of them?"

Hall looked at his niece with sad, watery eyes. "That depends on how much she knows. Or suspects."

"But, really—"

He held up his hand to stop her. "Do not make me remind you again, Isabel, that this is a war. The future of our nation and the free world is at stake. Mary Margaret is dear to me, too, so let us hope she hasn't learned more than she should have."

Isabel lowered her eyes. "But we take care of Browne first?"

"Find him and have him killed. Browne has been a disappointment, a waste of time and money."

"And Riley?"

"I'm turning Blue Man loose on the cowboy. I want to know what manner of man this Montanan is. Blue Man will dig in his subconscious for a few nights and we'll see what happens."

"But, how will we know? We have no one close to him now."

"Send Maintenance to Montana. Have him take care of Browne, then stay to keep an eye on Riley. Tell him to fly into Billings, not Miles City. While you are at it, have our computer man locate Browne. It will make Maintenance's work easier."

"And Ezra Riley, is it that important to break him?"

Staring at his niece with a will the Chinese, Koreans, Cubans, and Vietnamese could not subdue, Hall raised a bony finger and declared, "Ezra Riley will crack like a pinata—spilling his little secrets, including the contents of the President's dream.

"The breaking of Ezra Riley is now Blue Man's goal."

31

Thursday, November 11

The pained screeches of a bird awakened her. Was the kitchen staff killing a chicken? Gray Lady changed hastily from pajamas to black slacks, black blouse, and a gray woolen sweater, then moved quickly down the marble stairs to the landing by the doors to her uncle's study.

The noise wasn't a bird in pain; it was her uncle. She pressed an ear against the door.

"Idiots!" she heard him scream. "You are all idiots."

Was he berating his staff? Her worst fear hit her. Blue Man had escaped!

A tinny, wavering noise was in the background.

Television. Her uncle was watching TV.

"Fools! You're ruining the country. You should all be shot for treason, every last one of you."

Uncle Bill was watching the morning news.

Isabel Hall hurried back to her room, got her cell phone, and dialed a number.

The phone rang four times before a man picked up. "Yes?" he said solemnly.

"Operation Roadkill," Gray Lady said. "Mockingbird."

"Copy."

"Operation Spyglass. Meadowlark."

"Affirmative," the voice answered, and the man hung up.

It was a prearranged code: Locate Davis Browne and kill him. Then spy on Ezra Riley.

She called her highly paid contact at Hyde Field.

"Ready the smaller jet for our maintenance man," she told him. "Property problems out west require his services."

The man agreed.

"Any action on the other items?"

"The reporter was back," the man said. "I don't think she's getting anywhere. And your sister's jet arrived after midnight last night."

"Was she alone?"

"Just her and her pilot."

Mary Margaret owned a HondaJet HA-420, a single-pilot plane that cruised at 483 miles per hour. Isabel was privately pleased that her Citation CJ4, also rated for a single pilot, was faster at 508 miles per hour.

Speed issues aside, why had Mary Margaret been in Montana so long? What had Riley told her?

She ended the call. This information would have to be kept from her uncle if possible.

"Isabel!"

He was calling her from downstairs. She glanced at herself in the room's vanity mirror and regretted she hadn't time for makeup. Her face was as ashen as her sweater.

After a soft rap on the study door, he summoned her in.

"Take a seat," he snapped. "Need coffee?"

"Yes, please."

He grabbed a small bell from the table beside his chair and shook it as vigorously as he could. Moments later, a woman entered the room with a silver serving tray, set it on the table, poured two cups of coffee from a sterling pot, and left. Gray Lady turned her face toward the window so as not to look at her. It was a beautiful morning outside. She wondered, for an instant, what it would be like to awaken to simple chores: filling a bird feeder, raking a lawn, cleaning windows.

"Isabel, your coffee."

She turned to see a shaking hand, rattling cup, and coffee spilling on the floor. She grabbed the cup quickly.

"The idiots in Washington are rabid dogs," Hall said. "They'll destroy this nation in a week at this rate."

"There are new developments?" his niece asked carefully.

"They think they have a clear road to do what they like." The old man's eyes squinted with tension, and his brow was ribbed with wrinkles. "Open borders, destroy the oil industry, be partners with China. How can adults be so stupid?"

"Generations of brainwashing," Gray Lady said. "Thanks to our colleges and universities."

"Damn them all! I should have kept Blue Man focused on the President. He'd drive him raving mad until he threw himself off a balcony."

"There may still be time."

"No," he said sharply. "I'm committed to Riley and I will see it through. It's too late for the President. He's regained his strength and set things in motion. I wish I knew what his dream had been."

Hall tried to sip his coffee, but his head shook nervously, and coffee spilled down his chin and dripped onto his shirt.

"Besides," he added. "If we activate the President again, he's likely to call Riley. Or, more likely, he would contact *you* to get to Riley."

You. Isabel felt the emphasis. Was she a loose end, too?

William Anderson Hall sighed, and his entire being seemed to deflate. A softer countenance formed on his face.

"I apologize for my tone," he said. "Perhaps things are not as bad as they seem. The President's actions may initiate a total civil war. If we take care of the incidentals soon, we may still be able to influence the outcome."

"I've initiated Roadkill," she said.

"Very well," he replied tiredly. "But give Blue Man time to play with Riley."

His head slumped back into the chair.

"I'm curious about that cowboy," he said softly, the words barely escaping his lips. "I'm as curious as a cat."

32

It was helpful that Maintenance was a retired Navy jet pilot. He was airborne two hours after receiving the call, and once cruising, activated the plane's onboard computer that linked to servers at a private home in Arlington.

Wild Bill Hall's dismissal from the CIA had not affected his fans in other agencies, notably the National Security Agency and the Defense Intelligence Agency, where some considered him a national hero. One of those retired admirers had been a computer specialist at the DIA before taking Hall's bid to enter the private sector.

A very private sector, as he worked for Hall and no one else. Hall, Gray Lady, and Maintenance, the three people who knew of him, referred to him as Gyro Gearloose, or Gyro for short.

Maintenance and Gyro linked up over Illinois.

"I'm activating the six cameras in Browne's Ford pickup. Can you see it on screen?" Gyro asked.

"I can."

The two cab cameras showed the interior, both front seat and back, to be empty. The cameras embedded in the headlights and taillights confirmed what the GPS had reported: the truck sat in Ezra Riley's yard.

"I'm going to start the truck now," the technician said.

Maintenance smiled as he saw exhaust suddenly emit from the empty vehicle.

"This may be a risk," Gyro said. "I'm going to shift it into gear and slowly drive it around the yard. Keep an eye on the exterior cameras."

The pilot watched five separate small camera views at once, an overhead view provided by satellite, and the four pictures from the pickup.

"Did you see anything?" Gearloose asked.

"Just some horses in the corrals."

"Okay, let's see if I can draw Mockingbird out of the house."

Gyro maneuvered the Ford to the front door, stopped it, and sounded the horn twice.

Nothing.

"Park it where it was," Maintenance said. "And show me recent aerial photos."

A flurry of still photos soon flashed across the pilot's screen.

"Go back three days and give me a good overview."

Maintenance stared at the screen. Everything seemed normal except one thing: the old yellow truck.

"Go through the tapes," the pilot instructed. "Find out what happened to that old yellow pickup."

Minutes later, Gearloose responded. "There have been comings and goings the past few days," he said. "A man and a woman came out twice. I believe that was Gray Lady's sister and her pilot. There was an older cowboy, some friend of Riley's, I presume. It was dark when our new truck arrived with Browne driving. It was parked and hadn't moved again until I moved it minutes ago. But, twenty minutes after Browne parked, a rear camera caught the taillights of another vehicle departing the yard."

Maintenance smiled. "Smart," he said. "Mockingbird traded trucks."

"The records show the other truck is a 1978 four-wheel drive. How far is he going to get in that?"

"Bring up Mockingbird's file. Where does his mother live?"

Gearloose hit a few keys. "Plainview, Texas."

"Where the heck is that?"

"About halfway between Amarillo and Lubbock."

"No wonder they call it Plainview. Chart the most direct path, including secondary highways, between Miles City and Plainview."

"That's easy."

"Then hack into the security cameras of truck stops along the way."

"That's not so easy."

"He has a jump on us, but he can't be traveling very fast. Look for that truck in Douglas and Wheatland, Wyoming first. Work south until you see it. If you confirm he's southbound, jump down to southern Colorado. Look at truck stops in the smaller towns. He can't have much range in that old beater. He'll gas up often and he has to catch some sleep sometime. Access rest areas if you can."

"You're not asking for much, Mister Janitor."

"It's Maintenance, wise guy."

"Mr. Gearloose to you. This could take a while."

"Roger that. I'll let the folks at home know I'm rerouting south. I'm going to refuel in Pueblo. Who knows, if the airport is near Interstate 25 I might see Mockingbird drive by."

"He'll be hard to miss. He'll be the only one going under eighty."

"Get back to me when you have something."

"One more thing, Janitor Man."

"What's that?"

"I'm looking at the notes on Meadowlark. He gave that old truck a name. It's Old Yeller."

"Good to know," said the pilot. "If I whistle, maybe it'll come."

33

Ezra stepped off Quincy and stared up at the sky. An airliner going west had sketched a contrail that crossed the trail of an aircraft going east. The intersection appeared like the crosshairs in a rifle scope.

The westbound jet, Ezra guessed, was destined for Seattle. The eastbound, perhaps Chicago. He liked to imagine the passengers in those seats. How different was his life from theirs? He'd flown enough to dislike flying, and he detested airport terminals. You didn't need to watch zombie movies to see half-dead, gray-faced humans stumbling mindlessly after nothing.

Cynical, but true. Few people in airport terminals looked healthy, especially the traveling businessmen. The advantage they did have, other than speed, was perspective. Having seen his ranch from the air many times, Ezra knew how small, brown, bare, and valueless it could look. You had to lie on the dirt to love it or trod it horseback and hear the rhymic hoofbeats hitting the soil.

The weather remained atypically warm for November. The pundits blamed Climate Change, and radicals blamed cattle for that. Cow flatulence, they said. Ezra had never heard a cow pass gas. Belching, perhaps. Once he caught the Wildebeest, he'd ask her about cow biology.

Anne would love this weather, Ezra thought. She'd happily call it Indian summer and give God the glory while walking the creek, playing in her flowerbeds, and raking leaves. The nights were mild, so reservoirs only skimmed with ice—which a cow could break with its nose. The Wildebeest was not going thirsty.

He thought about Barney Wallace. His friend was sharp enough to realize the truck trade—and the *deer hunter's* reason for it—was legitimate. But Barney was also wise enough not to dig too deep. If

Ezra needed help, even a gun hand, Barney would be there. Until then, Barn Wall preferred a life uncomplicated by serious chaos. Not-so-serious chaos was different. He thrived on that.

Ezra thought of Mary Margaret Hall and wished he and Anne could have met her under better circumstances. Anne and Mary Margaret would blend like Coke and rum. As it was, he knew Ms. Hall was not immune from her uncle's retributions. He hoped she'd keep her distance from Ezra, the ranch, and discussions about jets and dreams.

Finally, there was Davis Browne. Browne would arrive at the destination he needed, Ezra knew, but he'd fall short of his hoped-for goal. That was the problem with gamblers: they had trouble distinguishing between needs and desires.

Gyro texted Maintenance: "I got him. Where are you?"

"Call me," Maintenance Man texted back.

Moments later, a cell phone buzzed, and the pilot picked it up. "Whadya got?" he asked.

"Where are you?"

"I just fueled up in Pueblo and I've been waiting for your call."

"Good news and bad news," said Gearloose. "The good news is I caught him and the truck on a security camera at a truck stop in Cheyenne."

"And the bad news?"

"The timestamp was screwed up. It's not the Fourth of July, is it?"

"Hardly. How did he look?"

"Hard to tell—it was grainy and dark."

"But it was him, for sure?"

"I got a good shot of the truck and matched the plates. It's Old Yeller."

"He must be ahead of me. The guy isn't sleeping much. Have you pinpointed any phone calls?"

"None. He may be using an untraceable burner, or he's smart enough not to make calls."

"How about NSA chatter? Is anyone talking about him?"

"Yes. Cecily York."

"The reporter?"

"She's trying to locate him, too. With less luck than us."

"What do you have on the mother?"

"Imogene Archibald Browne, widow, age eighty, lives on Social Security."

"Send me her address."

"Will do."

"Anything else about her?"

"I've scanned her phone records. She hasn't heard from her son in a long time. And no records of flowers being delivered on Mother's Day or her birthday. Something ironic there."

"What?"

"Her birthday is May 9th, so her birthday sometimes falls on Mother's Day."

"Spare me the irony. Anything else?"

"Judging by the available data, she is a lonely woman. UPS is her best friend."

"Any pets?"

"Doesn't look like it."

"No yippy little dogs? Old women like yippy little dogs and nasty cats."

"No pets. She spends her money on television ministries and pyramid schemes. Have you ever used Essential Oils?"

"What?"

"If you need any, she'll have them. How's your libido? I bet she'll have something for it."

"I'm signing off, Gearloose."

"What's your next stop? Plainview?"

"Too small. This bird would be noticed. The airport in Lubbock is much larger. I'll rent a vehicle there."

"Copy that. I'll be here if you need me, and Maintenance?"

"Yes?"

"Happy hunting."

Happy hunting, indeed.

34

It was late afternoon in the little white house on the side street of Plainview, Texas, in a neighborhood that was less than safe for an elderly woman living alone, but Imogene Browne never sensed danger. In her mind, the west Texas town of twenty thousand had not changed since she and her husband moved there and purchased their home fifty-five years ago. Yes, the drug problem was immensely worse, but Imogene did not see people as addicts but as souls that needed Jesus.

The same was true for the homeless, illegal migrants, unemployed single mothers, and elderly shut-ins, many of whom were younger than her. Still, she took meals to them because Imogene didn't consider herself old.

Pleasant neighborhoods existed in Plainview, a town that generally held an optimistic and enduring attitude, but Imogene did not live in those parts of the city. *Enduring* and *hopeful* lived in her mind, like ribbons in her salted and peppered hair. Imogene saw life through rose-colored glasses, but her manufactured gaiety was as welcome as her onion and cauliflower soup: at first glance, her slathering religiousness was off-putting, but given time and seasoning both the woman and her soups were nutritious.

How she afforded her generosity, no one knew. She was a pensioner who wasted money on telemarketing schemes and televangelists, but her rolls and soup multiplied like biblical loaves and fishes. Her joy was manic, her laugh a high-pitched cackle that slid through listeners' ears like fingernails on slate, but the sparkle in her dark eyes silenced the doubters, and she left people smiling. In a world of desperation and craziness, she seemed a beacon of serenity and sanity.

Twice a week, Imogene walked three blocks with fresh rolls for the Graham sisters, Dolores and Betsy. Today she left her little house with the purposefulness of a front-line general.

She marched with anticipation toward the Grahams' house because the sisters always were the only neighbors who asked about Imogene's family.

She rang their doorbell, and two voices cheerily called her in.

"Have you heard from your granddaughter, Destinee?" Dolores asked.

Imogene answered, "No, but she is very busy with school. She's at Bennington, you know."

And Betsy: "Have you heard from your son, Davis?"

"Oh, he doesn't dare contact me," Imogene explained again. "He's a secret undercover agent for the government."

The two sisters nodded with understanding. Then, the three ladies prayed for the government, church leaders, the persecuted in China, Besty's aching knee, and Dolores's gout, and ended with prayers for Davis and Destinee.

They'd met for seventeen years, and Betsy's knee and Dolores's gout had not become any worse.

As Imogene walked back to her house that evening, an old yellow truck drove by and slowed to a crawl. She didn't pay any attention. Old pickups weren't uncommon in her neighborhood, but her attention perked when the truck stopped in front of her house. She watched a slender man in a military-style jacket get out.

"Davis!" she yelled, and she ran as fast as an octogenarian could on long, spindly legs.

Watching her, the son realized he had inherited his track excellence from his mother.

"My baby," she sobbed, throwing her arms around his neck.

She is still taller than me, Brown thought.

Her hug was fierce, and the tears torrential, until she broke away and stared adoringly at his face. "Come in, come in," she said. "I will fix you something special." She took his hand and pulled him toward the house.

The meal was memorable: stew with potatoes, carrots, onions, dark gravy, warm buns, and the promise of apple pie. All the while, she praised Jesus and declared her happiness to the universe.

Browne's mother asked about Destinee, of whom Davis could say little, and about his job, of which he could tell less.

With the meal finished, she retired them to her sagging couch, insisting on holding both his hands in hers, and he allowed it.

"How long can you stay?" she asked joyfully.

He looked at her and realized that his mother was as frail as a wicker basket, and he knew he had to break her heart.

"Mom," he said. "I can't stay."

Her face fell, but she summoned strength. "Oh," she said. "Are you in trouble?"

He nodded heavily as if his head might roll from his shoulders.

"It's your job, isn't it?"

"Yes, Mom."

"I knew it. God bless you for your service to our country, Davis, but secret agent work is dangerous. You could get hurt."

"Mom, it's not safe for you with me here. I can't stay the night."

"But, the old truck," she said. "Shouldn't you be driving something faster, like a sports car?"

"Mom, with new cars, people can track you. They can even listen to your conversations."

"Oh, I know. I don't have Internet, but my friends Betsy and Dolores do and they tell me the most terrible things. It's the End Times, Davis. The Lord is coming back very soon."

"You could be right," he said, then he looked at her sincerely and honestly as he'd never done before. "Mom," the son said. "I want you to forgive me."

"Oh heavens, Davis, what for? Have you had to kill people?"

"No, Mom, it's not that. I've been a bad son."

"No, Davis Browne," she said, scolding him. "You have been a wonderful son and I am very proud of you."

"I never write, I never call..."

"Well, you can't! It's your secret agent job. I understand that."

"Mom," he said, tears forming at the corners of his eyes. "I have to leave now. Would you pray for me?"

"Oh, honey, I pray for you every day, and me and the Graham sisters pray for you twice a week."

"No, I mean, right now."

And she did.

Then he rose and helped her to her feet and hugged her.

"I don't know when I'll see you again," he said.

"Just make sure it is on the other side," she said. "Where Jesus is."

He left and went to the truck.

35

Friday, November 12

William Anderson Hall got up early, dressed, skipped his muffin and coffee, accessed the tunnel, and tottered toward the sanctuary, stopping several times to catch his breath.

He found Blue Man in the solarium tending the herbal garden.

"You're fascinated with living things," Hall said, taking painful and deliberate steps to seat himself.

Blue Man moved to a shadowed corner and sat on the floor.

I like green things. Hall heard the words in his mind.

"Good, good. You're coming through clearly. May I test you?"

Think of something.

Hall folded his arms across his chest and held his chin in his right hand.

Dandelions.

"Ha! That's right. I don't know why I was thinking about dandelions."

Again.

"Okay, you won't get this one."

Persimmons.

"Yes, you are on your game today. Let's try again, more than one word." Hall bowed his head in thought.

Bowling alley.

"That's accurate. Now, three words. Are you ready?" Hall paused to think.

Evening in Paris.

Hall chuckled. "Very good, what shall we try next?"

I will give you a thought.

"Okay."

Hall heard *combinations* in his mind.

He looked at Blue Man with scrutiny. "Combinations?"

Combinations came again.

"Combinations?" Hall felt a probing force in his mind, one that directed a weakening chill down his spine.

Combinations! a voice demanded.

The four-wheeler left a spray of red dust as it sped down County Road 400 south of Plainview. Jimmy Garza checked stock ponds and fences on his little ranch east of I27 before commuting to work as a Lubbock machinist. He had no family and couldn't afford hired help, so his daily chore was a quick look-see through the property. He hadn't enough cattle to afford to lose any.

Sunlight that glinted off metal near his south pasture suggested something amiss. As he neared, he saw it was an old pickup in the ditch. Probably wrecked by teenagers the night before, he thought. Lubbock was far from the border, so Garza didn't worry about cartels or *coyotes*, but you could never tell. Drug smugglers and illegals could be anywhere. For that reason, he traveled armed with a twelve-gauge shotgun scabbarded behind his seat.

The truck was an old yellow Ford three-quarter ton. A '78, he guessed.

Garza unsheathed the scattergun and approached. The cracks in the windshield looked fresh as if something heavy—a human head?—had hit it. Oddly, there were no items left in the truck, making him think teenagers had likely stolen it. No license plates, either, but the keys were still in the ignition.

Examining the pickup closely, he found no structural damage, so he climbed in the seat and turned the key. The truck fired up.

Garza grinned. He wasn't a thief, but there wasn't any harm in taking the truck home to keep vandals from trashing it. Garza maneuvered the pickup to a bank, backed up, set the brake, then loaded his four-wheeler in the back. He had an old barn where he'd store the old Ford. If anyone came looking and found it, he'd explain things like this happened every once in a while. Drug smugglers and *coyotes* did make it this far north, after all.

In his haste and excitement, he didn't notice the silver dollar-sized splotch of dried blood on the passenger seat.

Maintenance was northbound over Cheyenne, Wyoming, when the cockpit's computer screen lit up.

"Talk to me, Gyro," he laughed. "Talk to me."

As signals connected, the computer expert appeared on the screen.

"I see you're in the air," Gyro said. "I picked up your signal fifteen minutes ago."

"I'm routed toward the land of Meadowlarks," the pilot said. "Unless you've received preemptive orders."

"Orders stand as given. Status on Roadkill, Mockingbird?"

"As you say, roadkilled."

"Any peck and scratch?"

"Total surprise. Mockingbird's mind wasn't in the game."

"Nothing left on the highway?"

"Just the old yellow truck. I couldn't do anything with it."

"Mockingbird's feathers?"

"Dropped in a deep lake along with its toys."

"Pity. Did you meet the bird's mother?"

"From a distance."

"She got to see him?"

"She did."

"That's good. I'm glad for her."

"Gyro, you're going all soft and gooey on me."

"Just respectful to mothers. Your new itinerary?"

"Billings, Montana. This bird is too shiny for small spaces. I'll rent an SUV there. Feed me info and updates on Meadowlark."

"Will do."

"And his wife? Is she still in Rio?"

"Still there. She flies out in three days if the weather is clear."

"Are there problems down south?"

"Just on radar. A heavy rain event could be approaching."

"Roger that. She should pray it rains. I'll keep channels clear until Billings. Silent running."

Hall's eyes snapped open. Had he been asleep? Focusing on the surroundings, he saw he was still in Blue Man's solarium, and Blue Man was still seated in the shadows.

"Did I nod off?"

For a moment.

"I must be tiring. It has been a long week. Did you focus on Riley last night?"

No.

"No? Why not?"

I was tired, too.

"Oh, okay. That's understandable. You've had an exhausting three weeks, but very productive. I'm very proud of you. Can you concentrate on Riley beginning tonight?"

I can.

"Is Mr. Riley going to be a challenge?"

I like challenges.

"His firewall will be strong."

I find cracks.

"Very good."

Or I make cracks.

"Excellent." Hall rose stiffly and supported himself with his cane. "Next time I visit early I'll have coffee first," he said, smiling.

Blue Man did not return the smile.

When Hall had left, Blue Man focused his thoughts on Gray Lady.

Mr. Hall is weakening.

He felt the energy sent and received.

Ezra Riley must go.

Again, sent and received.

A real threat must fracture Ezra Riley.

He heard the woman agree, and Blue Man smiled.

Blue Man rarely smiled.

After two full days of flying and driving, Maintenance was happy to settle into a Miles City motel that evening, kick off his shoes, and quaff a couple of cold Bud Lights.

He liked the word *quaff.* It reminded him of the *Peanuts* cartoon with Snoopy and Woodstock.

He knocked back two beers quickly, opened a third, and clicked on the television. More riots. He once found politics amusing, but someone had opened the cages in the human zoo, and all types of beasts and birds were ravaging one another. Fools, all of them. The Right was drunk on conspiracy theories—a few of which he knew to be true—and the Left was the puppet of the media. They couldn't have an original thought if you pounded it into their heads with a hammer.

Both sides were being played as far as he was concerned. Maintenance wasn't political. He admired Wild Bill Hall, but he served him for the money, not the cause. One more job and Maintenance would disappear to a temperate climate.

In Mockingbird's files, he found brochures touting Costa Rica. Maybe that little country was worth a look.

But, first, Meadowlark.

Opening his laptop, he watched a folder open on the screen.

The title page read: "Ezra Riley, Miles City, Montana, b. 1952."

The next page was a photograph of a cowboy on a horse.

36

At dusk, Gray Lady slipped from the brick mansion through the back door to get fresh air, be alone with her thoughts, and make a phone call. Overhead, the first stars shone brilliantly; the air was crisp and pine-scented, and for a few moments, all seemed right with her world.

But all was not right with her world.

In her bedroom dresser drawer, she'd found a photograph of her and Mary Margaret when they were twelve and fourteen. They looked happy and full of life. The girls were orphans, but Uncle Bill had raised them well if absently. His job kept him away most of the year, but their nanny was kind and fun-loving, and the country home in upstate New York was beautiful, quiet, and filled with young girl adventures.

She and Mary Margaret had never fought, not that Isabel would have dared. Mary Margaret was not only older, but she was also stronger, faster, and tougher. She once got a fishing hook stuck in her palm and never cried while removing it herself with tweezers and a razor blade.

That Uncle Bill would consider killing Mary Margaret was more than Isabel could bear, proving her blindness toward him. For years, Uncle Bill had been slipping, but Isabel had refused to see it. She was the dutiful sister, the one who paid debts.

And why shouldn't Uncle Bill slip? He'd been tortured by the Chinese and carried bullet wounds from the Cubans and the Viet Cong. What else he'd endured Gray Lady could only guess, but his deepest scarring came from the CIA canceling psychic programs and putting him out to pasture.

The old man was stubborn. Offered to return to service and oversee cutting-edge technology programs, he'd laughed, calling it a preposterous waste of time to embed computer chips in human brains and link nervous systems to operating systems.

"What will they try to do next?" he'd asked Gray Lady. "Shrink humans down to the size of ants."

"It is the trend of the future," she tried to tell him.

"Future? They are technological Darwinists. If you are not techy, you have no business living. There is no soul in technology. None. Anything that technology can do, the paranormal can do better."

How might his life have changed if he'd not died on a Chinese operating table and floated above his body, reading the minds of the workers below him?

Pulling a cell phone from her pocket, she tapped in Maintenance's number.

"Speak to me," she heard him say.

"Mockingbird's roadkill confirmed?" she asked.

"Mockingbird roadkilled."

"Meadowlark's Roadkill tomorow. Confirm?"

"Meadowlark's Roadkill? I understood Spyglass. Observation."

"Change of plans. Operation Roadkill, Meadowlark."

"Operation Roadkill, Meadowlark confirmed."

"Repeat. Tomorrow, no later."

"Tomorrow, no later."

"Must appear to be by his own hand."

"By his hand, confirmed."

She hung up, hoping the call had not been picked up or overheard. She'd gone against her uncle's orders. Ezra Riley would not be tested and observed. Maintenance would kill him, but it would appear to be a suicide.

Her uncle's obsession with Riley was getting out of hand. It had to end.

She was surprised, though, by her change in attitude. Until today, she'd been Riley's defender. Suddenly, she realized he needed to be removed. Ezra Riley was a distraction.

Ezra walked across the graveled yard from the corrals to the house at dusk, the setting sun slashing the hills and cottonwoods with golden light. The faint imprints in the dust would have escaped most eyes, but a lifetime in the hills, and years of looking at the familiar, taught Ezra to notice *sign*, whether it was a glint of a track or an object seemingly out of place.

He saw both.

The tracks were from new tires, and looking at Browne's fancy Ford, he observed the smallest details in where it sat. Inspecting the truck closely, Ezra saw someone had moved it, then attempted to repark it where it had been. They'd barely missed, stopping four feet short and two feet too far to the west.

Drawing his .357 Magnum from its holster, he moved cautiously to the house, grabbed a tactical flashlight from a shelf, cleared each upstairs room one at a time, then did the same in the basement.

Tomorrow, he told himself, he would remember to lock the house.

But would it make any difference?

He spent the entire day in the hills; intruders would have ample time to break a window and gain access.

Okay, he told himself, *things are getting real.*

He brought a ladder from the garage, locked the doors, and then positioned the ladder under the hallway's attic opening. With two ropes in one hand and the flashlight in the other, he climbed the steps, pushed away a square of plywood, squeezed through the narrow portal, and lifted himself into the attic. Every muscle in his shoulders, arms, and neck screamed with the effort.

In the attic, he swept away insulation until he located a black, nylon rifle case. Securing the handles with the rope, he lowered the gun case through the opening and down to the floor. Another quick look and he located a go-bag. He lowered it, too, then he carefully and stiffly followed, closing the attic entryway behind him.

Laying the case on the kitchen table, he unzipped it and removed a rifle—a Ruger Mini 14 semi-automatic, the civilian version of the military's M14—from a rust-protective silicon gun sock. From the case's side pockets, Ezra extracted three fully loaded thirty-round magazines.

Some experts claimed magazines left loaded caused their springs to weaken.

Other experts said that wouldn't happen.

Ezra tested the magazines by pushing down on the top round in each. The springs felt resilient.

Quickly shedding his chaps, jeans, and boots, he donned a pair of insulated pants, laced up Gore-Tex hiking boots, and squeezed into a camouflaged parka. Ezra checked the go-bag. It held an inflatable pillow, matches, first-aid kit, space blanket, winter-rated sleeping bag, and two boxes of .223 ammunition. He hefted the load and humped it out the door.

And into the hills.

37

Friday morning, November 13

Ezra, cold, stiff, sore, and tired, rose from a grassy swale, rolled his sleeping bag, and limped in the dark toward the house. He'd had better nights. Chill and discomfort Ezra could handle, but not accompanied by nightmares. All night he dreamt of being in the dirt cellar of his parents' old house, where bull snakes slithered after mice and salamanders splashed in muddy corners. Daylight, glimpsed between cracks in the foundation, provided the only illumination, and the air was thick with a damp, rancid mustiness. The mice not caught by bull snakes died by D-Con and decomposed into carcasses as light and fragile as dry leaves.

He hadn't dreamed about being locked in the cellar for years.

It was his older sister's doing. They were friends now, but she terrorized him when he was young.

He needed coffee.

Arriving at the gate to the horse pasture, he saw headlights coming from the highway, instinctively dropped to his knees, unzipped the gun case, and pulled out the Mini-14.

An hour earlier, Maintenance's cell phone beeped him awake. He showered, dressed, filled a tall mug with coffee in the motel's lobby, tossed his small travel bag in the rented SUV, and climbed in. Google Earth maps told him where to go, and his experience reminded him what to do when he got there.

No creeping around in the brush for a pilot. He was an aviator, not an infantryman; subterfuge rather than stealth.

Maintenance planned to drive to Ezra Riley's front door, knock, explain that he needed to make an emergency call but couldn't get a signal.

Do you have a landline? he would ask.

The Code of the West being hospitality—his research said it had something to do with *leaving the latchstring out*—Ezra would invite him in to use the phone. Maintenance would pull his Ruger Mark IV .22 pistol and shoot the cowboy in the right temple at the opportune moment, then drag the body downstairs, position it in the writer's office, place Riley's .357 Magnum to the .22's entrance wound, and pull the trigger. With gloved hands, he'd then position the revolver in Riley's right hand for prints, then let it drop naturally to the floor.

It would be days before Anne Riley found the body, but there was nothing the pilot could do about that. Bad things happen. As for forensics, how good was the science in Montana? Maintenance would collect the spent shell casing, so there'd be no suspicion Riley was shot first with a .22.

The logic was on the assassin's side. Writers were moody, so it'd appear to be suicide. Why would anyone murder Ezra Riley, anyway? He was not significant.

The plan pleased him. He'd soon be on a Costa Rican beach. Anticipating a payday had him speeding as he passed the airport and descended the hill on the north side.

Then, in the headlights, a form!

Ezra, his Mini-14 at the ready, watched as the vehicle stopped and a tall man in a big hat got out, climbed his front steps, and banged on the front door.

"Ezra! Open up!"

"What?" Ezra shouted, stepping from the darkness.

"Hurry," Barney yelled, get in the truck. There's been an accident and a fire."

Ezra dropped his baggage, ran to Barney's pickup, and jumped in. 'What's going on?"

"I was just moments behind an SUV when it went off the road up on the hill." Barney's truck rolled from the yard, shooting gravel in all directions.

"Where the embankment is so steep?"

"Right there. It must have rolled several times. I stopped and checked, but the guy's dead. A fire was starting but I pulled the body away and called 911."

"How bad's the fire?" To the east, Ezra could see a rising red glow.

"Not bad yet, and fire trucks are coming."

"What were you doing coming this way?"

"Anne wanted me to check on you."

"Again?"

"Yeah, she said she called last night and early this morning and there was no answer."

"Yeah, I slept in the hills."

"You look like it. Why were you sleeping in the hills?"

"Long story. I'll tell you after we take care of this."

Emergency lights at the scene, flashing from emergency responders' vehicles—Fire, Police, Sheriff, Highway Patrol, and Ambulance—lit the stage in eerie flashing colors.

"Shoot, this looks like Las Vegas," Barney said.

Barney parked at the entrance to a pasture gate, and they approached on foot.

"Stay back," a highway patrolman yelled at them.

"I'm the landowner," Ezra said. With the fire spreading down the borrow pit toward his pasture, no one was keeping him away.

Ezra and Barney removed their coats and beat at the flames. The Fire Department's focus was on the inferno consuming the wrecked SUV.

The two cowboys were only stalling the flames, beating as they retreated toward the fence line.

"If it gets in that thick brush, we won't stop it!" Barney said. The fire's heat was reddening their soot-speckled faces.

With flames mere inches from tall sagebrush and the fence line, a small Rural Fire Department truck roared up, stopped, and two men jumped out and went to work with hoses. Volumes of water doused the fire's lead, leaving it a cold, smoldering ash heap. The firemen then turned the spray on the fire's edges.

Barney and Ezra collapsed, exhausted.

"I'm too old for this," Barney said.

"Is it too late to become accountants?" Ezra asked.

The sun rose, painting the sky pink. With the body loaded, the ambulance sped away.

The highway patrolman who'd yelled at Ezra walked up to them. "Either of you witness what happened here?" he asked.

"I sorta did," Barney offered. "I was coming over the hill when I saw his lights suddenly veer, and he went off the road. I stopped, but the driver was dead. I pulled him out of the car, called 911, and raced to get Ezra."

"The driver was veering like he was avoiding a deer?"

"Yeah, I think that was it."

"You're Barney Wallace, the cartoonist?" the officer asked.

Barney nodded.

The officer then looked at Ezra. "And you're the writer?"

"Yeah," Ezra said. "But the rancher in this case."

"What do you make of this?" the patrolman asked, showing Ezra a plastic evidence bag with a piece of paper in it.

"What is it?"

"It's a map from Google Earth with your house circled."

Ezra tried to hide his alarm, but his face gave him away.

"Why was this guy coming to your place?"

"I don't know," Ezra said. "Who was he?"

"The man had no identification, and the fire consumed the interior of the vehicle. The map must have fallen from a pocket when Mr. Wallace moved the body. The SUV is a rental from the Billings airport," the patrolman said. "But the map isn't all we found."

Ezra looked at him expectantly.

"The deceased had a loaded .22 semi-automatic pistol in his jacket pocket."

The officer and Barney both stared at Ezra.

"I have no idea what's going on," Ezra said.

Both men knew Ezra Riley was not good at lying.

Ezra was thinking of Mary Margaret's words: *There is death on the highway.*

38

"Maintenance is dead."

The voice was Gyro's.

Gray Lady's hand went to her mouth in shock, and she nearly dropped her phone. "What!"

"I tried getting a confirmation from him this morning," Gyro said. "But neither his phone, tablet, nor laptop would respond so I tapped into Eastern Montana law enforcement networks. He was killed early this morning in a one-vehicle accident."

"Do they think it's suspicious?"

"The official report is he swerved to avoid a deer and went off the highway."

"This is unfortunate, but it's nothing that points back to us."

"Maybe. Maybe not."

"What do you mean?"

"I hacked into emails between the Sheriff's Department and the Highway Patrol. They found a pistol in his jacket and a map with Meadowlark's house circled."

"He printed a map! What was he thinking? Can they trace his car?"

"They already have."

"And the jet?"

"He used a different identification for the car rental. I can hack into an airlines passenger manifest and put him on a commercial plane."

"Do it immediately."

"And the jet?"

"Dispatch pilots to bring it back."

"What about the gun and map?"

187

"Create a solid identity for him using the name he used at the car rental. Social media, bank account, driver's license, Social Security number, the works."

"Place of residence?"

"Los Angeles. They won't track anything down in a city that large. Did the pistol have a serial number?"

"Yes."

"Good. It would be suspicious if it didn't. Do you have the number?"

"I do."

"Create a provenance for it. Run it through gun shows and pawnshops."

"Gun shows may not work."

"Hint at it somehow. Make it confusing, but make it look legal."

"And the map?"

"Make him a fan of Meadowlark's books. Can you postdate the Meadowlark's answering machine?"

"I should be able to."

"Leave a message pretending to be Maintenance. Say you're a fan passing through and would like to meet him."

"Meadowlark will know it's fake."

Gray Lady paused. "He might, but try it anyway. If nothing else, it will keep him off-balance."

"I can inject a message to the Chamber of Commerce. An email from Maintenance wanting to know how to reach Meadowlark."

"Good. Slow email might be expected out there."

"I'll postdate it last night."

"We're dealing with small town cops. I'm not too worried about them turning a pistol and a map into a contract hit."

"What about Meadowlark?" Gearloose asked. "Is he still an ongoing operation?"

"I don't know," she said. "I'll have to let my uncle make that decision."

Barney stopped his pickup near where Ezra had left the semi-automatic carbine lying on his sleeping bag.

"I don't think that's a lever-action .30-30," Barney said.

"A Mini-14. I bought it forty years ago and stored it away. Totally legal firearm today, but maybe not so tomorrow. If the ATF comes for it I'm going to tell them I traded it to you for a new pickup."

"I thought you wanted barn cats?"

"I'd rather have three German shepherds, a Doberman, and a Belgian Malinois."

"My mother-in-law has a mean toy poodle."

"That might work."

"All kidding aside, Ezra, what's going on? You're sleeping in the hills, and a stranger with a gun and a map dies in a car crash."

"I need a shower, coffee, and breakfast, Barney."

Cleaned up and fueled by stout coffee, Ezra sat at the kitchen table with a bowl of cold cereal and the new Ford's title.

He slid the title across the table to Barney. "Take a look at who the truck is registered to."

Barney held the paper up and squinted. "I don't have my reading glasses, but it looks like Zebulon Associates Limited. What's that?"

"I've no idea. I can't find them on the Web. It must be a dummy corporation."

"Who's Zebulon?"

"A Hebrew patriarch in the Bible. The name means 'Dwelling of Honor.'"

"Why are they after you?"

"I gave my word not to talk."

"So what can I do to help?"

Ezra looked sternly at his friend of many years. "You can help by staying away."

"What? You want me to abandon a longtime friend?"

"I know it goes against your principles, but do it as a favor to me."

"You're going to fight this alone?"

"It's my fight, Barney, not yours."

"So who was that Benny Davis guy? At least tell me that."

"His real name is Davis Browne. He's a private contractor for some powerful people."

"What did he want?"

"I can't tell you."

"Where is he?"

"That might be a question for eternity. If he's lucky, he's in Mexico."

"If he's unlucky?"

"He's dead. They got him."

Barney scowled. "What are you going to do when Anne gets home?"

Ezra shook his head sadly. "I'm hoping this will be resolved by then."

"Go to the sheriff," Barney insisted. "The cops are already suspicious about that gun and map."

"I have a feeling those suspicions will evaporate."

"You can't make me walk away from this."

"Barney, if that car hadn't crashed and you'd pulled into the yard minutes after that guy—whoever he was—you're the one who might have caught a bullet."

"I don't abandon my friends."

Ezra sighed and folded his arms across his chest. "Fine," he said. "Check on me by telephone and drive the highway, but do not pull into the yard."

Barney didn't like it, but he nodded his assent.

"And on the phone," Ezra added. "Don't talk about anything except cows and weather. We have to sound like normal cowboys."

Gray Lady took her chair across from her uncle in his study. The old spymaster looked especially tired, and she hated bringing bad news.

He fidgeted, waiting for her to speak, but his nervousness was little more than a tremble.

"Maintenance has been killed in a car accident," she reported.

Hall coughed. "Near Riley's ranch?"

"Yes. He was on his way to complete the job."

"Complete what job?"

Isabel lied. "Observing Riley."

"What caused the accident?"

"The authorities think he swerved to miss a deer."

"A stupid reaction," Hall said. "He was smarter than that and he was in a rented SUV. Why would he swerve?"

Gray Lady had no answer to the rhetorical question.

"Have the necessary details been taken care of?" he asked.

"Yes. There shouldn't be any problems."

"Did he have any family?"

"An ex-wife in England and parents in Boston."

"Spin it as necessary. Say he was a courier for one of our corporations who took a fateful sightseeing trip."

"And what about Riley?"

Hall's jaw clenched. "We'll turn up the pressure," he said. "I'll give Blue Man a workout. We'll find out what both Blue Man and Ezra Riley are made of."

"You still want the dream?"

"I demand it."

"May I offer you a suggestion?" Gray Lady asked.

"What is it?"

"Maybe you are underestimating Blue Man. Maybe he can bypass the subconscious with a man like Riley."

"What do you mean?"

"Blue Man targeted the President and Davis Browne while they were asleep. Ezra Riley is an imaginative person who spends most of his time alone. Perhaps his normal day is like a sleeping state."

"Daydreams," Hall said. "Like Browne's fantasies?"

"Probably more realistic than Browne's fantasies."

"But possible. I will have Blue Man get on it. Daytime and nighttime, for that matter, if Blue Man can take the rigor."

"As you have said, Uncle. We must learn what both Riley and Blue Man are made of."

39

Sheriff Andy Royce knew about Ezra Riley's rebellious past, but when Ezra was a wild young man, the sheriff was in grade school. In the years Royce had been sheriff, he never knew Riley to look for trouble. Trouble, though, did have a way of looking for him.

Royce saw a light in the barn, so he parked his squad car near the corrals and found Ezra unsaddling a roan horse.

"Evening, Sheriff," Ezra said.

"Evening, Ezra." The lawman looked at the gaunt horse. "Looks like the roan saw some miles today."

"We rode a quick big circle. I have an old cow I need to find. We call her the Wildebeest. Barney and I got her calf gathered the other day, but this old cow can really hide. Either that or she's dead."

"I came out to talk to you about the accident," Royce said. He was a ruddy and rawboned man who eschewed convention and packed a .44 Magnum revolver on his hip. He looked like Dirty Harry's older brother.

"I figured that."

"The deceased was named Scott Pennington. Have you heard of him?"

"Nope," Ezra said, turning the roan loose to feed on hay.

"He flew into Billings two days ago but didn't rent a car until yesterday. It seems he might have been one of your fans."

"I could use more fans."

"Did he call here asking to meet you?"

"I wouldn't know. I haven't checked the answering machine."

"Even with Anne in Brazil?"

Does everyone know my wife is in Brazil?

The sheriff awaited an answer.

"Anne knows how I am about phones," Ezra said. "So we mostly use email. When she does call, it's early, around five."

"Can I check your answering machine?"

"Sure." Ezra led the way to the house.

The answering machine's flashing light indicated three unheard messages. Ezra pressed the Play button.

Hello! We are calling you about your car's ext—

Ezra canceled that one.

Did you know that you can qualify for low-interest cred—

He canceled that one.

Mr. Riley, my name is Scott Pennington. I'm in the area, and I'm a big fan of your books. Would you autograph a couple for me? I'll call later, or if you don't mind, I'll come out tomorrow morning. Thanks.

The sheriff looked at Ezra. "That call was last night?"

"I guess so."

"That explains the map," Royce said. "It doesn't explain the pistol in his pocket, though."

"Where was he from?"

"Los Angeles."

"He probably thought Montana was still the Wild West."

"One problem with that. All he had was a carry-on. If he flew commercial how did he get the pistol on the plane?"

"I've no idea," Ezra said. "Have you contacted the next of kin?"

"There doesn't seem to be any. We got a strange call, though, from a guy claiming to be his boss. He said Pennington hadn't checked in and he was concerned. He heard about the accident from the Billings police."

"I guess that solves part of the mystery."

"There's been talk about private jets flying in and out of Miles City the past two weeks," Royce added.

"Really? I suppose they fly too high to find my cow for me?"

The sheriff rolled his eyes. Old cowboys could be exasperating. "If you're in trouble, Ezra, I can help."

"Thanks, I appreciate that, Andy."

"So, are you in trouble?"

"Can't say that I am."

"I see you have a new truck in the yard."

"I do. What about it?"

"Seems a little odd, doesn't it? This Pennington fellow didn't look like the literary type. All he had in his carry-on bag for reading material was an aviation magazine and brochures about Costa Rica."

Ezra laughed. "You're thinking drugs, aren't you?"

The sheriff shrugged. "There was a day—"

"Fifty years ago," Ezra interrupted.

The sheriff shrugged again. "I'm just passing on other people's suspicions."

"People who don't know me," Ezra said. "You know me, Andy. Do you really think I paid for a new pickup with drugs flown in from Costa Rica? Of course, maybe Anne is bringing some home from Brazil."

"No, I don't think that, Ezra, but you have to admit this looks odd. A fit man in his late thirties dies near your place. He has a gun in his pocket and a map with your house circled."

"You've seen stranger things, Andy."

"I have, but would you mind telling me about the truck?" He pointed at the kitchen table. "Is that the title to it?"

"It is."

"May I have a look at it?"

"No, you may not."

"It's not like you to be evasive, Ezra."

"If I told you the truth, you wouldn't believe me."

"Give me a crack at it."

"You know my '78 Ford?"

"Old Yeller? Yeah, I know Old Yeller—why?"

Ezra couldn't contain his smile.

"Some guy traded me straight across," he said. "That new truck for Old Yeller."

Sheriff Royce frowned. "Well, hell. Why didn't you say so?"

A handler escorted Blue Man through the tunnel to Hall's study, rapped once on the door, then opened it for Blue Man to enter.

Blue Man glided across the room as if his feet were winged.

"Have a seat," Hall said.

Thank you.

"I'm too tired for telepathy tonight, Blue."

As you say.

"I'm too tired to think, so I'll talk. You can telepath if you want."

Blue Man nodded.

"We've had some misfortune. A colleague I sent to keep tabs on Riley was killed in a car accident. I've no one on the ground there."

Send me!

"No, no. You know that isn't possible. Your system cannot withstand the outside pollutants."

Blue Man stared passively at his creator.

"What I need you to do is dial up the intensity on Riley."

You want the dream?

Hall waved a thin hand. "Yes, yes, I want the dream, but I also want to know what he can take, what he can endure."

How will we know?

"You must make him do something dramatic, something that will make the news even if it's his own death."

Montana is a long way.

"This isn't about distance—you know that!" Hall snapped. "This isn't quantum mechanics. This is quantum physics. There is no space or time."

Minuscule anger sparked in Blue Man's eyes.

"Riley is the test. It's not how high you can levitate or putting your hands through solid walls. It's about dominance, of breaking the adversary. You are an invisible warrior, Blue Man. You are the ultimate invisible warrior."

Yes, Mr. Hall.

"Total and complete focus on Riley day and night. Nothing else."

Day and night?

"As long as your energy lasts. Hit him and hit him hard." He waved Blue Man away. "You can go now. Get to work."

Blue Man rose and left. His feet did not touch the floor until his hands touched the door.

The phone rang as Ezra was getting in bed. He picked it up on the third ring.

"Hi, sweetheart," he said.

"Hi, my love. How are you?"

"I'm fine."

"Are you sure?"

"I'm sure."

"What's new up there?"

"Not much."

Anne paused. She'd punch him if she could reach across the globe. "You're not telling me anything."

"There's nothing to tell."

"Did Barney stop by this morning?"

"He did."

"Where were you? I tried calling at five your time."

"I was already outside." Ezra smiled. That part wasn't a lie.

"So, nothing new is going on."

"Same ole same ole."

"Well, I have some news. I'm stuck down here."

"You're stuck?"

"We're having a large tropical storm. The airport is damaged and flights are grounded."

"You don't know when you'll be getting out?"

"No, it could be three or four days. Maybe more."

"But you and the kids and grandkids are okay?"

"Everybody's fine. Gabby and Garris miss you and want to be in Montana riding horses."

Garris has not even met me.

"Tell them I miss them too, and I wish they were here."

"Okay. I better go. I read to Garris when I put him to bed. He insists on it."

"Okay. I love you."

"I love you, too."

Anne hung up the phone. For being the most honest man she knew, her husband was such a liar.

40

Gray Lady sat in her bedroom in her uncle's small country mansion, staring at the floor.

Small mansion? Was that an oxymoron? Manor?

Mansion or manor, it didn't matter.

She didn't like it here, didn't want to be here, but couldn't leave because she was practically a prisoner.

I have been his prisoner for thirty-five years, she thought. And would be more so when he passed, for her inheritance would be Blue Man.

Adding to the dynamics was her uncle's increasingly irrational behavior, part of which she attributed to the national news.

The President was on a tear. He'd issued more executive orders in the past two weeks than any president had in three months. When haunted by the nightmare, the President had been depressed, exhausted, and ineffectual. Since Riley's dream interpretation—and her uncle calling off Blue Man—his behavior had become manic, and the actions so opposite her uncle's principles, you'd think the President had a vendetta against Hall.

In fact, the President didn't even know who William Anderson Hall was.

Uncle Bill should be using Blue Man now to disrupt this administration, Isabel thought. *Instead, he's using Blue Man against a Montana cowboy.*

She'd hoped killing Ezra Riley would solve the problem, but instead, the killer was dead.

It's the gunfighter in my uncle, she decided. *Uncle Bill has created a psychic top gun and needs to prove it: Psychic Shoot-out at OK Corral.*

Kung Fu Blue against Old Cowboy.

How silly.

But what could she do?

If she fled her uncle, he would find her—unless he died first.

And what if that happened?

The staff would desert, wouldn't they? They didn't know her, and she didn't know them.

She couldn't inherit the property because she already had, but the title was buried deep in paperwork to deceive those who suspected Hall hadn't died eleven years ago.

The property was hers, but it wasn't, but Blue Man certainly was, or was he?

Would Blue Man accept her, and what would she do if he didn't?

Isabel missed Mary Margaret and wished she could talk to her, but that wouldn't happen.

She'd insist I come live with her, Isabel thought.

She would want me deprogrammed.

She might even try to cast demons out of me.

Gray Lady got up, went to the window, and looked toward the evergreen trees that hid the sanctuary. Their trunks and limbs looked like knife blades thrusting up from the earth. She wondered what Blue Man was doing at that moment.

I am in the house.

The thought was not hers, but she'd heard that voice in her head before.

I am in the house.

Gray Lady rushed to the bedroom door and cracked it open.

It looked like smoke. A cloud drifted down the dark hallway leading to her uncle's room, then stopped. When it ceased moving, it took human form. Barely human. It was vapor as much as it was flesh.

No, it was flesh. It was Blue Man, and he turned and looked at her.

Be quiet.

She was too terrified to speak.

Blue Man entered her uncle's room. Did he open the door or merely pass through it? She couldn't tell.

William Anderson Hall, eyes closed, reclined in his king-sized bed against a bulwark of pillows.

Blue Man floated like smoke to the edge of the bed and took a pillow in his hands.

The action disturbed Hall and awakened him.

His weak, watery eyes took a moment to focus.

"You," he said.

Me.

Blue Man pressed the pillow down firmly upon the old man's face.

41

Sunday, November 14

Early, early morning. Ezra is sleeping.

He is swirling in blue.
It's his favorite color.
Blue roan.
He'd always wanted a blue roan horse.

Johnny Riley's herd of range mares gallop across the prairie, led by his father's favorite, a blue roan named Blue Rocket.

Ezra and his parents are crowded into the small cab of the 1949 GMC pickup. The mares aren't wild, but they're not gentle; they run from the truck, and Johnny Riley drives fast, chasing them. Bouncing over the brush, the GMC seems held together by its rattles.

"Slow down, Johnny," Pearl Riley scolds, but once Johnny's blood is up, he can't hear thunder if it cracked in his ears.

A long blue line of horse rolls before the boy like a bubbling stream. Blue Rocket begets Blue Sister, who bred to a Shetland stud, begets Blue Baby. Blue Baby births a blue roan horse colt with a mottled-white face and two black streaks in its tail.

The foal is named Ribbon Tail.

Ribbon Tail is two, Ezra is ten. It is a warm spring day. His father fore-foots the colt and ties the four legs tight up against the belly. Ezra, undersized and thin, holds the tail of the rope. His dad pulls out a Case pocketknife, swishes it a time or two in a bucket of iodine-tainted water, then lays the thin, keen blade against the colt's scrotum.

202

Ribbon Tail is castrated. "He's yours now to break," Johnny tells the boy.

Ezra isn't happy, nor is he sad or afraid. He is accepting.

His world is ruled by those who can "whip" others. Ezra knows he can't whip anyone except his little sister, and it isn't right to hit girls.

He looks up at a vast blue sky fleeced with white clouds, cottonwood leaves rustling sweetly in a soft breeze. He sees his father's brown, knotted hands, the fingers, sized like sausages, stained with iodine and a colt's blood.

Blue.

Ezra sits on a tattered blue cloth that covers a ragged couch. The opposite wall, coated greenish-blue with peeling paint, is lined with framed displays of Indian arrowheads.

"Ezra's gonna break the blue roan colt," he hears his father boast to his six bachelor brothers.

Ezra memorizes the arrowheads in the displays.

"Bah," spits Solomon. His salt-and-pepper eyebrows knit together like two spaniels fighting.

"Is he now?" laughs Sam, the youngest of the seven Riley boys. Sam's cheeks glow from pink to scarlet with his moods.

"The hell he is," chuckles Willis, his rolling belly striped by red suspenders.

"Hrrmmph," grunts Archie and Rufus in harmony.

"A real bronco-buster," Uncle Joe says as if saying something last was better than saying nothing.

Blue. The wall would look better, Ezra thinks, if it were a solid blue and not a greenish blue that looks like a sickness.

Black.

The blue roan has hard black eyes like coal or obsidian.

"That colt doesn't have a good eye," his mother warns him.

A good eye is large, round, soft, and sparkles with willing intelligence.

Ezra is born reading the eyes of horses.

The eyes mean nothing to Johnny Riley. The wilder the eye, the better.

The blue roan never bucks. It balks.

Barn sour is what cowboys call it.

Day after day, Ezra crawls into the saddle, and day after day, the blue roan throws itself into the corral's creosoted timbers. Johnny Riley's pens—constructed of bridge plank and railroad ties—can hold wild, untouched range horses. Ribbon Tail cannot escape them.

The blue horse scrapes its little rider against the planks, prickling the boy with long, dark slivers.

"Spur 'im, quirt 'im," his dad hollers.

Ezra's thin arms bring the rawhide quirt down, time and time again; its leather lashes only anger the roan.

Months go by, and the first year comes and goes.

In the evenings, Ezra's mother, Pearl Riley, lectures her sullen husband while his fierce form molds into his reading chair like a king on a granite throne.

"Give the boy a good horse to break," his mother demands. "Give him a chance."

Johnny Riley has good horses, but those foals are sold every fall and sent to Canada.

You sell the good ones to make a living. You ride the rest to make a life. A hard life.

Ezra fights sleep. Sleeping means awakening to the blue roan standing in the corral glaring, declaring itself half-horse, half-demon.

Ezra awakened thinking he was ten years old.

I'm six decades past ten, he thought.

He looked at the clock. It read 3:33.

Unusual for him, he rolled over and went back to sleep.

The two-hour time difference meant it was 5:33 in Virginia.

Isabel Elizabeth Hall, with a coffee cup in her hands, entered the study and sat down.

Blue Man sat in her uncle's chair. Taking a large pad of unlined paper, he wrote: "We will bury Mr. Hall in the garden."

She looked at the paper but not at him, and her nod was a tremble.

"Look at me," he wrote.

She slowly turned her head and met his blue eyes; intense, but not savage. The silver-blue skin and flowing musculature gave him the appearance of being made from water.

With a black Sharpie, he wrote, "I am a human."

"Yes," she said softly.

"I would send you thoughts, but your grief and shock would block them. I will write until your mind is clear."

"Okay," the Gray Lady said.

"I am in charge now."

"Yes. What would you like to do?"

He wrote in a fast, fluid cursive. "You would like me to torment the President."

"That would be my choice."

"I must complete my assignment to honor Mr. Hall."

He tore off sheets of paper and let them float to the floor like bird wings.

She waited as he wrote.

He held up the paper. "I am going to my chapel. I will finish Ezra Riley."

"Okay," she said.

What else could she say? Blue Man was in control.

Ezra hears the sounds of hooves and smells horse sweat. The horse's feet stomp at flies, and it swishes its tail back and forth.

The boy moves onto the top plank of the corral. The horse, unsaddled and unbridled, stands below him. He eases himself down upon the animal's back.

The horse looks back curiously but doesn't react, so Ezra stretches forward and holds the horse around the neck. Its hair smells sweet.

Ezra is thirteen. The paint horse has never been ridden.

Ezra says softly, "Gusto."

His consciousness ascends through the hypnopompic state between sleep and wakefulness. A blue form fights to emerge behind him in roiling darkness, a sparse mane behind reddened eyes, a blue roan striving to break free from the ebony depths.

Ezra grips the mane of the sorrel-and-white paint in both hands, and the young horse lunges and carries him to a surfaced wakefulness.

Ezra opens his eyes and looks at the clock. It is 4:38.

Now he understands!

The gift of spiritual discernment tells him that what just happened wasn't natural. It was supernatural. The dreams and memories were not the organic processing of his mind but had unnatural origins.

There was someone somewhere creating nightmares by excavating memories.

Ezra had sensed this when interpreting the President's dream but hadn't been sure. Now he was.

The President had been targeted by...a weapon? A person?

And Ezra was the target now.

Blue Man emerged from his chapel, confused. He'd sent forth energy, but the power had returned.

Mr. Hall was not present to guide him through this new situation. He'd killed Mr. Hall to be free, to be human.

But what did being human mean? How did one do it? Perhaps he needed Mr. Hall's niece more than he'd thought.

And how should he respond to this unique development with Ezra Riley?

42

Blue Man summoned Isabel to his chapel.

She'd never been in the sanctuary and was awestruck by its massive quartz monolith surrounded by gold and silver tiles outlined in diamonds. She instantly realized her thoughts seemed magnified.

Is it impressive?

She looked at Blue Man and realized he was quite handsome— she could barely look at him earlier in the study. He was six feet tall, 170 pounds, blond hair, blue eyes, and a beautiful body.

I am five-eleven and 168 pounds.

A faint blush covered her cheeks. It was easy to forget someone could read thoughts.

You can hear my thoughts?

"Yes."

Pure telepathy must be practiced, so you will need to speak out loud until you are adept.

"Why am I here?"

I want you to dismiss the staff. Pay them well, but send them away.

"But, who will do the work?"

You.

She fidgeted.

He smiled.

No, Isabel. Remember, I can read your thoughts. There is no way for you to escape.

"I won't try."

He moved closer, and she stiffened in response. An aura about Blue Man was colder than his skin color.

I am sure you have questions, and I will answer a few.

She raised her face, her nose tilting slightly upward. She was a Hall, after all: Isabel Elizabeth Hall, a woman of means and influence.

"Why did you kill him?" she demanded.

To be my own man.

"Can you really levitate four feet in the air?"

He gurgled a laugh, and the guttural sound resonated in the chapel chamber until it wrapped around Gray Lady like heavy lace.

I have, once.

"How did you escape the sanctuary and enter the house?"

I demanded the lock combinations from Mr. Hall's mind. It took time. He had a strong will and was well trained. His bedroom is lined with lead. Lead inhibits my energy. Did you know that?

She shook her head.

What else would you like to know?

"Are you going to kill me?"

No, why would I? You will be helpful.

"You said you wanted to complete the mission and destroy Ezra Riley to honor my uncle. Is that true."

He beamed, and his face shone like snow-covered ice painted by a low-angled sun.

It is. Partially.

"What do you mean, partially?"

I want to do it to prove I can.

"Mr. Riley is not our enemy."

I have my mission.

"What else would you have me do?"

Fix my morning drink. The ingredients are in the kitchen.

"Where do I stay?"

It is safer for me if you stay in the house. Do not attempt to leave or communicate with others.

"There are people within this organization that I may need to talk to."

Blue Man had to think for a moment. He'd never used a phone or a computer.

You may keep one computer and one cell phone. Destroy the others. You may go now. I need my drink.

Blue Man closed the door to the chapel. He was eager to get to work.

The phone rang as Ezra was going out the door. He came in and answered it.

"Cows and weather," the voice said.

"You're checking on me?"

"Weather and cows."

"Okay, Barn Wall, I get it. We're going to talk about cows and weather, just like I instructed you."

"Are you going looking for the Wildebeest?"

"Yes, I am."

"Did you know a big shift in the weather is coming in a few days?"

"Is this code? You never know what the weather forecasts are."

"The magpies have moved into the junipers all around my house. That means a big storm is coming."

"Are the magpies talking to you?"

"No, not yet, but I keep hoping."

"I don't think we have to use the cows-and-weather code, Barney. I believe the physical threat is over."

"Why? Did you kill somebody?"

"No." At least, not yet.

"Then how do you know it's over? Did you learn any more about that Pennington fellow?"

"No."

"I used to be a reserve deputy. Maybe I'll have a visit with Andy Royce."

"Andy stopped by yesterday just before dark. He had a few questions."

"Did you have any answers?"

"None that thrilled him. The new truck isn't a blessing. It attracts attention."

"I'm still looking for a bagful of barn cats. What else is new?"

"Anne got delayed. There's a big storm in Brazil."

"Do they have magpies?"

"What?"

"I was just wondering how they forecast storms? Do magpies fly backward south of the equator or upside-down?"

"Barn Wall, have you been in cartoon-land?"

"All night long."

"What sparked this burst of creativity?"

"I dunno. Maybe it had something to do with flashing lights, sirens, fires, and pulling a dead man from his car."

Isabel found a recipe book in the kitchen with detailed lists of Blue Man's drinks and meals. Most of it was predictable: organic fruit juice and vegetable juice, non-soy protein powder, honey, nuts, and enough vitamins and minerals to keep a fleet of horses running for months.

Where was the colloidal silver?

On a blank page at the back of the book, she found a hand-drawn map of the kitchen dotted with numbers and a map key below.

Number 14 was Silver Hydrosol.

She found its location but decided not to use it. Without daily doses of colloidal silver, the effects would diminish. Let Blue Man turn white, she thought, and we will see how he handles that.

Numbers 18 and 19 confused her: Mscln and Pslbn.

Mscln and Pslbn?

She discovered their drawer and opened it. Number 18 was a tray with scores of vials holding a green liquid.

Number 19 was a tray with vials containing a blue liquid.

Mscln and Pslbn?

Mescaline and psilocybin, she realized. Organic hallucinogens. Her uncle had not abandoned the MKUltra Subproject 58 pursuits but had developed his own "sacred mushroom" formulas. What quantity of the drugs had he been giving Blue Man, and when? Surely, it couldn't be every day, or Blue Man would be toast. This made Isabel wonder: If Blue Man could read minds, why didn't he know about the colloidal silver and the hallucinogens? It was true his psychic development was ongoing, but there had to be another reason. Her uncle's bedroom was lead-lined; could his study be lead-lined, too? Was the exposure to lead the reason he'd become increasingly erratic?

And what kept Blue Man from reading her uncle's mind in the sanctuary through these many years?

Uncle Bill's iron will. That had to be it. Blue Man was like a son who'd not grown past his father's willpower until the father grew old and frail.

Am I that strong? she wondered.

I had better be, she realized.

43

Ezra was on a high ridge posting a trot on Q-Tip and thinking about Barney Wallace and his invasion of magpies. Surfing the religious channels early in the morning was the only television Ezra allowed himself. The news programs angered him, and he found the reality shows stupid and the sitcoms disgusting. It seemed to Ezra that televised sports and even the Weather Channel were intent on pushing propaganda.

Television was not relaxing, but Eastern Montana's delightful temperatures were. Still, if Barney's magpies were correct, Ezra needed to quit searching for the Wildebeest and bring his cattle home for the winter.

He'd seen drastic changes in the weather before; the election year of 2000 was one example. October had been mild with rain at the end of the month, but overnight the rain froze, turned to a foot of snow, and temperatures plunged to thirty below zero.

The year his father died, 1978, was another case in point. One November day, Johnny Riley, in light clothing, was replacing a gate post in the corrals. The next day the wind chill was seventy below. Ezra's father never saw that hard winter as Johnny Riley had died of a massive heart attack before the first storm struck.

Ezra pulled Q-Tip to a stop on the pinnacle of a gumbo butte, reached into his cantle bag for binoculars, then surveyed the landscape.

A small herd of antelope grazed in the sagebrush on a flat far below him. If bitter north winds came, he'd have pronghorns by the thousands as they drifted from as far away as Alberta to pick at the sagebrush on Sunday Creek.

Further to the north, he glimpsed a single massive mule deer buck traveling with its nose to the ground, seeking a doe in estrus.

Ezra did not feel his thoughts drift away.

One moment he was admiring the mule deer, then moments later he was thinking of his trip to the White House.

He, Ezra Riley, had to be one of the essential Christians in America, wasn't he? Wasn't he the one chosen to interpret a dream for the most powerful man in the world? If Ezra hadn't been sworn to secrecy, imagine what would be possible: a book, a movie, interviews on television, and countless invitations to speak to thousands. His face would adorn the covers of magazines. He would see himself on early morning religious programming.

He shook his head hard to dispel the vain imaginings.

Where did those thoughts come from?

Ezra spun Q-Tip in a slow circle until the colt faced directly to the north.

"And do you seek great things for himself?" he said out loud, quoting from the forty-fifth chapter of Jeremiah. "Do not seek them; for behold, I will bring adversity on all flesh, but I will give your life to you as a prize in all places, wherever you go."

The vain thoughts were not him, not even from the darkest recesses of his flesh, for Ezra had long ago repented for wanting to be a famous Christian professional.

Famous, no; effective, yes.

He nudged Q-Tip back to a steady trot, thinking he'd left vanity behind. A mile later, Ezra dismounted to open a gate. Its five wires were stretched tight, so he pushed hard with his right shoulder while lifting with his left hand to loosen the wire loop.

The heart is deceitful above all things and desperately wicked; who can know it? Behold, I am against the prophets; I am against those who prophesy false dreams. Do not let the prophets and the diviners deceive you nor listen to your dreams, which you cause to be dreamed.

Ezra gripped the gate post, and the intruding thought seized him.
Condemnation.

When self-exultation failed, the next arrow sent to his soul was tipped with the poison of condemnation.

Pushing with new fury, he popped the gate open, led Q-Tip through, closed the gate, and remounted.

This time he turned and faced the south.

And again, Ezra quoted Jeremiah: "Refrain your voice from weeping, and your eyes from tears; for your work shall be rewarded, and they shall come back from the land of the enemy. There is hope in your future, that your children shall come back to their own border."

He reined Q-Tip north and spurred the colt to a gallop.

Blue Man summoned the Gray Lady to his chapel.

She entered and sat on a carved bench padded with crushed velvet. She noticed Blue Man's face looked pinched and pensive.

I need your help.

"Yes?"

I again sent energy to Ezra Riley, and again it came back to me.

She sat silently, not knowing what he wanted from her.

You know him.

"I met him for only a few minutes in Washington and he was blindfolded. He did not see me."

Blindfolded?

"Yes, he insisted on it."

What manner of Master is he?

"I don't understand your question."

He stared at her intensely, then dismissed his question.

She waited for the next thought.

You have read his books and articles?

"I have."

What is a common thread in his writings? What is his weakness?

"When he was young, it was drugs. Especially hallucinogens."

I can use that. What else?

Gray Lady thought for a moment.

"Land," she said.

Land?

"He's Irish," Gray Lady explained. "The love of land is in his DNA. The Irish have always felt dispossessed."

Dispossessed? Land is only soil.

Isabel paused, remembering Blue Man had never been outdoors.

"Riley has a love for creation, for the natural world, especially for the ranch he grew up on," she explained.

Blue Man frowned, trying to process the sentiment.

"For Riley, land is freedom with responsibility," Isabel continued. "The freedom to roam and explore, but also the duty to care for and tend."

And this is a weakness?

"It is for Riley. The land is the skin of the world, but it is more than that. It is a recording device. It holds memories from the beginning of time, as well as hopes and dreams.

The land holds dreams and memories?

"Riley thinks so."

Blue Man smiled.

Dreams and memories. I can work with that.

44

Ezra had shortened his ride and was nearing home when he saw the figure approaching.

Barney Wallace on horseback.

Ezra slowed his colt to a walk so Barney could catch up.

"Barney," Ezra said as the tall cowboy reined his draft-cross gelding beside him.

"Ezra."

"What brings you to the hills, Barn Wall?"

"Magpies."

"The magpies told you to come?"

"Yup."

"So you finally heard a magpie talk to you?"

"No, not really, but I decided if winter was on its way I better get horseback and enjoy myself."

"My sentiments exactly."

"I did stop in town and see Andy Royce."

"The sheriff tell you anything new?"

"Nope. They released the dead guy's body—"

"Pennington?"

"Yeah, Pennington. The coroner's inquest didn't show any evidence of foul play."

"Someone already arrived and claimed the body?"

"Yup. It was gone this afternoon."

"That was quick."

"I thought so, too. I think Andy was just glad to have the case over with."

They rode their horses to a high cliff that overlooked Sunday Creek and Ezra's ranch. The leaves had fallen from the cottonwoods, but a setting sun bathed the valley in quiet beauty.

"Shoot, it's peaceful out here," Barney said.

"Sure is," Ezra agreed.

"I mean, besides a car wreck killing a mysterious man and you sleeping in the hills armed like a Ninja, it really is peaceful here."

Ezra looked at his old friend. "You got something on your mind, Barn Wall?"

Wallace brought a hand to his face and stroked his thick mustache. "You really did go to the White House, didn't you?"

"If I told you, I'd have to kill you."

"No, I mean really, you did. That Benny Davis character leaving a brand new truck in your yard, and this Pennington dying with a gun in his pocket and your place circled on a map—that all adds up to something."

"Adds up? Are we being accountants again?"

Barney looked half-steamed. "You aren't going to tell me anything, are you?"

"You don't want to know."

"But you said the threat was over."

"I said the physical threat was over."

"What's that supposed to mean?"

"Something more has piqued your curiosity?"

"Yeah, well..." Barney paused and chewed on the ends of his mustache. "I had a dream last night."

"You? You only dream about pizzas."

"And outhouses. I dream about outhouses a lot."

"Only because you failed toilet training. So what was the dream?"

"You know I'm the security officer for our church."

"I know you pack heat with your Bible."

"I often forget my Bible."

"And what does this have to do with your dream?"

"In the dream, I was sittin' in my pew trying not to scribble cartoons on the church bulletin when I smelled smoke. I looked around and saw flames. I thought I saw people outside settin' fires so I tried to reach for my gun, but I couldn't."

"Why not?"

"I was frozen. I couldn't move. I looked around, and everyone else was frozen, too. I figured we were all going to die."

"Then what happened?"

"I had to pee really bad."

"In the dream?"

"No, in real life. I made myself wake up because I was afraid I'd try to pee on the fire."

Ezra looked at his friend and shook his head. Barney Wallace never ceased to amaze.

"I didn't think Mrs. Wallace would appreciate my fire suppression efforts."

"So you got up, went to the bathroom, came back, and went to sleep. Did the dream reoccur?"

"How did you know?"

"So it did?"

"It did. I was back in the pew, only the fire was hotter, and the smoke was thicker."

"And then?"

"Well, the building burned down around us, and when it did, embers fell on our heads. But they didn't burn us. Instead, they thawed us out."

"Thawed you out?"

"Yeah, remember, I told you we were all frozen in our pews, but the burning embers thawed us out and we could move."

"What did everyone do then?"

Barney scowled. "That was the odd part. We all started dancin'."

"You were all dancing."

"I must have been doin' so in the bed 'cause I kicked Mrs. Wallace and woke her up."

Ezra smiled. "You never cease to amaze, Barn Wall."

"So what does it mean?"

"It means the Frozen Chosen are goin' to the Dancin' Mansion."

Barney scowled again, his upper lip pushing through the brush of his mustache and almost caressing his nose. "Well, shoot," he said. "That doesn't make any sense at all." The old cowboy stared at the distant horizon as if wishing he could slip over its lip and land in a better place.

"It's a good dream, Barney."

Barney continued to stare. "When you were nineteen, did you ever think the world would ever be in such a mess, especially America?" he said finally.

"Actually, I expected it."

"When I was nineteen, all I wanted to do was ride saddle broncs as well as I possibly could."

"You rode them as well as anybody."

"What makes you say you were expecting this mess?"

"Remember, I was a hippy. Most of the kids I hung with wanted America brought down, and the college professors encouraged it."

"We're headed for a civil war, aren't we?"

"Yes, unless the Lord intervenes."

"This trip to Washington you joke about and this business with Benny Davis and Pennington, if you gave your word not to talk about it, then that's good with me. I won't ask any more questions. All I want to know is how do you think this will all turn out?"

Ezra shrugged. "Pray for falling embers," he said. "Pray for falling embers."

Dreams or memories. Blue Man repeated the thought to himself, but Isabel heard it in her mind.

Which is Riley's greater weakness? he asked.

"They are entwined. The memories are Riley's foundation, the legs of his being. His dreams are his vitals, his chest, arms, and head."

Blue Man scowled. *That confuses me.*

"Yes, because you are unable to leave this sanctuary and go places."

His thought snapped back quickly. *I have gone places you can't imagine.*

What does he mean? she thought.

Again. What is his more significant weakness, memories or dreams?

"What I'm trying to tell you is they are one body. With Riley you can't separate them, but you can isolate the attacks."

Blue Man nodded. *I understand. Kicks to the knee before a punch to the face.*

"As you say."

I find all of this very interesting. If I did not have to destroy Ezra Riley, I believe I would like to meet him.

I would like to see that, Isabel thought.

Blue Man looked at her quizzically.

You have communications on your mind.

"I need to go to the main house. There are details that need to be checked on."

The employee who was killed in Montana?

"Yes, a tragic accident."

Not an accident.

Isabel's mouth dropped. "What?" she gasped. "What do you mean, not an accident?"

You may go.

Blue Man's abrupt statement—"not an accident"—and Isabel's sudden dismissal felt like slaps across Gray Lady's forehead.

45

Monday, November 15

Ezra awakened, sensing it was early, and rolled over to look at the clock: 3:23. He lay back, wishing he could go back to sleep but knowing he wouldn't. He wasn't wired for rest.

Anne was supposed to be home today, but she wouldn't be. In another hour, perhaps, she'd call.

He found himself thinking about his mother. She'd been dead forty years, and he hadn't thought of her much lately.

He remembered the time in the kitchen when she looked out the window and saw a car approaching. "Oh, gracious," she'd exclaimed. "It's the Hofers." She looked down at her eight-year-old son and saw dread trickle through his body. The Hofers had five daughters, ages five to twelve.

Ezra spun and raced for the back door. He'd rather hide in the hills than entertain five girls.

"I wish I could go with you," his mother called after him as she snubbed out a KOOL cigarette in an ashtray.

Another time it was the Hansons. His mother, Pearl Riley, saw them coming, shook her little bird-like frame, and said, "I hate visiting with Lillian Hanson," she said. "She talks nonstop. Chatty, chatty, chatty. I'd rather be in the living room talking horses with your father and Fred Hanson." Ezra took the cue and raced for the back door.

The hills received him warmly. Some days he packed his single-shot .22 rifle, the second-best present he'd ever received from his father. The best gift came the Christmas morning when he was thirteen and found a bill of sale for Gusto in his stocking.

He often traveled light—no gun, just a pocketknife and a gunny sack for gathering rocks and exploring the badlands' canyons, pinnacles, sandstone walls, caverns, and deep, narrow creeks. There were mysteries in the wonderfully carved hills.

Ezra would strip down to his shorts and sneakers and practice stalking game like an Indian, getting so close to bedded deer he could see their eyelashes. Many times he'd watched coyote pups at play and once observed a fox and hawk battle over a freshly killed rabbit. The boy gave a wide berth to badgers, skunks, and porcupines but killed rattlesnakes when in the mood; other times, let them be, and once, he'd found the tracks of a mountain lion.

The hills were secure and consistent.

His home was unpredictable. His older sister, Diane, might be nice to him, or she might not. Usually not. His little sister, Lacey, was small enough to need attention, and if Ezra was home, his mother expected him to babysit. Pearl Riley was a bundle of nerves. She reminded Ezra of an open-faced fishing reel backlashed with knots tangled in self-pity and negativity. Still, her intelligence and creativity recognized the same in her son, and she saw a future for him beyond cursing drought and fighting blizzards. The nickname she gave her sole surviving son was "The Dreamer." He was their second chance. Pearl and Johnny had lost their first baby to crib death.

Ezra's father was the real uncertainty.

Johnny Riley could be sullen and withdrawn—"Your father has a lot on his mind," his mother would say—or playful and fun. Johnny's eyes carried a mischievous sparkle suited best for poker games, horse-trading, and bare-knuckle fights—none of which were activities for little boys.

His father had grown up fast, leaving school after the fifth grade to work for one notorious wagon boss after another at a time when motor vehicles were an oddity and horses still ruled the plains.

Mealtimes were the hardest for Ezra in the Riley household. His mother complained about not being appreciated; his father coughed nervously and stared out the window; Diane mocked him for whatever reason pleased her; and little Lacey spit out her peas and corn.

Canned peas and canned corn. Ezra smiled to himself. Every meal except breakfast had canned peas and corn.

He remembered his mother's sad, soft brown eyes staring through him when she called him The Dreamer, and he wondered then, and now, what did she see?

The phone rang. It was Anne calling early.

"Did I wake you?" she asked.

"No, I've been awake."

"How are you doing?"

"Fine."

"How's the weather?"

"Great. When are you coming home?"

"I'm on call. There is a lull coming between storms. Some flights might be allowed to leave today."

"So it could be today or it could be a week from now?"

"Yes, I'm afraid so."

"The kids all doing fine?"

"They're doing great. Are you still looking for the Wildebeest?"

"I am."

"Take Barney with you," Anne pleaded.

"He's with me most days," Ezra lied.

"And nothing new is going on?"

"Quiet as can be."

"Okay, I better get off the line in case the airlines call. Love you."

"Love you, too."

Blue Man left Isabel for his morning ritual of martial arts and yoga. It was a discipline he couldn't break.

Recharging his *chi*, Uncle Bill had called it.

Isabel walked to the tunnel's entrance, tried the door, found it unlocked, and hastened down the long corridor to the manor. Rushing upstairs to her bedroom, she rummaged in her purse for her cell phone. She'd lied to Blue Man and gotten away with it: Pennington's death was not her concern; Mary Margaret's safety was. She found her phone and hurried to her uncle's bedroom to avoid Blue Man's mental probe. If Blue Man was fulfilling missions, her sister might be on the list. Isabel had no idea what orders Blue Man was following.

She punched in Mary Margaret's number. One ring, two, three.

"Hello?" a voice said.

"Mary Margaret, it's me, Isabel."

"Isabel! How nice to hear from you."

"Listen, I don't have much time. I wanted you to know that Uncle Bill is dead."

There was a quiet pause.

"For real this time," Isabel added.

"What happened?"

It was Isabel's turn to pause. Did she dare tell the truth? "He died in his sleep," she said.

"I suppose there will be no funeral."

"No, no funeral."

"Isabel, you sound worried. Are you okay?"

"No, I mean, yes. Yes, of course, why wouldn't I be?"

"You don't sound okay."

"Mary Margaret, listen, do you remember the code Uncle Bill had for us when we were kids?"

"The traffic light colors?"

"Yes. Red light, yellow light, green light."

"I remember, why?"

"Do you remember what the yellow light meant?"

"With Uncle Bill it was his way of saying 'wait and see.'"

"What else can a flashing yellow light mean?"

"A flashing yellow traffic light is a warning. Isabel, what's going on?"

"And a red light?"

"Stop, of course."

"What I told you about Uncle Bill's death, Mary Margaret? Red and yellow, Mary Margaret. Red and yellow."

"Isabel, you're not making sense. Are you in danger?"

"I can't say any more. Just remember red and yellow."

Mary Margaret was in her car doing errands in Burlington, Vermont, when her sister had called. As the call suddenly ended, Mary Margaret looked down at the phone's screen in bewilderment, then quickly looked up. The traffic light in front of her flashed yellow, then changed to red.

She hit the brakes.

Then the light instantly changed to green.

The light indicating *Go* did not stay steady as traffic lights do. It started flashing.

She stared up at the flashing green light.

Go!

46

After his meditations, Blue Man summoned Isabel to the chapel again.

Are you distressed?

"I don't know what you mean," she said.

Are you ill at ease?

Gray Lady broadened her stance and crossed her arms across her chest. "Am I distressed, you ask? You killed my uncle, made me release the staff, and give me orders on my estate. I own all of this."

I do not understand ownership. What bothers you?

"I am not pleased with this arrangement. You need me more than I need you. Yes, you could kill me, but where would you be then?"

Your focus is not on the mission.

"I am Mr. Hall's heir and successor, remember?"

So you are the boss?

"I didn't say that."

We need to complete our mission.

"Tell me again why you killed my uncle."

I already told you. I wanted to be human.

"You were selfish. Killing him was not part of the mission."

Yes, it was. Mr. Hall's instability was threatening the mission.

"Did you discuss your concerns with my uncle?"

Mr. Hall would not have understood.

"How was the mission defined to you?"

The mission was to expose corrupt leaders in the government, beginning with the President.

"But the mission was sidetracked because of an old cowboy in Montana?"

Yes. He is a threat to the mission.

228

"Direct your energy back to the President. You can bring him down. Do you have proof of his wrongdoings?"

Do you understand remote viewing?

"Remote viewing? Of course, my uncle helped develop those programs. His viewers repeatedly gathered valuable intelligence from foreign enemies by using their psychic vision."

I can do more than that.

"More than remote viewing? What do you mean?"

His viewers only received perceptions. I can travel.

"Soul travel? Astral projection?"

Whatever you wish to call it.

"What have you done? Where have you been?"

Russia, China, North Korea, Iran. My time abroad is limited. My main journeys have been to Washington, D.C.

"You were in rooms with people, but they couldn't see you?"

They could not see me, but I could see and hear them and read their thoughts.

"Are you psychokinetic?"

To some degree.

Gray Lady frowned and moved a step closer to Blue Man. "But you are not able to bring back physical evidence?"

I am not. But what I learned was recorded on videotape by Mr. Hall.

"You know who is guilty of perjury, treason, and taking bribes?"

And murder. Many murders.

"Human trafficking?"

Yes.

Gray Lady paused and stared at the floor. "Without physical evidence, I can understand the strategy of driving them mad through nightmares. But why did my uncle want a dream interpreter if he already had psychic evidence? A dream interpretation is not any more valuable than remote viewing, is it?"

Mr. Hall called it "stirring the pot."

"Stirring the pot?"

Mr. Hall wanted to know if the enemy had a person like me.

"He shared those suspicions with me."

Mr. Hall knew the Communists had powerful psychics, children they had trained since their birth.

"Like you," she said.

Not like me. Mr. Hall adopted me because of my special needs. The training was to develop my extraordinary giftedness.

"Have you wondered about your birth parents?"

No. I look forward, not backward.

"Did my uncle have a name for you? Something besides Blue Man?"

Blue. Just Blue.

"There is one thing I must know. Is my sister on your target list?"

Your sister? I did not know you had a sister. Is she relevant?

"You didn't know it was my sister who had recommended Ezra Riley?"

No. Does it make a difference?

Gray Lady shook her head, moved around a chair, and rested her arms on the backrest. "No, it makes no difference," she said. "I think we can redefine our relationship."

How so?

"We will be a team. You will have much more independence, but we will continue the mission."

Blue Man didn't answer.

"We will put the focus back on the President, only this time we'll break him. I will help by using my influence with his staff to find more weakness for you to exploit."

He will ask for the dream interpreter.

Gray Lady gripped her hands together. "He might."

Riley needs to be eliminated but you are uncomfortable with this.

"Ezra Riley is not a bad person."

Good or bad means nothing.

"Targeting Riley will drain your strength."

He is my mission. Do not argue.

"I thought we were a team," Gray Lady insisted.

We are not a team.

"My advice and opinion mean nothing?"

That is correct. His eyes flared angrily. *And you are beginning to waste my time.*

Isabel stepped back as if pushed.

Do you want to know how I will destroy the cowboy?

She didn't respond.

I will go to him.

"Go to him? You can't leave—it's dangerous for you."

I will go my way.

"You will soul-travel to Montana?"

Yes.

"And then what? You won't be physical. You can't pull the trigger on a gun."

I have a plan.

Blue Man left the room.

Gray Lady crossed her arms, gripping herself tightly, and thought of Mary Margaret. Why had she called her sister? She didn't dare call Mary Margaret back to reassure her. Not yet.

Isabel Elisabeth Hall feared for her life. She knew she might soon awaken to see a pillow lowering onto her face.

47

Ezra took a step outside and breathed in the fresh air. The atmosphere was spring-like, but it was November, and winter was coming with cold white teeth that bit to the bone. He glanced at an insufficient woodpile. He should be cutting wood for cold weather, not pursuing an old cow that might already be dead.

But the hills were calling him. He could cut wood when it was forty below—he'd done it many times. But he wouldn't be horseback at forty below unless it was an emergency.

Perhaps today he'd start his main cow herd home and look for Wildebeest, too. No, bringing the cows home was a commitment, a two-day job. He'd best wait until Anne was home.

Ezra was tired. He could have easily gone back to bed, but another hour of sleep only limited the remaining daylight.

Simon, Quincy, and Q-Tip stared at him as if they were tired too.

Something in the air. Had it been two weeks ago that he'd rode home to find a stranger blocking the gate and scaring Wildebeest and her calf?

Two weeks ago, when he boarded a jet, flew to the White House, and interpreted a dream for a president he hadn't supported? Could he ever tell anyone, even Anne, about the experience?

What had happened to Davis Browne?

Ezra caught Quincy, saddled the roan colt, checked his gear, and realized he'd forgotten a firearm. It was hard to kill a horned cow with one's bare hands. He sighed deeply and was walking wearily to the house for a gun when Barney pulled into the yard.

"Morning, Ezra," Barney chirped.

"Morning, Barney."

"You look tired."

"I am tired. Anne called really early."

"Is she on her way home?"

"I don't know. She's on a call list."

"Are you still after the old cow? Don't you think she probably died?"

"What would have killed her?"

"The same thing that's going to kill us. Old age and orneriness."

"Yeah, it could be, but I'm going to look one more time."

"You're riding a colt?"

"Yeah."

"And you're riding from here? You're not trailerin' somewhere?"

"That's the plan."

"Bad plan," Barney said.

"And why is that?"

"You're tired, the colt is young, and you're headed into badlands where you'd be hard to find if something happened."

"You're sounding like Anne."

"I'm sounding like common sense."

"And that's scary coming from you, Barn Wall."

"What if I told you I had another dream?"

"You? Well, I'd say the prophet Joel had nailed it."

"Who nailed what?"

"In the Book of Joel, the prophet says in the Last Days the young men will have visions and the old men will dream dreams."

"I'm glad I'm old. A vision would scare me."

"Let me guess, you dreamt I was sitting in an outhouse, eating a pizza, and thinking about becoming an accountant."

"No, actually, I don't remember the dream, but I know I had one, and it involved you, the Wildebeest, and Simon. I woke up thinking you shouldn't ride a young horse today. You should ride Simon."

"Okay," Ezra said. "If my friend, Barney Wallace, is going to start having dreams and thinking they mean something, then I'll oblige. I'll ride Simon."

"And take the pickup and trailer."

"The pickup and trailer were in your dream?"

"No, that's just common sense. The days are getting shorter. You don't need to be riding home in the dark."

"Common sense from a cartoonist twice in one morning?"

Barney looked over at the new Ford Davis Browne had left. "I don't suppose it has a gooseneck ball in it," he said.

"I don't know why it would."

"I'm going to go look." Barney walked off in strides built from planks and hinges, each part moving separately from the others.

Ezra shook his head and continued to the house.

"Hey," Barney yelled. "It's got one."

"It has a trailer ball?"

"Yup, and all the wiring. You're good to go."

"I don't want to take it," Ezra said.

"Why not? It's yours, isn't it?"

"Yeah, it's mine."

"Have you even driven it yet?"

"No, I haven't."

"Go get your firearm," Barney shouted. "I'll hook this truck up to your trailer. You need to ride in style."

Gray Lady was mixing Blue Man's drink in the sanctuary kitchen when she received a telepathic summons.

Come to the chapel.

She poured the drink into a large glass and took it with her.

He accepted the concoction, and she watched him consume it.

Blue Man handed the glass back to her.

I need more help with Riley.

"What do you want?" Isabel asked.

I need eyes on him.

"I don't know how to do that," she said. "Uncle Bill controlled the access to the drones and satellites."

You have a technology expert.

She paused for a moment. "Yes," she said. "But the drones and the satellite require codes. I don't know those codes and neither does he. Only Uncle Bill did."

Think. I know there is something.

Isabel tried to resist the force that pounded her mind.

You are stalling. You know something.

She relented. "Yes, the truck. There are cameras in Davis Browne's truck."

That's all?

"It is still parked in Riley's yard."

But does Riley use it?

"I don't know."

Contact your expert. Have him activate the cameras.

"Why do you need eyes on Riley?"

If I know his location, I can direct my energy more accurately.

Gray Lady went to the house, took her laptop to her uncle's bedroom, and contacted Gyro Gearloose.

"Gyro here," he said.

"Did you get everything resolved with Pennington?"

Both stayed off-screen. Neither knew what the other looked like.

"It's all squared away," Gyro said.

For a moment, Isabel was tempted to ignore the command about the cameras, but she knew Blue Man would discover her trickery. She could not match him.

"I need you to activate the cameras in Mockingbird's truck," she said.

"You mean Meadowlark's truck," he corrected her. "They traded."

"Just do it and hurry."

"It's on my screen and here comes your screen-share."

Four boxes appeared on her computer's desktop. One showed a man in a hat, a second showed an empty back seat, and the other two displayed a moving gray highway surface with intermittent yellow stripes.

"Where is he?" Gray Lady asked.

"According to the GPS, he is seven miles north of Miles City and approaching a county road. He's pulling a trailer, the temperature is fifty-four degrees, and he's getting seventeen miles to the gallon."

"Too much information."

Gyro rolled his eyes. He missed Maintenance. At least he had a sense of humor.

"He's turned onto the gravel road."

"I can see that," Gray Lady said. "Activate the truck's homing beacon and keep the cameras on. Stay with him."

"Roger that." *It's going to be a long day,* Gyro thought.

Isabel took her cell phone and texted her sister: *Everything fine here.*

She returned to the sanctuary and knocked softly on the chapel's door.

Yes?

"The truck cameras are on. Riley is in the truck, and the homing beacon is activated. He appears to be going to the corrals at the back of his ranch."

Excellent. My trap is already set.

"Your trap?"

Last night's work.

"Oh. Do you need anything else?"

I need another drink. The blue one this time.

"The blue one?"

Yes. Set it outside the door, then leave me alone. I will be busy.

The blue one? Isabel hurried to the kitchen and grabbed the recipe book.

Did Blue Man know about the colloidal silver and needed it? No, certainly silver hydrosol had no mystical powers. Thumbing through the booklet, she found two pages stuck together at the back. She separated them; on one page was written: Blue Drink.

The ingredients shocked her: four cups of dark coffee, a cup of cream, two blue vials, and one green vial. Stir vigorously.

Blue vials and green vials. Psilocybin and mescaline.

Blue Man *was* going on a trip.

48

Ezra breathed in the new-truck smell deeply. He'd never owned a new vehicle and found the dashboard intimidating with gauges, dials, and plug-in sockets fighting for space.

He wondered how Old Yeller was doing.

He turned onto the county road and traveled five miles enveloped in the cab's luxuries and mysteries—how would he explain the pickup to Anne, who would be home any day?—then turned onto the two-track pasture road that led to the corrals. The first mile was a gradual ascent to a ridge high enough to see in every direction. It was one of Ezra's favorite places on the ranch. He slowed the shiny Ford to a stop, put it in park, and got out. The weather forecast that morning said a change was coming, so Ezra stopped to take a few minutes to enjoy the view. A final pleasant November day was like kissing a loved one goodbye, knowing the absence could last through April.

As he stared at the twisting path of Deadman Creek, the velvety grassy plains, and a rugged rampage of badlands, he felt a toxic sensation in his bloodstream that traveled from his limbs and organs toward his brain.

Something was wrong in his body! Hit by a stampede of panicked thoughts—stroke, heart attack, poison—he reached for the truck's hood to steady himself.

Ezra breathed deeply over and over again. Good air in, bad air out, but his nerves refused to settle—they flared like Christmas lights, like the running lights on the semi-trucks, like sunsets on sequential planets, like...

He was *tripping*.

His hippy days were decades behind him, but Ezra knew the sensation of *coming on* to a drug.

How could this have happened? He'd seen no one except Barney. Was it the truck? Had Browne's handlers infused the seat covers, the steering wheel, the air freshener—was there even an air freshener in the rig?—with a hallucinogen?

Paranoia. Ezra was getting paranoid.

Ezra had a reason to be paranoid!

The sky and clouds' colors began to scintillate as if coated with tinsel: *Lucy in the sky with diamonds.* He'd flashbacked to the '60s.

Flashback?

Was he having a flashback?

After all these years?

He gripped the sides of his head, wanting to scream, wanting to repress the scream, wanting to wake up and have this be a dream.

It wasn't a dream. Don't panic. Breathe. Relax.

If he'd been poisoned by LSD, he would come down. He might crash, but he'd come down. Trips lasted eight, ten hours. Maybe twelve.

I can handle this, he told himself. If any cowboy my age can handle this, it's me.

Jesus.

Acid trips—if that is what this was—peaked. They were an intergalactic rollercoaster. You started, you climbed, there were ups and downs, and then there was a pinnacle. After that, who knew?

Use your brain while you have it.

What was happening? Who was doing it?

Reason and deduction were sliding away. He had to catch a rational thought and hold it.

Repressed memories.

The President's nightmares had been repressed memories that took on current, symbolic forms.

I'm not on acid, he thought. *I am remembering acid.*

239

Psilocybin and mescaline.

That's it, he thought. *The effect is not LSD; it's mushrooms.* The sensations he felt were identical to organic hallucinogens, not a synthetic substance.

But, this trip is not organic, he thought.

It is not in my *blood. It is coming from outside of me.*

Where was Anne? He needed Anne.

It's a spiritual attack. I let my guard down. I was seduced by the shiny new truck.

Two long, distant ridges morphed into muscled arms, and a gray gumbo butte became a head with eyes, nose, and a mouth. The hills became his father. Young, strong, and handsome.

The ravines and creek bottoms melted below him, then reshaped as the face of a pretty, young woman in a gingham dress—his mother.

"Oh, you don't need that," his mother said, her face rising from the sagebrush and grass, a slender hand pointing at the truck. "You don't *need* that."

One could never desire what they wanted, only what they needed.

His father's badland face stayed expressionless, and the arms immobile, but swirls of dust rose from the hardpan flats and ghosted into herds of horses; hundreds and hundreds of wild horses chased by a lone figure: Johnny Riley, the wild horse man.

A tiny Johnny Riley rode down the arms of a giant badlands Johnny Riley like a moving tattoo.

Then a voice boomed behind Ezra Riley:

"Today is a good day to die."

Ezra whirled at the sound and saw an Indian warrior standing yards away wearing only a breechclout; his chest painted in blue lightning strikes, his face halved in red and black, and a braid tumbling down his back. In his muscled right arm was a tomahawk.

"Today is a good day to die," he said again.

Isabel Elizabeth Hall sat by a window in her uncle's study, looking toward the sanctuary hidden behind a copse of evergreens. She shook her head in bewilderment, trying to imagine what was transpiring in the chapel.

Three vials of organic hallucinogens! She couldn't grasp their effect on Blue Man.

Four cups of stout coffee would have been more than enough for me, she thought.

Her uncle's death and Isabel's imprisonment by Blue Man had her at the edge of catatonia. Why hadn't she expected and prepared for this situation? She couldn't have, she told herself. Her uncle had assured her Blue Man would eagerly accept her leadership, but Uncle Bill had not predicted Blue Man smothering him with a pillow.

A part of her felt sympathy for Blue Man and hated Wild Bill Hall for what he'd done. Who would create a baby and train the child to be a paranormal monster? Blue Man was handsome. If Isabel had ever married and had children, she might have a son his age. What was it like for Blue Man not to have a real name, know his parents, or play outside?

Sadly, she accepted that her life was similar to his. People called her Gray Lady for her penchant for wearing clothes colored like ashes and soot, color choices she couldn't explain. Had her uncle created this obsession? Had he meant her to blend in and not attract attention, even be unattractive?

And Ezra Riley! She'd stood near him on the tarmac and sat by him in the limousine but hadn't seen his eyes. His presence had comforted her—peace and protectiveness radiated from the man— but she shared the blame for his coming murder.

Isabel stared vainly at the vehicles parked near the estate's garage. She knew where the keys were and was confident she could drive away without Blue Man stopping her. He was terrified of the outdoors, though it held no threat to him whatsoever.

Physically, she could escape easily. Psychically, she had no escape at all. No matter where she went, Blue Man could enter her dreams, maybe even materialize in her home.

She pondered suicide. Her life had been eventful but meaningless. She had no husband or children to mourn her—only her sister, Mary Margaret.

Blue Man's mission was encoded within him. He neither needed nor wanted her advice or orders. She was kitchen help that doubled as secretary.

That status hurt her pride. After all, she was Isabel Elizabeth Hall, friend to presidents, senators, industry captains, international leaders, and movie stars. In fact, she was Dr. Isabel Hall, should she add the title of her Ph.D. in Political Science.

Now she was mixing concoctions for a miscolored misfit who'd murdered her lifelong guardian.

Suicide. How would she do it?

The simplest way was to drive two of the vehicles into the garage, close the doors, and leave the motors running.

How long would it take for the carbon dioxide to kill her?

Should she bring a book along in case it took longer than she anticipated? What book?

She rose, walked to the bookcases where leather-bound first editions lined the walls. So many books, so little time.

Little Women? Not her style.

1984? The Red Pony? The Old Man and the Sea? Narcissus and Goldmund? Brave New World?

She chose *Brave New World* and then went to her uncle's desk to leave a note.

Not your typical suicide note, but a message to Blue Man.

Why was she writing this memo? Was it revenge on her uncle? Was it compassion for Blue Man or hatred?

She wrote in large block letters:

Blue Man, you are not ill.

Your coloring is artificial and the outdoors will not harm you.

Isabel.

She went to the door, stepped outside, turned toward the garage, but paused when she heard a distant but familiar sound: the *whup-whup-whup* of helicopter rotors. To the north, just above the treeline, she saw it, coming like a slow, ponderous bird.

Was it hers? she wondered. Had her pilot come for a reason she couldn't fathom?

No. As it neared, Isabel saw this helicopter was trimmed in red. Hers had blue trim. It touched down on the helipad, the rotor wash rippling grass, leaves, and well-manicured bushes.

Mary Margaret stepped out and waved her sister forward.

Isabel walked to her wearily, one foot falling in front of the other.

Brave New World dropped from her hands to the ground, the pages rippling in the turbulence.

Wordlessly, Mary Margaret assisted her sister into the helicopter and belted Isabel into her seat.

Gray Lady watched numbly as the aircraft lifted off, banked north, and gradually sped away. She caught a brief glimpse of the sanctuary. Deep underground, resting in a seat carved into a massive crystal, the Blue Man was at work doing his duty.

Weak as she felt, Isabel released what she thought was a prayer, projecting the plea at the pine trees like a missile:

God, if you exist, save us from foolish zeal.

49

"Today is a good day to die."

Ezra approached the Indian warrior, reached out, and put his hand through the native's chest.

The apparition vanished.

Ezra was facing toward the west fork of Deadman Creek and stepped out on a graveled knoll to feel the sun. The sun felt peculiarly warm, but a north breeze prophesied a change. He looked down, mesmerized by the variety of small stones, and began picking agates. Within minutes he had a pocketful.

He heard the sound of *bellering* cattle. Ezra smiled because, throughout his writing career, editors routinely edited that to the proper *bellowing*. The editors were wrong. Cattle bellered.

The sound pulled his vision south to a herd of Hereford cows and calves churning through the deep sage of the creek. There were horsemen. One man rode *point*. Johnny Riley.

That's odd, Ezra thought. *I saw my father on the other side of this hill on the east fork of Deadman Creek.*

He reminded himself that he was stoned.

Other riders rode *swing*. Uncles Sam, Willis, and Archie.

Two men and a child rode drag. Uncles Joe and Solomon and...

Him.

Ezra saw himself, a ten-year-old boy, on a blue roan. The cattle suddenly milled and turned and became a red-and-white flood of hoof, hair, and horns. The little boy was caught in the turbulence while the adult riders whipped, spurred, and yelled, their vulgarities and obscenities seen in bursts of yellow, black, and red eruptions like exploding land mines.

The men raced, but the little boy was drowning in the herd.

How do you drown in a herd, Ezra wondered.

Then the cattle, horses, and men were out of sight.

Ezra looked back at the ground and saw an arrowhead. Excited, he bent and picked it up. It was an atlatl point knapped from moss agate and was as beautiful as any he'd seen.

He held it to the sun and admired the colors.

Then it was gone. Ezra looked in his hands, but it wasn't there. He searched the ground beneath his feet but couldn't find it.

Where did it go?

I never had it, he told himself. *This isn't real. None of this is real.*

Ezra looked at the new pickup and the attached gooseneck stock trailer. He wondered if it was safe for him to drive.

Did he remember how to drive?

"Today is a good day to die."

Behind him, the Indian warrior reappeared and pointed to a hill to the southeast where a lone figure led an animal. It was a slender youth with wavy hair reaching his shoulders. He wore a fringed leather jacket and knee-high moccasins.

The animal was a paint horse.

Ezra at eighteen and Gusto.

The youth hugged the horse around the neck, then unfastened its halter and set it free. Gusto slowly trotted away. Ezra sat on the ground and stared at shadowed badlands.

The day before leaving home. I said goodbye to my horse and the hills, but not to family or friends.

Memories of hitchhiking washed through his mind: lost in the streets of Seattle, alone in the dusty deserts of Arizona, arrested in Kansas, sleeping on the beach in Oregon, a knife at his throat in San Francisco. Communes, dope, riots, demonstrations, psychics, New Age gurus, living on a dollar a day, fending off male and female predators, training in the desert mountains of Nevada, and meeting a very strange man.

He heard music rippling through the clouds above him: Crosby, Stills, Nash, & Young, Credence Clearwater Revival, James Taylor, Bob Dylan, Sly and the Family Stone. The puffy cumulus clouds vibrated with purple, orange, and yellow highlights drawn in paisley patterns.

He missed the music.

Paisley is an Indian pattern inspired by pinecones, Ezra remembered.

"Today is a good day to die."

Ezra faced the warrior apparition and thought of Anne. "It is not a good day to die," Ezra said.

The specter vanished.

I am not stoned. I am under a spiritual attack.

This is metaphysical, not physiological, Ezra told himself. *The attack is in the air, not in my blood.*

Blood?

"I plead the blood of Jesus," Ezra said, his voice pushing through the counter-reality that enveloped him.

The spell broke. As suddenly as the counterfeit experience had hit him, it left. Ezra breathed deeply and looked around. The hills and creeks were regular again.

How long did the *trip* last? Thirty seconds? Two minutes. Twenty minutes?

Ezra had no idea. He looked in the stock trailer where Simon stood patiently. "I don't know what just happened," he said to the big bay. "If I were still tripping you'd probably give me an answer."

After getting off the phone with Ezra early that morning, Anne was contacted by the airlines. A flight had been cleared to depart if she could make it to the airport immediately. Dylan rushed his mother to Galeao International Airport. Anne hadn't had time to say goodbye to her sleeping grandchildren.

Now, eight hours from Billings, Anne was anxious. If the plane only had pedals, she thought, she'd help it get to Montana.

In his seat carved from quartz, Blue Man shuddered violently.

The sent energy had returned with force. He massaged his temples to relieve a pounding headache.

I should call for Mr. Hall's niece, he thought.

I need another blue drink.

No. He hadn't time for drinks.

Ezra Riley had weathered the first storm, but the bait still awaited him. The hallucinations were a feint. Now he would strike with purposed reality.

Blue Man closed his eyes in concentration, knowing this feat would take all the energy he had.

50

Isabel sat on a bed in a five-star hotel suite in Washington, D.C., her eyes staring vacantly at the floor, hands twisting a handkerchief. She'd been silent since being pushed into the helicopter.

"Isabel," Mary Margaret implored. "Tell me what happened back there."

Her mind was remote, and her words slow. "It...still...happens," she said, dragging the sentence out like a wagon through sand.

"What do you mean, it still happens? What happened to Uncle Bill?"

"He was murdered."

"Murdered? Who killed him?"

"Blue Man." She said the name flatly and with finality, like pronouncing the word *death* in a eulogy.

Mary Margaret helped her sister to her feet. "Come," she said, leading her to an overstuffed chair. "Sit where you will be more comfortable."

Isabel tried to settle slowly, but gravity collapsed her heavily into the seat.

"Do you need a doctor, Isabel?"

The younger sister shook her head.

"Who is Blue Man?"

"Someone Uncle Bill created. He took him as a baby."

"Was this a CIA project?"

"No. It was his. He paired two government psychics and kept the child." Her voice was flat and droning.

Mary Margaret looked at her sister incredulously. She'd never known Isabel to drink or use drugs, but this story seemed too bizarre even for Uncle Bill.

"Why did Blue Man kill Uncle Bill?" she asked.

"Blue Man wanted to be treated like a human."

"Why is he called Blue Man?"

"Because he's blue."

"I think you need a doctor."

"No, no doctor."

"Your face is drawn and white, Isabel. When did you last eat?"

"I don't know."

"Do you want room service sent up?"

"Maybe."

Mary Margaret frowned. "Isabel, you're not making any sense. What is Blue Man doing now?"

"His duty."

"What is his duty?"

"He brings up people's darkest memories to torment them."

"Who has he done this to?"

"The President."

"The President of the United States?"

"Yes. And others."

"What others?"

"Davis Browne. Uncle Bill had him killed."

"Who was Davis Browne?"

"He was an employee."

"Did Blue Man do it?"

"No, Maintenance did it. But Maintenance is dead, too."

"You need coffee," Mary Margaret said, reaching for the phone. "I'll have room service bring up coffee and a Danish." She made the call. Her sister had been traumatized by something, but the idea of a blue man stirring memories was more than Mary Margaret could accept.

"Do you need a shower, or maybe a hot bath?" she asked.

"No, I'll be okay."

Isabel made eye contact with her sister. Her senses seemed to be returning.

"Everything happened so quickly," she continued. "Blue Man smothered Uncle Bill with a pillow. I knew he was going to kill me next."

"Did you see Uncle Bill's murder?"

"No, but I saw Blue Man go into the room."

Did my sister murder our uncle? Mary Margaret wondered. *Is that why she is in a state of shock?*

"Isabel, you said Blue Man was doing his duty? Is he on an assignment?"

"He is in the chapel."

"What chapel?"

"The underground chapel with the giant crystal."

A soft knock sounded at the door, and Mary Margaret rose and answered. A waiter brought a covered silver tray into the room on a cart. Mary Margaret thanked him with a generous tip and hurried him out the door.

"Where is this chapel?" Mary Margaret asked, pouring her sister's coffee.

"Underground."

"At the estate?"

"Yes."

"Where was the staff? I didn't see anyone when we landed."

"Blue Man told me to release them."

"Eat some Danish, dear."

Isabel brought the roll slowly to her lips. "I'm responsible too," she said.

"For what? For Uncle Bill?"

"No. For Davis Browne and Ezra Riley."

"Ezra Riley!" Mary Margaret exclaimed. "What about Ezra Riley?"

"He's Blue Man's new target. That is his duty."

"His duty to do what?"

"To kill him." Isabel bit into the roll, and crumbs fell on her sweater. "Blue Man's duty is to kill Ezra Riley," she said.

"What? Why?"

"Uncle Bill said he was a loose end. He knows too much."

Mary Margaret got on her knees and took her sister's hands in hers.

"Isabel," she implored. "Are you telling me the truth?"

"Yes," Isabel responded, almost angrily. "I am telling you the truth."

"How do we stop Blue Man?"

"We can't. The assignment is set in motion."

Mary Margaret shook her sister's hands briskly, the tremors traveling up Isabel's arms and into her shoulders.

"We must go back to the estate," Mary Margaret said.

Isabel's eyes widened. "No!"

"Is Blue Man armed? If you are afraid of him, we'll take bodyguards with us."

"He's not armed," Isabel said with contempt. "He's never held a gun. He can't even cook or go outdoors."

"What are you saying? What do you mean he's never been outdoors?"

"Uncle Bill convinced him he has a deadly auto-immune disease. He's blue because Uncle Bill poisoned him with colloidal silver."

Mary Margaret let that information settle. Had her uncle turned someone blue?

"What do you think we should do?" she asked Isabel.

"Wait. We stay away from the estate."

"But we must warn Ezra Riley." Mary Margaret grabbed her cell phone and punched Ezra's landline number. Riley's answering machine came on, a woman's voice:

You have reached the residence of Ezra and Anne Riley. We are probably outdoors. Please leave a message after the tone and we will get back to you. Have a blessed day.

"Ezra," Mary Margaret spoke to the machine. "This is Mary Margaret Hall in Vermont. You are in serious danger. When you get this message please call me immediately."

"It won't do any good," Isabel said.

"Why not?"

"Ezra won't be home until dark. It will be too late by then."

"Has his wife returned from Brazil yet?"

"I don't think so."

"Maybe she has and she will hear the message. If you won't go to the estate with me, give me instructions and I will go alone."

Isabel shook her head. "No. It's too dangerous."

"Isabel, what else can we do? I can't call the police and say a blue man in an underground chapel is killing a cowboy in Montana by sending bad energy."

"Gyro."

"What?"

"Gyro Gearloose. Our computer expert. He's watching Ezra through the cameras in the truck. He knows where Ezra is."

"Call him. Have him pinpoint Ezra's location, and we'll contact the local sheriff."

Mary Margaret scrolled through Isabel's phone, found a number for "Gyro," hit the dial button, and handed the phone to her sister.

Moments later: "Gyro here."

"This is Gray Lady. Do you still have eyes on Meadowlark?"

"That's an affirmative."

"His location, please."

The computer expert paused. "I'm sorry," he said. "I don't know."

"What do you mean, you don't know?"

"Whoever installed the signal beacon in Billings messed things up. Both the beacon and the GPS are burnt. That's the problem with using local talent."

"How about the cameras?"

"They are up and running."

"Can you see where Meadowlark is?"

"He's high on a hill somewhere—that's all I can tell."

"What is he doing?"

"Good question. He seems to be just wandering around."

"That's it? Just walking around?"

"That's what he is doing."

"Keep eyes on him. Call me if you see any type of landmark."

"Roger that. By the way, when I said he was high on a hill?"

"Yes."

"I mean, he is *high* on a hill. Meadowlark is acting like he's stoned."

51

It wasn't the *cowboy* in Ezra Riley that led him to recklessness, nor the *hippy* streak that made him adventurous. It was the writer's instincts—indelible ink flowing through his veins—that took him where the cautious wouldn't go.

After what he'd just experienced, a prudent man would return home, unsaddle his horse, and lock himself in the house.

Not Ezra. The reporter's blood demanded he observe, the novelist required knowing how stories ended, and the warrior in Ezra Riley wanted to fight.

Someone, or some *thing*, was trespassing not just on his land but in his soul.

How powerful was a person or a spirit that induced hallucinations, activated forgotten memories, and altered one's dreamscapes?

Ezra had gone willingly to the White House, told the President his dream, and gave the President a distasteful interpretation. Ezra knew there would be spiritual retribution he couldn't hide from, but who was behind it, and what was its source?

He had been targeted and had no choice but to stand and fight.

But how did one fight this invisible enemy?

If it meant to kill him, as Ezra suspected, then his best tactic was simply to survive.

But who wanted to kill him?

Ezra could understand the President silencing him if he were talking, but he wasn't. If the President wanted to punish him, a bullet through the head would suffice. There was no need for a politician to waste time with metaphysical sparring.

If Mary Margaret's uncle, William Alexander Hall, was behind this, what was his purpose? Ezra was not a threat to expose anyone.

What news reporter would believe an old cowboy had gone from his horse to the White House to interpret a dream?

Don't overanalyze it, he told himself.

The enemy will expose himself. He always does.

I will win by staying alive.

Pulling up to the corrals, Ezra parked behind the loading chute, got out—annoyed by the truck beeping a reminder that the keys were still in the ignition—and unloaded Simon from the gooseneck trailer.

Ezra was awed again, looking at the big bay. So much muscle, power, and athletic balance in a spirited but charitable package.

"If you were a white horse," Ezra told Simon while tightening the saddle's cinch, "the Lord might choose you to ride upon His return." He led the big QuarterHorse to a cottonwood stump—Simon patiently put up with Ezra's awkward efforts—and pulled himself aboard.

"Sixteen hands closer to heaven," Ezra said, quoting a song by Wylie & The Wild West. "Actually, more like sixteen-two."

From Simon's back, which was similar to being on a hill, Ezra gazed to the eastern landscape where an apron of rising prairie broke over a ridge into gnarled, fisted badlands. The divide.

Stories were deposited in this soil.

Ezra couldn't help but love the land and imagine its stores: nomadic natives with domesticated wolves carrying packs and pulling travois.

What a difficult existence that had to have been.

Then natives horseback, free and mobile, firing arrows into stampeding buffalo.

A parade of white men: trappers, traders, and miners. Then buffalo hunters littering the grasslands with blood and bones.

Cattlemen funded by European barons and cowboys riding dangerously for a poor man's wages.

Sheepmen herding the woolies and horsemen supplying herd power to farm fields, city wagons, and the world's armies.

Johnny Riley leaving school at ten, wrangling for an infamous cowboy, then later, riding roughshod with the CBCs, sweeping the plains of feral horses.

And the homesteaders. Hungry with dreams and filled with sorrow.

Housewives like pretty Pearl Riley, pining to be outdoors but chained to children and chores.

A brittle but tenacious land had given Ezra more than it had taken from him.

The costs to his soul, spirit, and body had been enormous, but the rewards of silence, solace, legacy, and history were greater. The land had made him what he was: stubborn and stoic to some, generous and noble in the eyes of others.

Ezra sighed, knowing his days on fine horses in a big country were limited.

The land and the cattle were the Lord's, but when it was your blood and bone as well, it was hard to let it go.

He thought of a dream he'd had many years ago, shortly after his father died. He was alone and on horseback around red cattle. He rode as far as the divide, stopped on a high hill, got off, hobbled his horse, and sat down. He saw something on a distant skyline. He didn't pay it any attention at first, but it kept getting closer. It was a coyote coming toward him. The wind chilled, and Ezra sensed evil as the coyote came closer. Ezra couldn't move. The animal approached, and Ezra felt its hot breath on his face. He heard a voice from within the coyote. It was his father's voice. "Release me," the father was saying. Then the coyote smiled and spoke. "I have him and soon I will have you, too."

Ezra trembled. He'd not thought of that dream in years.

"Whoever you are," he said to the air. "Stirring that memory will not help you. You are an illusion, and you are a liar."

Then a noise came from the corral. Simon heard it first, and the bay's head swiveled, and its ears pointed.

Ezra turned in his saddle to stare at a shaded corner in the corral's largest pen.

He could hardly believe what he saw staring back from the shadows.

"What the..."

52

May Margaret let her sister finish the Danish, then poured her another cup of coffee.

"Isabel," she said. "I need to know as much as you can tell me about Blue Man and his abilities."

Isabel took a sip of coffee and then lowered the cup. "Why?" she asked. "I want to forget about him."

"Whatever you tell me might help Ezra Riley."

"How? Riley is in Montana and we can't reach him."

"Please. Start first with the President. I know you've been close to him. What was Uncle Bill planning to do?"

"I would like another Danish, please. Or breakfast. I'm really hungry."

"Okay, I'll order from their lunch menu. While I'm doing that, you start telling me what you know."

"Okay," she said. "I spent years getting close to this President. It wasn't easy."

"Why him?"

"Uncle Bill said the fix was in, that he'd be president no matter what and this man had to be stopped."

"I hate his policies as much as anyone," Mary Margaret said. "But what in particular was Uncle Bill worried about?"

"China. He said this man was owned by the Communists."

"I don't doubt that," Mary Margaret said, holding her hand up to pause Isabel while she made the brunch order.

"Okay," she said. "Go on. How was Uncle Bill going to bring him down?"

"The President is feeble," Gray Lady said. "Anyone can see that. Uncle Bill was using Blue Man to drive the President off the edge, and the Vice President and congressional leaders were next."

"He was doing this with repressed memories?"

"Memories that become nightmares. The President was teetering on the brink when Uncle Bill decided he had to know what those memories were."

"Hence, a dream interpreter."

"I thought it was an unnecessary risk, but Uncle Bill insisted."

"And I gave you Ezra Riley."

"We sent Davis Browne to Montana to get Riley, and I escorted him to the White House."

"Did you hear the dream and the interpretation?"

Isabel shook her head. "No, Uncle Bill wanted me to, but the President met Riley alone, which is very unusual."

"I should think so, but I guess presidents have been able to meet mistresses alone."

"Something unexpected happened," Isabel said, the flatness returning to her voice.

"Unexpected?"

"Riley told the President the dream."

Mary Margaret's head tilted. "Let me get this straight," she said. "Ezra told the President the dream first?"

"Yes. That's what the President told me."

"But the President didn't tell you the dream or the interpretation?"

"No."

"How did Uncle Bill react when you told him what Riley had done?"

Isabel's mouth wrinkled at its corners. "Uncle Bill seemed very curious, even challenged by that."

"How was the President after the interpretation?"

"He was much better," Isabel said. "He got his energy back and began working furiously. I think that made Uncle Bill suspicious of Riley."

"Suspicious, why?"

"If the President had guilty memories and Riley exposed them, we expected the President to be rattled. Uncle Bill was concerned that Riley's interpretation was encouraging."

"Not like Nathan and David," Mary Margaret said more to herself than to her sister."

"Like who?"

"King David in the Bible," Mary Margaret explained. "He lusted after Bathsheba and had her husband killed in battle. The prophet Nathan exposed him."

Isabel looked at her sister blankly.

"Enough about that," Mary Margaret said. "Tell me about Blue Man. What is he capable of doing?"

"He can levitate?"

"Okay. What good can that do?"

"I don't know. He's almost not human. He's childlike and handsome but also terrifying. He told me he could soul travel."

"Astral projection?"

Isabel nodded. "He said he'd even been to other countries."

Mary Margaret paused, seriously considering her line of questioning. Isabel sipped her coffee while waiting.

Finally, Mary Margaret asked, "Isabel, do you believe witchcraft was involved with Blue Man?"

"Witchcraft? Uncle Bill didn't believe in witchcraft," she said. "He believed in good energy and bad energy. Blue Man's energy was good because our mission was worthy."

Mary Margaret expected that answer and dropped the subject.

"Why do you need to know all this?" Isabel asked. "It's safer for you to know nothing."

"I'm not worried about safety. I'm concerned for Ezra Riley and I'm concerned for you, Isabel."

"I'm going to build a house made of lead," Isabel said, staring absently at the floor.

Mary Margaret ignored the remark, thinking it nonsensical.

Again, a soft rap at the door. The waiter came in, left a tray, and exited.

"I will let you eat in peace," Mary Margaret said.

"Where are you going?" her sister asked, fearful of being left alone.

"It's okay. I will be in the bathroom making phone calls."

"Phone calls?" Isabel asked suspiciously. "Who are you calling?"

"People who pray," Mary Margaret said. "And pray with authority."

53

For an instant, Ezra thought it was a hallucination. The pseudo-psychedelic effects had returned.

Staring at him from a back corner of the largest pen was the Wildebeest, thin as a knife blade and angrier than a hornet. When the old cow felt the cowboy's gaze, she shook her head vigorously and pawed the earth.

"What are you doing here?" Ezra said.

At the sound of his voice, Wildebeest lowered her head and threatened to charge.

Ezra knew he was safe. A section of stout woven wire supported by railroad ties separated them.

"How did you get in there?"

Ezra checked every gate by riding slowly around the big set of pens while the cow followed his every movement. There were no unlatched gates or tracks from vehicles or horses.

She must have dropped from the sky.

Was it a prank? Barney Wallace went to extremes pulling practical jokes, but this didn't have Barney's prints on it. First, Barney knew Ezra was a serious person in a serious situation; second, Barney was fond of Wildebeest and would never abuse her. The cow looked as if she'd been run for miles then left in a corral without feed and water.

"No wonder you're mad," he told her.

Wildebeest wasn't in the mood for conversation.

It couldn't have been a rustling attempt because the old cow was the least valuable animal in Ezra's herd.

He stared at the pens and gates again, trying to imagine how this had happened. The Riley corrals had one large pen to the south and four smaller enclosures with three alleyways to the north. One alleyway funneled to the squeeze chute, another to an elevated chute for loading semi-trucks, and the third into a wing for loading stock trailers.

The corrals could be accessed through any of five gates, which were all securely fastened.

Ezra had no explanation. A pilot might have harassed the cow toward the corrals, but how was a gate opened and closed? The corral sides were six feet high with top rails. The cow could not have cleared the fence cleanly, and why would she try? Since when did wild cows break into enclosures?

Had she been looking for her calf?

Doubtful. Wildebeest had abandoned the steer. And looking for her calf didn't explain how she'd entered the corrals.

Ezra shook his head. Things happened in the hills that defied explanation—and this incident topped his list—but it was a blessing in the end: the Wildebeest was captured. All Ezra had to do was back the trailer to the loading alley and get the old girl on board.

Then what?

Ezra had planned to shoot the cow and let her bones bleach in the badlands. Hauling her to the livestock auction in Miles City could endanger their crew, and she'd only bring thirty cents a pound across the scale. Thirty cents times nine hundred pounds minus the commission might total $250. Hardly worth it.

Or, he could open a gate and let Wildebeest take her chances with surviving the winter. This option was the easiest but the cruelest.

"What do I do with you?" he said to the cow. "You were a family pet for years except for your shenanigans at brandings and shippings. You raised good calves. But opening the gate is condemning you to a slow death. You deserve better than that."

Ezra grinned, realizing he'd given a longer speech to Wildebeest than he'd given the President.

He chose to load Wildebeest into the trailer, then decide what to do. Tying Simon to a post, Ezra backed the stock trailer into the alleyway, opened the trailer's gate, propped it back with a post, then opened the gates that led to the alley.

There was now a clear path for the cow to the trailer. Wildebeest observed Ezra's every move.

"You know what's going on, don't you?" he said. "I hate to see you go, old girl. I think even Simon hates to see you go."

The cow was fifty yards away and shaking her head. Ezra stayed near the corral panels knowing she might charge at any second. In his younger years, he'd outrun cows and bulls, climbed corral planks, and vaulted over gates, but his cowboy athleticism was long gone. A simple chore thirty years ago was a dangerous task now.

He needed to be on horseback to move the cow into the small pen, but that was no guarantee of safety. If Wildebeest got on the fight, she might run a horn through Simon's ribs. If he had to, he'd rope her. Simon could easily drag the small cow into the pen. Once in the smaller corral, he'd play matters as they came.

Ezra led Simon into the big pen, keeping the bay between himself and Wildebeest as he tightened the girth, back cinch, and breast collar.

Pawing dirt in the corner, Wildebeest looked like a cloud of hide and horns formed from a dust devil.

Ezra pulled himself into the saddle with a groan, shifted to adjust his seat, and unfastened his lariat from its keeper.

He shook a loop open and then patted Simon on the neck.

"Showtime," he whispered to his horse.

54

Ezra approached the Wildebeest from his left, hoping he could slowly herd the cow to the open gate.

She was having none of it. The thin cow backed into the corner until she was wedged against wire and planks, then she lowered her head and shook it in rage.

"You're not bluffing, are you?" Ezra said. "I apologize for whoever tormented you into this condition, but it was your fault for hiding the last three weeks."

Why am I talking to a cow? he wondered. *It's as if she is not an animal.*

The cow's sides heaved like bellows, snot dripped from her nose, and her eyes rolled in their sockets like loose marbles.

Ezra squeezed his legs as a cue to Simon to be ready.

Then the Wildebeest came, exploding from the corner with deadly purpose, her corkscrew horns aimed like gunsights. Ezra neck-reined Simon to the right, brought his left leg up, and spurred him in the shoulder. The bay sat back on his hocks, then pivoted quickly as the cow's horns grazed his left shoulder.

Wildebeest rushed by, slid to a stop, and turned to face her adversary.

Ezra could feel Simon's tension vibrating through the saddle pads and saddle.

The cow glanced around, looking for an escape she'd not earlier noticed. Satisfied there wasn't, she pawed twice, then charged again, her head tilted slightly up—better to see the horse's movements.

Ezra gave Simon free rein. As the cow charged, the horse jumped back and viciously bit the cow's neck as she passed. Wildebeest slammed into the corrals, faltered, and regained her footing but not before Ezra's loop sailed through the air and settled around both horns.

Ezra took two quick dallies around the saddle horn then braced for action. As Wildebeest attacked, Ezra nudged Simon diagonally to her path and jerked the cow sideways.

The cow kept her feet but let out a bellow of rage.

Again, Wildebeest rushed the horse, and again Ezra jumped Simon out of danger, the taut rope jerking the cow laterally. This time Ezra spurred Simon forward toward the open gate. The big bay threw 1,350 pounds of muscle against the breast collar and pulled. The cow followed with stiff-legged lunges, but as they neared the open gate, she stopped resisting and charged.

Ezra was expecting this, and he spun Simon aside and threw his dallies free. The cow rushed by him, through the open gate and into the smaller pen. Ezra sprang off his horse as if he were young and closed the gate as the cow stopped, turned, and charged it. The piston latch clicked into place as two horns threaded through the gate's bars, tearing Ezra's jacket.

"Dang, girl," Ezra said. "I like this coat."

Wildebeest pushed with all her strength, but the gate wouldn't budge, so the cow dropped to her knees and tried to go under it.

Ezra laughed at her. He was exhausted, but the adrenaline was surging, and he found the cow's predicament funny. He reached down quickly, grabbed the loop around her horns, and held it tightly. As the cow backed away, slack ran through the lariat's honda until the rope dropped harmlessly to the ground.

Ezra let out a big breath and turned to Simon.

"We have her in the little pen," he told his horse. "But she's still a long way from the trailer."

The pen was a small square that curved into a channel that straightened to the left into the loading alley.

Ezra recoiled his rope and assessed the situation. The old cowboy adage to never leave your horse seemed applicable. He was not going into that pen on foot. He considered going outside the corrals, climbing on the planks, roping Wildebeest as she charged him—only this time around the neck, not the horns—and securing her with wraps around the corral pole.

It was a good idea in theory, but theories have a hundred holes.

If he roped her around the neck, Wildebeest would lose air and choke down. He could feed her enough slack for her to recover, but she'd get hotter and wilder in the process.

It was the old cow's horns that had Ezra worried. If the Wildebeest was hornless, he could ride Simon into the pen with her. The stout bay could take a few hits but still crowd the cow into the trailer.

But horns were horns, and Ezra wasn't going to get his best horse hurt over a $250 cow. He'd first shoot the cow in the corral and drag the carcass some distance from the pens.

That made the most sense.

But, there was one problem.

It wasn't a challenge.

55

Blue Man was fatigued. He moved from his chambered seat within the crystal to the door of the chapel, opened it, and looked up and down the hallway, hoping to see Mr. Hall's niece.

He could neither see her nor feel her thoughts, but his nearby sensitivities were often dulled after a session of long-range projections, so he assumed she was somewhere in the manor.

In an adjoining foyer were a chair, table, and a small refrigerator. Blue Man got a bottle of energized water from the fridge, chugged it down, then grabbed a second bottle, poured a portion into a cupped hand, and splashed it onto his face. Blue Man didn't know what time it was, but he sensed he'd been *in the ethers* for hours.

In the ethers was Mr. Hall's term.

Blue Man stretched luxuriously like a large cat, his spine and limbs moving like molten plastic. Today's duty had robbed him of his kung fu and Kundalini yoga workouts, and his *chakras* felt depleted.

There would be no levitating for fun today, he thought.

Where was Mr. Hall's niece? He tried again to access her consciousness, but his energy wandered into a void tinted with mere hints of her presence.

He had to get back to work. Being absent from the crystal too long could break his distant connections, and he hadn't the strength to reframe the links.

He walked back to the chapel, breathed deeply, and opened the door. It was time to finish his assignment.

Mary Margaret had commitments from eight of the eleven ministries she'd called to activate prayer intercessors on behalf of an unnamed dream interpreter.

"Jesus, Jesus, Jesus," she said softly to herself, stepping from the bathroom to check on her sister after dialing the twelfth organization.

Isabel had finished her meal and was sitting in the chair as if asleep.

"Jesus, sweet Jesus, oh, Lord Jesus," Mary Margaret continued praying as she waited for her call to be answered.

She did not notice her sister's eyes slowly opening.

"Jesus, Jesus, we implore you, Lord," Mary Margaret said, glancing out the hotel window at a brightly lit world where people went about a typical day.

"Jesus." She turned and glanced down at her sister.

Isabel's eyes widened with a black fire of hatred.

Mary Margaret recoiled from the sight.

"Don't say that name," came a low, guttural demand from Isabel.

"Jesus," Mary Margaret said absently.

Isabel sprang from the chair, gripped her sister around the throat, and pushed Mary Margaret back against a wall. Mary Margaret gasped for air as Isabel's fingers tightened.

"Don't say that name," Isabel repeated, the voice deepening to a growl.

"I rebuke...I rebu..." Mary Margaret tried to speak but couldn't, and her face slowly turned blue.

"Don't...say...that...name." With unnatural strength, Isabel collapsed her sister toward the floor.

With one last flailing grasp, Mary Margaret's hand found the empty sterling silver coffee decanter. She gripped the handle, then windmilled the pitcher up, striking Isabel heavily on the temple.

Both sisters fell to the floor.

Mary Margaret breathed heavily and involuntarily, her sister lying across her chest. As she revived, the older sister reached to feel a pulse on Isabel's neck and was relieved that Isabel was only unconscious. Mary Margaret waited a few moments to collect herself, then pushed Isabel off and climbed to her feet.

Her pilot had a room down the hall. Mary Margaret found her phone and dialed his number.

"We need to leave immediately," she said. "I need help getting Isabel to the car. Alert Hyde Field to have the jet ready. And find a nurse to accompany us."

Mary Margaret sat down. The first aid kit in the jet was well stocked. She could keep Isabel out until they arrived at her estate in Vermont.

And then what?

If Isabel was willing, she would need weeks of therapy.

If she were unwilling, what could Mary Margaret do?

One day at a time, Mary Margaret told herself. One day at a time.

56

Patience had never been Ezra's long suit, but he did know enough about mad cattle to understand giving them time to cool down.

And time for the cowboy to cool down, too.

One corral post was particularly tall and broad. Ezra climbed to the top of it, sat down, and rested his feet on the corral's top rail. He was close enough to the cow to watch her but not so close as to make her more nervous.

"I should've brought alfalfa pellets," he said to Wildebeest. "How did I forget to bring pellets? You probably would have followed me right into the trailer if I had a bucket full of pellets."

"How did I forget them? Well, I suppose it could have something to do with being distracted. Life hasn't been normal lately."

The cow cocked her head and looked at him curiously.

"When I was sworn to silence, I don't think that meant I couldn't tell a cow."

The cow cocked her head to the other side.

"So, I'll tell you I went to the White House two weeks ago. I was flown there on a private jet to interpret a dream for the President."

Wildebeest shook her head.

"So, you don't believe me. You're a cynic like Barney Wallace. What I should do is put you in Barney's corral. You two could entertain each other all winter. Some great cartoons could come out of that."

For the first time, the cow looked down the curving alley that led to the trailer.

"You'd rather be loaded than listen to my stories, wouldn't you?" Ezra asked.

Where the corral angle curved, there was a gate. If Wildebeest would venture that far, Ezra hoped to jump down and close that gate behind her, trapping the cow closer to the trailer.

"On the trail drives from Texas, the night herders sang to the cows to keep them quiet. I would sing to you but my singing may not have a calming effect."

The cow took one tentative step forward.

"You know, Wildebeest, they say people are what we eat. I've probably eaten a dozen of your steer calves, so I guess you and I are related."

Wildebeest took one more cautious step.

"That would mean Anne was related to you, too, and she hasn't shown any of your orneriness. But, you can be a very sweet ole girl when you want to be. And that's how we'll remember you."

Ezra suddenly had an idea.

One more hesitant step.

"I have a plan," Ezra said, lowering his voice. "When I get you home, I'll have to put you down, but it'll be quick and painless, and I'll bury you on the creek next to my three best horses, Gusto, Shogun, and Shiloh."

Another wary step forward, her head up and eyes darting.

"That's quite the honor," Ezra continued. "Those were great, great horses and if we can be a little more prompt about this, we can get it done before Anne gets home."

The cow made the turn.

Ezra eased lower onto the corral planks, then jumped, his knees almost failing when he hit, but he reached the gate and closed it before Wildebeest could escape.

She turned and glared at him.

Now to get her in the front compartment, Ezra thought. *I need Simon loaded in the back.* He went for his horse.

Ezra unhobbled Simon and led him into the small square pen that had held the cow, and then he climbed back up on his post.

"Step in the trailer," Ezra said told the cow. "And I will take you home and feed you all the alfalfa pellets you can eat for your last meal."

The cow turned from watching him and stepped closer to the corral wings that opened to the trailer.

Ezra knew that when Wildebeest decided to step into the trailer, he'd have to jump to the ground, run down the alleyway, and close the trailer gate. That would be the most dangerous move.

No wonder Anne doesn't like me working alone, he thought.

The cow took two steps and looked at the trailer. Ezra saw a ripple of tension go through her body.

"Don't be concerned," he whispered. "You've been in that trailer a dozen times."

Ezra glanced at Simon. The bay was standing "hipshot," one hind leg bent and relaxed, and his head down, asleep.

Wildebeest made her decision. She walked confidently down the wing and stepped up and into the trailer.

Ezra was instantly off the post, and forgetting his age and injuries, he opened the gate and raced down the alleyway and into the wing. Ahead of him, the cow was in the trailer's back compartment, and he only had to slam the end-gate to have her trapped.

As he reached for the trailer's back door, he saw something shimmering in front of the cow.

Something blue and shiny.

Wildebeest wailed like a tortured woman.

The blue and glistening particles took the shape of a person.

The cow spun and lunged for the gate Ezra was closing. Her leap put one horn under each of Ezra's arms, lifting him up and backward.

Ezra caught a flash of spotted cowhide, a dark trailer entrance, and a blue translucence floating toward him.

57

Instinctively, Ezra tried to roll away from the cow but was prevented by the horns catching in his coat, so he grabbed the horns and hugged Wildebeest's head. She crushed him into the corral planks. Ezra's beaver-felt hat cushioned the blow, but he was stunned just the same. The cow whirled to her right, naturally seeking escape by leaving the way she'd come, but dragged Ezra with her. His hat fell into the dirt.

Wildebeest pulled the cowboy around the corral's curve, her hooves striking him repeatedly as she struggled with the burden of the man's weight.

Simon snorted and jumped sideways at the commotion. Ezra desperately tried to roll away or gain his feet, but the cow's strength and momentum carried him toward the gate that blocked Wildebeest from the larger pen.

She hit the gate hard, throwing Ezra forward, and she turned her wrath on the cowboy with increased rage.

Ezra knew the danger of being caught in a corner by a crazed cow. Men, dogs, children, and baby calves had been crushed or gored in a mad cow's fury.

The weight and force of Wildebeest's head, one horn to each side of Ezra's body, smothered him and contorted his body. A sharp jabbing pain in his left shoulder was a collarbone breaking. He twisted, trying to reach the pocketknife clipped in his right front pocket, but his right arm was pinned against the gate, and the cow stood on the other.

The cow's wailing engulfed Ezra, drowning him in the noise of primal panic. Her snot and slobber coated his face, her breath blasted him like an air hose, and Ezra's nose, stuffed with dirt, was swelling with blood.

The cow backed off a few inches, the horns clearing Ezra's coat. Ezra moved to roll under the gate. The motion set Wildebeest off again, and she lunged forward. Ezra felt a horn pierce his side. The copper scent of blood fueled the cow's fury. She dropped to her knees, ground her head against her enemy, and shook it back and forth, widening the wound in Ezra's right side.

And this is how I die, Ezra thought. *Crushed and gored by a family pet and nobody within miles to help.*

My body will be a mangled mess when Anne or Barney find it.

Streams of memories flowed through his mind. He saw himself as a boy, a teenager, a young husband, as a father; he saw horses, cattle, friends, churches, and books, but mostly he saw Anne.

Anne's face at its kindest. He heard her music at its finest. He felt her tenacity as she labored beside him in drought and blizzard, her encouragement and pride when he was writing, her principles and faith...

Ezra caught a glimpse of the sky. So blue, so pretty, so pure.

He saw the blue of Anne's eyes.

Then, for an instant, he envisioned something blue and vibrating riding the cow's back like a swarm of cerulean gnats.

Wildebeest's forehead struck Ezra's chin.

The blue sky, the blue of Anne's eyes, the cloud of azure insects were gone.

Everything went black.

Blue Man saw blue colors. The blue of the sky, the blue of a person's eyes, and then everything went black.

I did it, he said to himself. *The cowboy is unconscious, and I have accessed his memories.*

Brown and gray colors washed past, then dim greens and subtle reds. Blue Man knew he was viewing landscape and sunsets.

Very pretty, Blue Man thought.

More colors trickled in, little streams merging to larger creeks, creeks flowing into rivers.

Hurry up, he willed.

Finally, bright lights in a dark sky. A small jet plane landing. A large white house lit by outdoor lighting.

A dim figure in a black cowboy hat talking to a man half-hidden in shadows.

I am there, he thought.

I will have the President's dream and Ezra Riley's interpretation.

58

The cow hit the unconscious cowboy repeatedly, rolling Ezra halfway under the gate, which protected him from her horns. Still, Wildebeest's forehead and face pummeled Ezra even though the man appeared lifeless.

Then Simon attacked. His ears pinned flat to his neck, he charged, his jaws open wide. The horse gripped the old cow by the neck and lifted her up and back, but the cow shook loose, lowered her head, and hit Ezra again. Simon lunged back, bit the cow near her spine, and pulled, but hide, hair, and muscle came loose in his mouth. The cow spun, hooking with her horns. One horn traced a red slash across the big bay's chest.

Simon backed, bracing for a charge, but the cow turned back to Ezra, lowering her head for a better angle.

Simon pivoted and kicked with both hind feet, his massive hooves striking Wildebeest in the ribs, knocking her sideways into the gate. The bay took another step back and kicked again. The cow bellowed painfully and turned toward her aggressor, but the pounding hooves stopped her. Wildebeest faltered but didn't crumble. Simon struck, again and again, each blow delivered with murderous deliberation.

Then the cow's ribcage cracked, and splintered ribs thrust bony shards into her heart and lungs. Wildebeest emitted a last dying wail and collapsed dead on Ezra's legs.

It was twilight when Ezra regained consciousness. Dirt and blood packed his mouth, nose, ears, and eyes and an enormous weight lay on his legs. He struggled to move, but crippling pain shot through his entire body. Rubbing his face against a coat sleeve, he shook enough dirt free to see and breathe.

Yards away, Simon stood watching, a jagged wound scissoring his chest.

Ezra craned his head and saw the dead cow's head and neck lying on his legs. Reaching with his right arm, he grabbed a gate board and struggled to pull his legs free, but stinging pain in his ankles stopped him. Sweat beaded his brow.

You have to do this.

He pulled again, forcing himself through the pain, and one damaged ankle popped free.

One more time.

He screamed as the second ankle bobbled from beneath the cow and lay limp on the ground.

A cold breeze picked up from the north.

Time to take inventory.

Ezra assessed his injuries the best he could. Both ankles felt broken—he wouldn't be standing or walking. He had broken ribs and a snapped collarbone. Feeling an oozing from his side, he reached a hand beneath his coat and felt the wound. The hand returned bloodied.

Darkness was descending, and the weather was turning cold.

I live or die in the coming minutes, he thought.

Could he roll beneath the gate and crawl to the truck? The gate had sagged on its hinges, and while the cow's force had almost pushed Ezra under, he saw he'd have to remove his coat and vest, and maybe his shirt, to squeeze below it.

And he still might not.

Pinned shirtless at night in a storm did not sound appealing.

He had to open the gate.

Secured by a horizontal piston rod, the gate was tightly closed. Ezra had to reach the vertical handle to unlatch it. He looked up at the rod. It seemed as distant as the moon. With his best arm, he pulled himself up, careful not to put any weight on his feet. Pain screamed at him to quit, but he wrested himself higher, hooked an elbow over a board for support, and slowly raised the other arm, but shooting pain in his shoulder and ribs dropped him.

He lay face down in the dirt.

One more time. Ezra reached for a board, hoisted himself up, then grasped for the next plank, his fingers barely catching it. The latch assembly was iron, and though it was heavy, it was well greased. Gritting his teeth, Ezra raised the other arm quickly, hoping to push past the pain, but the reflex was immediate. He let loose and fell.

One more time. Rising to the third plank, Ezra braced with his elbow and reached with the same hand, his sore arm dangling at his side. His fingers barely gripped the handle. He tried to pull but teetered, almost losing the support of his elbow.

Then he thought of Simon. It was crazy but worth trying. Simon was notorious for opening any gate when he set his mind to it. By now, the horse would be thirsty, hungry, and ready for home.

"Here boy," Ezra said, mimicking the tone that called the saddle horses for oats.

The call was shallow and weak. Ezra's ribs barely allowed a whisper.

"Here boy," he called again, a begging inflection in his voice.

"Here boy."

Simon stepped forward, pushed the handle with his muzzle; the gate swung open, swinging Ezra onto the ground. Rising painfully on his right elbow, Ezra inched toward the outside man-gate near the squeeze chute.

Simon stepped into the big pen and nosed about for grass.

By the squeeze-chute was a table with veterinary supplies.

Crawling to the table, Ezra found an old branding iron propped against the fence. Using it, he hooked a plastic storage box and pulled it to the ground. The lid sprung open, and vet supplies tumbled out. A small LED flashlight rolled to his hand. Ezra turned it on and scanned the ground. Syringes, needles, a bottle of bovine antibiotic, blood-coagulating powder, a can of pine tar, iodine, and antiseptic spray lay within his reach.

His concern was the open wound. There was nothing he could do for his ankles, collarbone, or ribs.

The antibiotic was a long-acting medication Ezra primarily used for foot rot in cattle. Was it safe for human use?

Probably. Ezra fitted a needle onto a plastic syringe, drained 4cc from the bottle, pulled down his pants, and jabbed the needle into his thigh. The jab hurt, but pushing the plunger down and injecting the medicine was worse.

Then, grabbing the iodine bottle and the antiseptic spray, he rolled over onto his back and pulled his coat and shirt up.

"Lord, have mercy," he whispered and poured the iodine into the wound.

Hot coals seemed dropped into his belly, and agony in black and red waves washed over him. Ezra breathed deeply and rode the pain.

Like body-surfing in the Pacific, he thought.

That was a topless beach, he remembered.

What a strange thought at a time like this.

As the burning waned, he took the spray bottle and coated the wound generously.

Finally, he pried a can of pine tar open and dabbed a gob over the hole in his side.

"A little dab will do me," he joked. He started to laugh, but the ribs protested. "I love shock," Ezra said softly. "The body going into shock is a wonderful thing."

Simon stepped over and stood above him.

Ezra looked up at the horse.

"One more gate," Ezra whispered. "This one's mine."

This gate was smaller, designed for people, not cattle, and the piston latch was simpler to reach and handle. Ezra pushed the gate open and crawled through it. In the dimming light, he could barely see his pickup and trailer.

Could he drive?

If I can pull myself into the cab, I can drive, he decided.

And if nothing else, the truck offered protection from the weather.

"Here we go," he whispered, reaching with his forearm and elbow and pulling himself forward inches at a time.

Now, if nothing else goes wrong...

59

Minutes after deplaning in Billings, Anne Riley phoned home. The answering machine picked up. It was already an hour after dark; where was Ezra? Anne's night blindness made her a habitually cautious driver, but she sped out of the airport's parking lot and down a frontage road, then took the first entrance to the interstate.

Many thoughts rushed through her mind, and she fought to control them. In their phone conversations and emails, Ezra had seemed particularly cryptic. He was hiding something.

Anne knew it wasn't another woman, so it was likely cattle or horses.

Or the hills. With Ezra, the hills *were* the other woman.

She was two hours from home.

Isabel Hall was sleeping soundly, sedated by a flight nurse, in a guest bedroom in her sister's Vermont home. Mary Margaret covered her with a blanket, closed the door quietly, and stepped into the hall.

The older sister needed a hot bath and a change of clothing, but there wasn't time. Isabel was safe for the moment, but after repeated calls to Montana, Mary Margaret still couldn't reach Ezra Riley, and no one returned her messages.

She didn't have Anne Riley's number and knew none of Ezra's friends, so she called the sheriff's department in his county.

"Dispatch," a woman answered.

"Hi, my name is Mary Margaret Hall and I have reason to be concerned about someone in your county."

"Where are you calling from, ma'am?"

"Vermont."

"And the reason for your concern?"

Mary Margaret paused. She hated to lie, but she could hardly tell a stranger in Montana that a cowboy from her county was under attack by a blue man in Virginia.

"He was supposed to call me hours ago, but I haven't heard from him and no one picks up at his home."

"Who are you trying to reach, ma'am?"

"His name is Ezra Riley."

The dispatcher rolled her eyes. She knew Ezra often ignored phones. "Perhaps Mr. Riley is just outside," she said.

"It's after dark there, isn't it?"

"Yes, but he could be in his barn or his shop."

"Could you please have someone check on him?"

"Yes, ma'am. I will see if a deputy can swing by."

The call ended as Sheriff Andy Royce walked past on his way home.

"That was an odd call, Andy," the dispatcher said.

Royce stopped. "Who was it?" he asked.

"A woman in Vermont. She gave her name as Mary Margaret Hall. She can't reach Ezra Riley and is afraid he's in danger."

Royce thought of the man called Pennington and the gun in his pocket. "Did she say what her business was with Ezra?"

"No. Actually, she was a little elusive."

"Where's Harmon?" he asked, referring to the deputy who was on duty.

"He's south of town responding to a dogs-running-at-large call."

"Okay. I'll swing into Ezra's place on my way home and check it out," the sheriff said.

Mary Margaret wasn't hopeful about getting help from the authorities in Miles City, and why should they help? It wasn't like she could tell them the truth.

Then she remembered Isabel's computer friend, the man with the strange name. She had Isabel's phone in her purse, pulled it out, pulled up the last number called, and hit Redial.

"Hello, Gray Lady," a voice answered.

Gray Lady? Then she remembered her sister using that term. "Excuse me," Mary Margaret said. "Are you Isabel Hall's friend?"

The man hesitated. "I don't know anyone by that name," he said.

"I'm her sister," Mary Margaret added. "You call her Gray Lady but to me she is Isabel Hall. Now are you Isabel's friend?"

"Yes," said Gyro. "I am Isabel's friend."

"Are you still watching the truck as Isabel requested?"

"Yes, I am."

"Is anything happening? Can you see anything?"

"It's dark outside and it's dark inside the cab. I've seen no sign of activity for hours."

"What was the last activity you observed?"

"The truck was put in reverse and backed to a set of corrals. Meadowlark got out and entered the corrals."

Meadowlark? Yes, a code name for Ezra Riley, she remembered. "We are concerned for Meadowlark," she said.

"Excuse me," Gyro said. "But where is Isabel?"

"She is sound asleep."

"No offense, but I probably should not be talking to anyone except Isabel."

"Yes, I understand, but Isabel cannot be disturbed."

"Is it possible for me to get verification of your identity from Mr. Hall?"

"My uncle is dead."

Gyro was stymied. Hall's death had been a false-flag operation eleven years ago. Was that this woman's reference?

"My uncle died a few nights ago," Mary Margaret added. "And Isabel is not at his estate in Virginia. She is in Vermont with me."

Dead silence.

"Are you well-paid, Mr. Gyro?" Mary Margaret asked.

More silence.

"I assume you are," she continued. "And I am sure you would like a generous severance check, which I will make certain Isabel sends you, if you help me now."

She heard him clear his throat.

"What do you need?" he asked.

"This person you call Meadowlark is a friend of mine. We are concerned for his safety."

"When you say *we*, are you referring to yourself and Isabel?"

"Yes, I am."

"Again, what can I do to help you, Ms. Hall?"

"I'm not sure," Mary Margaret said. "I called the Sheriff's Office, but they don't act concerned. Is the GPS working yet?"

"No, the GPS and the signal beacon are still down. I do not know Meadowlark's precise coordinates, but I know he's at a set of corrals. A map of the area shows pens at the back of Meadowlark's ranch. He must be there."

"Perhaps he's disorientated and lost," Mary Margaret said.

"A cowboy lost on his own ranch?"

"In this case, anything is possible."

"In that case, I can turn the truck lights on," Gyro said. "Truck lights and trailer lights. I can even move the truck if that's helpful."

"Do it," Mary Margaret said.

Ezra moved by centimeters and held Simon's bridle reins in his right hand. He needed the horse for emotional support if nothing else.

His approach faced the passenger door of the truck. Climbing from the passenger seat into the driver's seat meant going over the seat's middle console. Not an option. It added distance, but he had to crawl around the truck to the driver's door by the front.

Not to worry, he told himself. He didn't have anything better to do, and the exertion helped take his mind off his pain.

Only minutes to go, he thought, *and I will at least be in the truck and out of this cold wind.*

Just as he reached the front tire, the truck growled alive, and the night exploded with lights. Dazed by the sudden brightness, Ezra paused, his head against the right front tire.

Then the truck began to move.

60

Sheriff Royce pulled into Ezra's yard. The house was dark. So was the bunkhouse, barn, and shop. Using the spotlight on his pickup's roof, he counted vehicles.

The truck Ezra generally used, a 2005 Ford, was there. Old Yeller was who knows where? The new truck and Ezra's stock trailer were gone. Royce took out his cell phone and punched in Barney Wallace's home number. No answer. He tried Barney's cell phone. A recording said this number's mailbox was full.

That explains it, Royce thought. Barney was always saying Ezra lived like a hermit. Ezra never did anything, and he never went anywhere. The new truck and Ezra's trailer being gone likely meant Barney had talked Ezra into a short road trip. The sheriff guessed if he'd checked Barney's house, he'd find no one there, either. Mrs. Wallace volunteered nights at the hospital, and Barney was certainly with Ezra.

If Barney was with Ezra, the cartoonist wouldn't answer a cell phone.

Ezra's life in danger? If Ezra was with Barney, the only threat to his life would be dying from hilarity.

Good detective work, Royce told himself, and he decided to go home.

Anne was an hour from home, and her repeated calls to her husband still went unanswered. She'd left two messages telling him to call her the moment he came into the house.

Even her attempts to reach Barney had failed.

Could Ezra and Barney have gone somewhere together?

Anne doubted it. Ezra knew she might arrive that night, and he wouldn't let her return to a cold, dark house.

Barney was at a weekly bull riding at the college arena, where he'd tried calling Ezra twice but got no answer, which worried him because of the dream he'd had the night before.

I should run out and check on him, he told himself.

As he got up to leave, Barney bumped into an old rodeo buddy he hadn't seen in thirty years. The two had even traveled together one summer.

Barney and his friend sat down and started rehashing rodeo days: Barney's ride on Brookman's Tequila Sunrise at Wolf Point; his buddy's ride on Cervi's Al Capone at Denver; the Tooke-bred Desolation bucking them both off in separate performances at Sidney, Iowa. An hour of fun and laughter slipped by until Barney and his buddy were saddle sore from the re-rides.

When the bull-riding ended, his friend suggested a brew or two at the Bison Bar. But since Barney didn't drink, the cartoonist offered ice teas at McDonald's.

"So, it's come to that," the buddy said, slapping Barney on the back. "Two old cowboys drinking tea at McDonald's."

Barney laughed, and they left for the Golden Arches.

Blue Man's head throbbed, his stomach was cramping, and his mouth tasted like dirty wool. Weakened from hours of concentration and projection, he crawled from the crystal and stepped into the hallway.

Where was Isabel Hall?

Blue Man had lost contact in Montana. He wanted to remain there and deal the death blow, but his body and mind demanded a respite. Blue Man reeled down the hallway, bracing himself against a wall more than once, but determined to find Isabel. If he couldn't locate Hall's niece, he'd discover sustenance on his own. He staggered past the sanctuary's kitchen because Blue Man's conditioning kept him from considering it.

Isabel! he screamed in his mind.

She was gone. He knew it. In the manor's kitchen, he found a loaf of bread and a pitcher of orange juice. He took both and started back to the chapel. Passing Mr. Hall's walk-in vault, Blue Man noticed the door was cracked open. That door's lock combination was not one he'd pilfered from Mr. Hall's mind, and he stopped and pushed the door open to see if Isabel was hiding there.

She wasn't, but the room looked interesting.

I will come back and investigate this, he told himself.

The truck tire nudged Ezra's head, and the trailer tires grazed his injured side. Simon raised his head and snorted.

The truck and trailer—lit with lights—rattled on, leaving Ezra staring in disbelief. The new Ford and Ezra's gooseneck bounced over brush and rocks, clattering northeast until they disappeared after cresting a knoll.

Moments later, Ezra heard a crashing thud followed by a whirring sound. The truck had hit a hole, was high-centered in the front, and the hind wheels were spinning worthlessly.

Any chance of using the truck for either transportation or shelter was gone.

"Something's wrong," Gyro said over the phone.

"What?" Mary Margaret asked.

"I turned the lights on and moved the truck a few feet, but it wouldn't stop. It kept going."

"Kept going? Where?"

"I don't know. There are clouds of dust obscuring the cameras. The truck's computer is indicating the vehicle is stuck but trying to move, and warning of a system failure if corrections aren't made. I'm shutting it down before it overheats and blows the engine. If your friend is lost, he may have seen the lights. Maybe the truck is still usable."

"Can you leave the lights on for him?"

"That would run the battery down."

"Okay. Did you see anything when you started the truck?"

"I thought so," Gyro said. "Just for an instant from the camera in the front right headlight. It looked like a form at the side, just under the camera's view."

"Was it a person? Was it Ezra Riley?"

"I don't know. Maybe."

"Okay. I'm hanging up but stay within reach. I'm going to call the sheriff again."

Moments later, the call went through.

"Dispatch, how may I help you?"

"This is Ms. Hall again. I may know where Ezra Riley is."

The dispatcher sighed. "Ms. Hall, the sheriff says Ezra Riley is with Barney Wallace. His guess is they are at the bull riding at the college arena. I got ahold of someone out there minutes ago and they said Barney just left with someone about Mr. Riley's age and size."

"It's not him. I'm sure it's not him."

"Ms. Hall..."

"Is your deputy back yet?"

"He's forty minutes out."

"Does he know the Riley ranch?"

"Yes, I think so."

"I'm sure Ezra is at the corrals at the back of the ranch. And he's hurt."

"Ms. Hall, how do you know this?"

Mary Margaret paused, then decided to tell the truth. "Because there are cameras in Ezra's truck," she said. "My sister's computer expert remotely started the truck, but he couldn't stop it. It drove off and crashed."

Whew, the dispatcher thought to herself. *It's only Monday!* She glanced at the calendar to see if a full moon lighted the night.

"One camera may have picked up something," Mary Margaret pleaded. "It could have been a person on the ground."

"Ms. Hall," she said. "As soon as the deputy returns, I will give him this report."

The call ended.

Mary Margaret quickly punched new numbers. She waited while Ezra's answering machine went through its spiel.

"Mrs. Riley," she said. "This is Mary Margaret Hall. Hurry to the corrals at the back of the ranch. Hurry. Ezra is injured."

61

Ezra lay in the dark, trying to make a decision. He'd just watched his best bet for shelter drive away and crash in a coulee.

He could try crawling to the pickup, but he wasn't sure what he'd find when he got there. *If* he got there. There was no chance he could drive a truck and trailer out of a ravine, but the truck's lights should still work, and if the engine started, he'd have heat. But would anyone find him there? No one was likely to look for him until Anne got home.

When would that be?

He could crawl back to the corral for shelter, but the corral offered little more than a windbreak.

If he could find matches he might be able to start a fire. A big enough blaze would surely attract attention, but Ezra wasn't ready to start a prairie fire.

Everything seemed to involve crawling and trying.

He didn't know the extent of the wound in his side. It was seeping blood, but Ezra didn't feel sick from infection or blood loss. The broken collarbone and ribs hurt, but he didn't consider those injuries severe.

His primary disability was the ankles. He couldn't walk or stand.

He'd kept the little LED flashlight and put the beam on Simon's wound. Ezra was relieved to see the rip was ragged but superficial. Simon would have a scar, but that would add to his appeal.

Crawl to the truck?

Crawl to the corrals?

Try to start a fire and hope it didn't spread and burn out the neighbors?

Okay, he thought, *where do I really need to be?*

He needed to make it to the county road. That distance was two miles by pasture road or one mile cross-country.

Cross-country was out of the question. Too many hills and gullies.

Monday night traffic on the county road was unlikely, but it could happen, and if he were lying on the road holding a large horse, he'd be seen, wouldn't he? Maybe not. A loaded semi-truck might run over him. *There's a cartoon for Barn Wall,* he thought.

If he were a better horse trainer, he would have taught Simon to lie down, and he'd try crawling on him.

Simon might still be the answer. In blading the pasture road, two- and three-foot banks were left at its sides in several places. If he could lead Simon to a bank, maybe he could crawl on him.

My night is filled with crawl, try, and maybes, he thought.

It was time for some *can* and *will.*

Could he crawl on his hands and knees? He hadn't tried that. Ezra put Simon's bridle reins in his mouth, and by using one fist on the ground, he slowly and painfully raised himself to his knees. Everything hurt, but he was tired of admitting that.

I'm not as injured as I think I am, he told himself. His ribs were cracked, not caved in. The collarbone was broken, but it wasn't piercing the skin. One ankle was broken, but maybe not the other—it might only be badly sprained. The wound in the side? That was his one concern.

He shuffled on his knees. *This is going to be slow,* he thought, *and it's really hurting the knees.*

Simon stepped up beside him. Impulsively, Ezra stuck his good arm through the stirrup, held it tight to his chest, and clucked several times, cueing Simon to move. Simon stood still.

"C'mon, boy." Ezra clucked and clicked, but having been trained to stand while Ezra mounted, the bay was as immobile as a rock.

Ezra let himself back down. He needed a stick to hold in his mouth and poke Simon in the belly. He felt along the ground and found one.

"Unbelievable," he said. "Praise God." He put the stick in his mouth.

Rising, Ezra, holding the reins in his hand, placed his arm through the stirrup again, hugged it to his chest, turned his head, and poked the horse.

Simon flinched, turned, and looked back at him.

Ezra poked him again.

Simon shook his head.

Again.

This time Simon took a step.

Ezra straightened his legs behind him and crooked the worst ankle over the better one. Then he poked the horse again.

Simon set off at a walk. Ezra steered him with the reins held in the fist that was tight against his chest.

Ezra kept poking. His mouth prickled with slivers. Pain in his shoulder, ribs, and ankles hit him like lightning strikes.

Stay conscious, he told himself. *Stay conscious.*

It seemed to take an hour, but Ezra finally felt a bank to his left. He spat the stick out and cued Simon to a stop. The bank was on his injured side. Upright on his knees, Ezra used his right arm to elbow himself up, and pushing off with the least-injured leg, he wallowed onto the berm. A tug on the reins brought Simon up beside him. Ezra rose, put the reins in his mouth, used his strong arm as a brace, pushed off with the least painful leg, and floundered into the saddle.

Did it, he thought. Systemic shock was a wonderful thing.

How long until the shock wore off?

He didn't want to think about it.

He lay across the saddle like a dead man. Gripping the saddle blanket with his right hand, he swung the right leg around.

His mind became a black canvas streaked with white, yellow, and red flashes as pain arced through his nervous system.

Better than mescaline, he told himself.

If I lose my sense of humor, I'm dead.

He raised his torso, letting the reins slacken as they slid between his teeth. The left side of his body was rigid with pain. The arm dangled, the ribs felt collapsed, and the foot bobbled like a toy on the end of a string. He reached up and took the reins in his hand.

I'm horseback. I can do anything now.

62

Ezra had lied to himself. Now that he was horseback, he couldn't do anything he wanted. Ezra felt as if fifty drunken leprechauns were poking him with electric cattle prods with each step Simon took. Hotshots! Hotshots to his ankles, ribs, shoulder, and the wound in his side.

And, horse and rider were traveling headfirst into wind-driven sleet. Simon tried turning sideways to avoid the blasting, but Ezra kept him on the pasture road.

Hotshots of pain, buck shots of sleet, and a night blacker than two crows in a cave. *If you like challenges,* Ezra told himself, *this one will do until something more exciting comes along.*

Ezra had a wool cap and a pair of gloves in the leather cantle bag behind the saddle's seat. He desperately needed both, but unzipping the bag would be a test. His left arm was almost useless, so Ezra put the reins back in his mouth and tried to reach behind the cantle with his right hand. He quickly found the zipper but labored to zip it open. Finally, he got his hand in the bag and felt around: binoculars, ammunition, wool cap. He pulled the cap out and onto his head.

Heaven! How wonderful to have warm ears.

Next, the gloves. Reaching to the far end of the bag, he snagged them, but he dropped the gloves as they cleared the bag, and they fell softly to the ground.

Goodbye, warm hands.

His boots felt tight. Both ankles were swelling, and Ezra suspected the ER technicians would cut them off with carpet knives. Goodbye to this pair of Tony Lama high tops.

Were carpet knives used to cut boots apart?

Anne would know.

Where was Anne?

Blue Man had hit a wall. His energy was depleted, so he rose stiffly from his seat within the quartz. Then he staggered when his feet touched the floor. His ankles ached, his ribs hurt, and his left shoulder barked with pain. His left side, just above the hip bone, stung, and reaching into his shirt, he felt sticky moisture. His fingers came back red with blood.

This type of pain was new to Blue Man. He was well acquainted with pain endured with training, but this was suffering caused by injuries. Blue Man had never experienced an injury.

And this pain wasn't his. This agony had returned with him from Montana, and Blue Man didn't know how to shed it.

Walk it off. That's what Blue Man's handlers had said when he was hurt.

So he walked, down the tunnel, back to the manor, not knowing where he was going or why.

His mission concerning Riley was finished. He had the dream and Riley's interpretation. Whether or not he'd finished Riley for good remained to be seen. In any case, Blue Man's energy was spent. All he had strength for was to record the dream and interpretation as proof of his success. He'd seen a journal in Mr. Hall's walk-in vault that would work ideally for his purposes.

The ranch yard was as dark as a tomb. Anne parked her car, opened the unlocked front door, and called his name.

"Ezra! Ezra, are you home?" No answer. She grabbed a powerful spotlight out of a cupboard and washed its beam over the vehicles and corrals. The truck Ezra usually used was there, but the stock trailer and Old Yeller were gone.

Why would he be using Old Yeller and the trailer?

On a hunch, she hurried across the yard and tried the white pickup. It fired right up. Ezra wasn't using Old Yeller because this truck was broke down.

The wind was fierce and bitter, and sleet pelted her face.

She rushed back to the house, turned on lights, and checked the answering machine. There were four messages; the third was from a woman named Mary Margaret Hall in Vermont asking Ezra to call her immediately because he was in serious danger.

Vermont?

Anne punched in her number, and a woman picked up immediately.

"Hello, is this Ezra?"

"No, this is his wife, Anne Riley."

"Anne, thank God. Is Ezra home?

"No, I just got home and Ezra is nowhere around. What do you mean about him being in serious danger and who are you?"

"Anne, I can't explain everything right now. Does your ranch have corrals back in the hills?"

"Yes, why?" An urgency was growing in Anne's voice.

"Do you have a way of getting there?"

"Yes, Ezra's main pickup is here."

"Ezra is up there and I think he may be injured."

"How would you know that?"

"Please, Anne, just go. I will explain everything later."

"But, injured, how? What do you mean?"

"Anne, please go now."

Ezra felt Simon move downhill. They were halfway to the county road.

Ezra was sick with pain and was tempted to fall from the saddle, curl up in a ball, and either be found or die. If the night got cold enough, freezing to death was not the worst way to go.

Hitting the ground would be a terrible experience, he told himself.

Find reasons to live, he thought. Only two came to mind. The first was Anne. Everything else—friends, grandchildren, horses, cattle, the hills—dimmed in comparison. Still, he had likely fulfilled his purpose in life. Years of preparation had taken him to the most powerful person in the world. What more could there be?

But, his second purpose for staying alive involved his encounter with the man in the White House.

"Damned if I'll let him win," he mumbled to the cold, dark air.

63

There was one chair in Mr. Hall's vault. Blue Man picked the journal off a table and sat in the chair. The journal was thin because Mr. Hall had ripped out hundreds of pages.

Blue Man was disappointed. He was hoping his life's story was written here, and perhaps Mr. Hall's true feelings about him.

To be human, Blue Man was realizing, was to love and be loved. Love was not an emotion he understood, and he'd hoped Hall's writings would shed clues.

It didn't. Hall's last entry was brief and not to Blue Man.

Isabel, if you find this, your father (and Mary Margaret's) did not die in 1968. He is presently very ill in a nursing home in Santa Barbara. Robinson did not abandon you. He sacrificed his happiness to serve our country in secret. He loved you both and frequently asked about your well-being. I sent him photographs as I could. When this country seems about to collapse, warriors will arise to save the republic. Please know that your father, Robinson Alexander Hall, will be a vital contributor in preserving America.

Who was Mary Margaret? Blue Man wondered. *Isabel's sister? And Robinson was their father?*

But, where was Blue Man's story?

Blue Man rose from the chair angrily. What part of his life was not a lie? And why was he alive at all?

Simon's hooves hitting gravel told Ezra they'd reached the county road. He reached down and patted the bay on the neck.

But what now? Getting off the horse would be painful, and he'd certainly never get back on. The wind would be at their backs if they rode toward the highway, but riding was difficult.

Standing still would be more difficult. Neither Ezra nor Simon was wired for waiting.

If this was the end of his story. Why not be discovered frozen to the saddle?

And what an odd ending it might be. The whole day had been like a psychedelic trip. What was real? What wasn't?

Soon, he was bent over, his good arm braced against the saddle horn, and his head slowly bobbing as if he were asleep.

Driven by panic, Anne flew over the tallest hill on the county road, and suddenly there he was in the headlights, Ezra on Simon, in the middle of the road. She braked hard, and the white truck skidded sideways toward the horse and rider.

Simon jumped to the side to avoid being hit, toppling Ezra from the saddle. He landed hard in the borrow pit.

The truck stopped diagonally on the road. Anne slammed it into park, jumped from the cab, and ran to her husband. "Ezra," she said, cradling his head. "Are you all right?"

His eyes slowly opened. "Where's Simon?" he asked.

"Ezra, where are you hurt?"

"Anne? Is that you?"

"Yes, it's me," she said, the first tear streaming down her cheek. "Where are you hurt?

"My ankles," he said. "And ribs. And collarbone. And I have a hole in my side."

She felt inside his coat. The wetness was thick and sticky.

"I'll help you up," she coaxed. "We have to get you to the hospital."

"I can't leave Simon."

"Ezra, you have to. Now, come on, let me help you up."

"Are we on a hill?"

"Yes."

"You have your cell phone?"

"Yes, I do."

"Call Barney. Have him bring his trailer for Simon."

"I'm calling an ambulance," she said. "Then I'll call Barney."

Anne made the calls—Barney had just gotten home from McDonald's—then moved the truck, so it wasn't in the middle of the road.

"I'm cold," Ezra called to her. "Look behind the seat."

Anne bent the seat forward, found a heavy coat, and covered Ezra with it.

"What happened to you?" she asked him.

"Wildebeest," he said.

"Okay," she said. "Don't talk. Save your energy." Laying her hands on her husband's chest, she prayed in a tongue known to angels.

The ambulance arrived minutes later. They rolled Ezra onto a backboard, loaded him, and sped away in a circus of lights.

Barney came minutes later. "What's happened?" he asked, getting out of his pickup. "I almost hit an ambulance. Is Ezra okay?"

"I don't know," she said. "But he was more worried about his horse than he was himself."

The sleet was turning to snow as Barney loaded Simon in his trailer.

"What happened to Ezra?" Barney asked.

"All he said was 'Wildebeest.'"

"I'll follow you back to your place," Barney told Anne. "I'll take care of Simon. You go to the hospital."

Blue Man walked from the study to the windows that opened to the outside. He'd always wondered if fresh air had a distinctive taste or smell. Should he step outside and find out?

How fast would the world's bacteria kill him?

It would be slow, he thought. Very slow.

He walked to the door, and as he reached for the handle, he saw a note on an end table. It was addressed to him.

Blue Man, you are not ill. Your coloring is artificial and the outdoors will not harm you. — Isabel.

He held it in his hands and read it several times.

Was it a test? A trap?

64

The moment the back doors of the ambulance closed, Ezra Riley died.

In an instant, his soul was flying through space. Stars whizzed by because he was traveling at the speed of light.

Warp speed, he thought. All he knew to relate this experience to was television reruns of *Star Trek.*

He was not afraid, but he was not at peace, either. His soul was traveling so fast its emotions could not keep up.

Then suddenly, it was daylight, and he was in the air far above the ranch. Below him in the distance sat the Deadman corrals. It was summer, and a huge sun hung in the sky, a sun far larger than the earth's sun.

He was not alone.

Ezra was yoked to a flying creature. He could not see the harness that bound them together, nor could he see the creature, but it was there.

He knew it was an angel.

Look at the sun.

The voice appeared in his mind. The voice filled his mind. It was not demanding, yet it radiated a quiet authority.

Staring at the sun did not hurt Ezra's eyes, and as his vision focused, it was evident this sun was many times larger than the sun Ezra had known while alive.

Do you see the shadow?

Ezra directed his eyes to where the number seven would be on a clock. There on the sun's border was a tiny black square.

Those are your fears.

His fears seem inconsequential, but the angel corrected him.

Look at the ground.

Ezra looked down and saw a small square shadow floating on the surface of the land.

When you are under the square, you walk in its shadow. The voice was still peaceful, but Ezra caught the slight inflection of a rebuke.

Looking north, Ezra knew his precise location above the ranch. Landmarks were clear and distinct.

Then, sky-lined on a distant pasture road, he saw motion. He was reminded of his dream about the coyote.

The object was moving in his direction. No, in *their* direction. The angel was not only still present, it still controlled his every movement. Where the angel went, Ezra went.

The object on the skyline gained speed.

Here comes the enemy.

Ezra was surprised there would be an enemy here, but then, he didn't know where *here* was.

I will show you the enemy.

Ezra tried to object. He didn't want to see the enemy, but he had no choice. The angel descended into a steep dive, faster than a fighter jet. The creature on the skyline stopped, sat on its haunches, and watched.

It was the coyote from the dream.

Diving to within feet of the beast, the angel positioned Ezra close to see the hair on the creature's face and the deep, glaring yellow of its eyes.

Look at the mouth.

Almost hypnotized by the eyes, it took effort for Ezra to look at the creature's mouth.

The enemy's mouth was tied shut with a clear monofilament, like a fishing line.

Never fear its bite. It has none.

Then the angel banked upward, rising with incredible speed.

Instantly, they were flying through space again, the stars streaking past with shimmering tails behind them.

Suddenly, he was above the earth again, but it was nighttime. It wasn't summer, and there was no giant sun.

Ezra began falling as if the angel had dropped him. There was no longer a binding yoke and linking telepathy.

He passed through a fluid level of warm, swirling colors and felt a radiant heat touch his side. Then he dropped into descending darkness.

Below him were the flashing lights of the speeding ambulance.

He awakened on a table with people alongside him, cutting his clothes off. He heard his boots fall and hit a linoleum floor.

Goodbye, Tony Lamas.

He was being washed with warm, soapy water that smelled of disinfectant.

Towels patted him dry.

He heard a nurse say, "Doctor, you need to look at this."

Anne rushed into the Emergency Room. She asked the first nurse she saw where her husband was.

"We just finished cleaning him up," the nurse said. "He's getting X-rays."

"Has a surgeon seen him yet?"

"No, I don't think surgery will be needed."

"But his stomach! He was gored in the side."

"You'll need to talk to the doctor about that," the nurse said, leaving Anne.

Anne sat in a chair to catch her breath. Digging into her pocket, she found the slip of paper with the woman's phone number in Vermont and dialed it.

"Anne," Mary Margaret said. "Is Ezra okay?"

"We're at the hospital and they're taking X-rays. I should know something soon."

"Thank God. I've been so worried about him."

"Who are you?" Anne asked. "Why have you been worried about my husband?"

Mary Margaret gasped. "Oh, of course, you don't know anything, do you. Don't worry. It's not what you might think. It's crazier. It's about Ezra, the President, my sister, our uncle—who is a dead spy—and a blue man."

Ezra, the President, and a blue man?

Anne was too stunned to respond. The woman had to be mentally ill.

"I know it sounds crazy," Mary Margaret said. "And Ezra is the one to tell you about it. I'm just so relieved that he's okay. Thanks for calling. I'll call you tomorrow."

Anne put her phone away and stared at the floor.

What in the world?

An hour later, a doctor came to see her.

"How is he?" Anne said, jumping to her feet.

"He's fine, but we are going to keep him overnight."

"But what about the surgery, the hole in his side?"

The doctor sat down, a cue for Anne to do the same.

"Your husband has a broken ankle, a badly sprained ankle, a broken collarbone, and a couple of broken ribs."

"The hole where he was gored?"

The doctor shook his head. "I can't explain that. The nurses washed off a layer of pine tar and the stains of iodine and an antiseptic spray, but there was no hole, just a long scratch that looked recently healed."

"But I felt under his shirt? My hand had blood on it.

"There are things I can't explain. Ezra was concussed. How long he was out, we don't know. He vaguely remembers his horse saving him by kicking a cow to death. The cow died on top of him. Maybe you saw the cow's blood."

"But the pine tar and the iodine?"

"Ezra remembers being gored. He says he crawled from one corral to a vet bench. He not only treated himself with vet supplies, he gave himself a shot of LA200?"

"LA200? The cattle antibiotic?"

"He thrust the needle into his thigh." The doctor shook his head. "Who knows what else he did to himself out in those hills?"

"So he's going to be okay?"

"He can go home in a day or two. He's bruised from head to toe. Your husband is the color of an eggplant." The doctor left.

The ER door burst open, and Barney rushed in. He saw the shock on Anne's face.

"Oh Lord," Barney said. "Ezra's going to die."

"Not unless the LA200 kills him," Anne said.

"LA200?"

"Ezra's going to be okay, Barney. He has some breaks and bruises, but he's coming home tomorrow.

"Oh," Barney said. "Well, I'll do the chores until he gets better. I'll get the cows home from Deadman."

"Thanks, Barney. We appreciate it."

Barney sat down and slumped back in the chair.

"What a night," he said. "What a night. Ezra's all beat up and then this deal with the President."

Anne looked at him and frowned.

"What deal with the President?"

"Oh, you don't know, do you?" Barney said. "I just heard it on the radio while driving here. The President had a massive heart attack. He died."

65

Blue Man read the note one more time. He wasn't ill, he wasn't blue, and the outdoors wouldn't hurt him.

He put the note back on the table. He was exhausted, but his body didn't hurt anymore. There was no wounding in his side or any sign of soreness.

He knew he should sleep, and this was his home, the only home he'd known, but if he slept, what would he awaken to? He'd not treated Mr. Hall's niece well, and if she returned, she would bring assistance. Her help would be men like his former handlers, dangerous men. Shooters.

What would they do to him? He was aware of prisons and sanitariums but doubted one could hold him. He thought of Mr. Hall's grave in the garden and suspected he'd soon be lying beside him.

He went back to his sleeping quarters and got two duffle bags from his closet. He filled one with clothing. He walked into the sanctuary kitchen for the first time and looked around. It was odd he'd been banned from this room all his life because he saw nothing that appeared threatening. He put two apples, two bananas, and a jar of grapefruit juice in the bag with his clothes.

Blue Man thought for a moment of the many handlers he'd had through the years. There had always been four, but the people changed through the years. As a small child, two of the handlers had been women, but he could barely remember their faces and didn't know their names.

He went down the tunnel and back to Mr. Hall's vault.

He left the journal on the table. He hadn't taken time to write down the President's dream or Ezra Riley's interpretation, and what did it matter? Who cared about that now? He thought of Riley and knew the old cowboy was alive because Blue Man could feel his energy. It was faint and interrupted by pain, but Riley lived.

Was that failure?

It didn't matter.

He looked around the vault for anything that'd be of value to him, though he scarcely knew how one survived outside the manor's door. He opened a large cabinet and saw shelves stacked with bound currency. Stacks of $100 bills. Blue Man had never used money, but he knew it was necessary, so he filled the other duffle bag with cash.

Also in the cabinet was a loaded .45 pistol.

Blue Man looked at it, but it scared him. He'd never handled a firearm.

He knew his talents and training was all the weapon he needed.

Blue Man left the vault and walked to the main door.

He knew this was the most significant decision of his life, and in many ways, this was the first real decision of his life.

Besides killing Mr. Hall, that is.

Should he stay and take his chances with Isabel?

Was this a trap, and the outdoors would kill him?

His hand, the color of glacial ice, touched the doorknob.

He pulled the door open and stepped outside.

Pine-scented air washed over him.

Blue Man looked around. The world was his.

He left to claim it.

Epilogue

"Please remove the blindfold," he was told.

Ezra unknotted the scarf and let his eyes adjust to dim, greenish lighting.

The President of the United States stood just feet away. He seemed smaller than Ezra had anticipated. His shoulders slumped as if his world was caving in on him and melting toward a molten core.

"You're Riley?" the President said.

"Yessir."

The President started to speak again, but Ezra held up a hand, surprising himself with the steadiness and authority of his voice.

"Mr. President," Ezra said. "Do not tell me the dream. Allow me to tell it to you."

"You are going to tell me my dream?"

"Yessir."

The President waved his hand as if flipping a stick to a dog. "Okay," he said. "Go ahead."

Ezra took a step closer.

"In the dream, you are ten years old," he said. "Your family lives in Connecticut by a narrow road. It is in the country, but other houses are nearby. You are outside in the yard. Your closest neighbors have a little girl. She's six years old and has a developmental problem. It might be Down's syndrome, I'm not sure."

The President's head perked up, and he took a step backward.

"The little girl has curly blond hair and blue eyes. She likes you. You always ignore her because she embarrasses you when your friends come over. Your mother says her family should have aborted her."

The President's eyes widened.

"It is Easter Sunday. The little girl is outside with her mother. They're about to go to church. The girl's father is already at the church. The mother hears the phone ringing in the house, and she tells the girl to stay where she is, then the mother runs up the steps.

"The girl sees you and runs to the fence. She says hi and calls you by name. I can't hear the name. It's a nickname. You try to ignore her.

"The little girl's name is Maggie. Maggie runs to a cage. No, it's more like a rabbit hutch. There are two baby chicks inside. She picks them up carefully and then runs back to the fence.

"They are Easter chicks, she tells you. One is mostly black but has yellow and white speckles. The other one is yellow, almost white. She stretches her arms out and asks if you want to hold them. You are angry. You have friends coming by soon, and you don't want them to see you with Maggie.

"You take the chicks from her but drop them on the ground. You stomp on the black chick first, then the yellow. They lie flat and dead on the grass. The little girl is too mortified to say anything. Realizing what you've done, you pick them up, run down the fence, and throw them onto the road.

"Maggie is crying now. You run into your house to hide. The girl runs toward the road. She climbs a short fence and stands in the street staring down at the chicks. A black sports car comes around a curve traveling too fast, and doesn't see her. The vehicle hits Maggie and kills her. Her mother runs screaming from her house.

"You are staring out the windows. Your mother asks what the commotion is outside. When she sees that Maggie has been struck by a car and killed, she says it's a tragedy, but it's better for everyone in the long run."

The President takes another step back, his face ashen and his lips trembling.

"That was your dream, Mr. President," Ezra says. "Now I will tell you the interpretation:

"The little girl represents the citizens you despise, and you want to take actions to crush two of their values. The speckled black chick is the freedom to bear arms. The yellowish chick is the church. You want to crush both under your feet, believing the citizens you resent will overreact and be crushed by further legislative actions, which are represented by the sports car."

The President stepped forward, his face reddened by anger. "I can do what I want," he said in a low, soft voice.

Ezra held a hand up to stop him. "There is more, Mr. President. If you step on the black chick, it will rise as a black eagle. There will be death in the streets as you have never seen. If you step on the yellow chick, it will lift and soar as a white eagle and revival will sweep the country."

"But I can do what I want," the President insisted.

"You can do as you will," Ezra said. "But there will be consequences."

"I am relieved to know what the dream means," the President said. "I feel like a burden has lifted from me, but I will do what I want to do."

"And there will be consequences," Ezra repeated.

"I am above those consequences," the President declared.

"No, sir, you are not."

"You, some *cowboy*, dare tell me the consequences are not in my control?"

Ezra didn't answer.

"I will make my decisions," the President said. "And you will see the consequences."

"Your scepter shall fall and be picked up by another."

"Are you threatening me?"

"No, sir. But another, not you, will have the choice of killing Maggie's chicks."

"You're telling me I will die in office."

"Your scepter shall fall," Ezra said again. "And be picked up by another."

"I will do what I want to do," the President repeated. "And we will see which one of us dies first."

Ezra nodded.

The President turned and left.

A Secret Service agent entered and escorted Ezra from the room.

The President went to bed. He slept well, and he never dreamt again.

John L. Moore is a third-generation Montana rancher who has won multiple awards for his novels and journalism. His fifty years of writing have resulted in his inductions into both the **Montana Cowboy Hall of Fame and Western Heritage** and the **Montana ProRodeo Hall and Wall of Fame**. Moore was active in prophetic ministry for over twenty-five years, and he and his wife, Debra, have pastored three home churches. They live on their ranch north of Miles City, Montana. His previous *Ezra Riley* novels are: *The Breaking of Ezra Riley, Leaving the Land, The Limits of Mercy,* and *Looking for Lynne.*

Praise for the Ezra Riley novels of John L. Moore

"If you want the real blood and bone of the West, read John L. Moore."

Shann Ray
Author of *American Copper*

"So many novels about the West are written by new westerners. For a refreshing dose of something different, try John L. Moore. Moore is a serious novelist unembarrassed by the cowboy way."

Steve Bodio
Author of *Tiger Country: A Novel of the Wild Southwest*

"*The Breaking of Ezra Riley* is like no other western I have read. American critics have actually compared it to Steinbeck. That should give some indication of the quality of his work."

Country Music People

"*The Breaking of Ezra Riley* deserves a medal for being poignant and honest and wholly free of the bogus Hollywood image of the American cowboy."

Denver Post

"In prose as lean and skillful as some of the cowboys he depicts, Moore portrays the depths of Ezra's soul...a literary achievement that leaves the reader wanting more."

Moody Monthly

"When history has its say, books like *The Breaking of Ezra Riley* will speak for the average American experience in the 20th century."

Milwaukee Journal

"John Moore is the most authentic Montana writer since Will James, only better."
Thomas Savage

Author of *The Power of the Dog*

"I've never known a cowboy with such verbal acuity and intellectual depth...this must be a cowboy on a higher plane, a philosopher and poet cowboy. John Moore delivers."
Margaret Jean Langstaff
Literary critic

"Moore is an authentic working cowboy in Montana, but more than that, he's the extremely well-read, and dare I say, intellectual, whose gift for words makes a good storyline. He knows the land, its history, and its people."
Kregg Jorgenson
Author of *Acceptable Loss*

"John Moore...has much of eternal importance to say."
Eugenia Price
Author of *Stranger in Savannah*

"*The Breaking of Ezra Riley* is breathtakingly good, and I look forward to a great deal more from John Moore."
Loren D. Estleman
Author of *The Eagle and the Viper: A Novel of Historical Suspense*

"An excellent novel, (*The Breaking of Ezra Riley*) vibrating with power and deep pervasive honesty."

Montana Magazine

"An amazing author, John L. Moore brings the West to life brilliantly."

Pastor Bill Johnson
Author of *When Heaven Invades Earth*

"*Leaving the Land* has characters so well rounded they appear to be sculpted."

Great Falls Tribune

"This novel (*The Breaking of Ezra Riley*) is a compelling and accurate view of what it is to grow up on the high plains, to strive to meet standards set by people who haven't an inch of give in the length of them."

Billings Gazette

"His love of the land shines through in his descriptive passages about the open prairies."

Helena Independent Record

"Moore has drawn wonderful, clear scenes and knitted them together in a riveting story that left me thinking about these modern-day cowboys and their country days after I put it down."

Christianity Today

"The author has a talent for painting pictures with words, and the whole book flows like you're watching a movie in your mind."

Western Horseman

"This is a story of the land and how deeply it can get into a person's soul."

American Cowboy

"Moore is such a gifted writer...the pleasure comes from his wonderfully constructed prose."

New Man Magazine

"*The Breaking of Ezra Riley* is a sincere, well-written book."

California Cattleman

"Moore is a master of suspenseful plotting."

Butte (MT) Standard

CPSIA information can be obtained
at www.ICGtesting.com
Printed in the USA
BVHW072237260621
610451BV00002B/127